★ THE SONS OF ★
LIBERTY

CREATED AND WRITTEN BY **ALEXANDER LAGOS** AND **JOSEPH LAGOS**

ART BY **STEVE WALKER**   COLOR BY **OREN KRAMEK**

LETTERS BY **CHRIS DICKEY**

Random House 🏠 **New York**

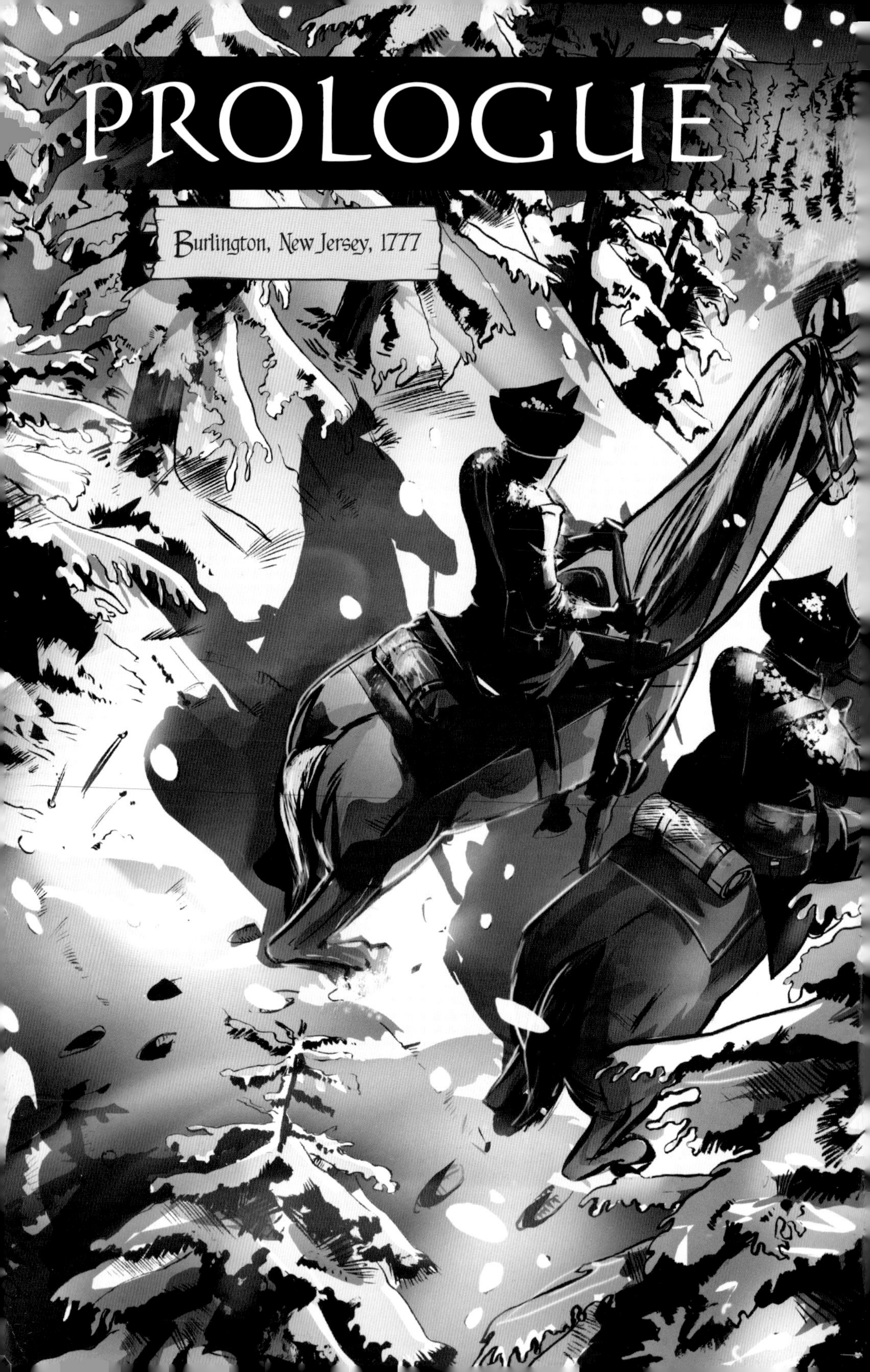
PROLOGUE
Burlington, New Jersey, 1777

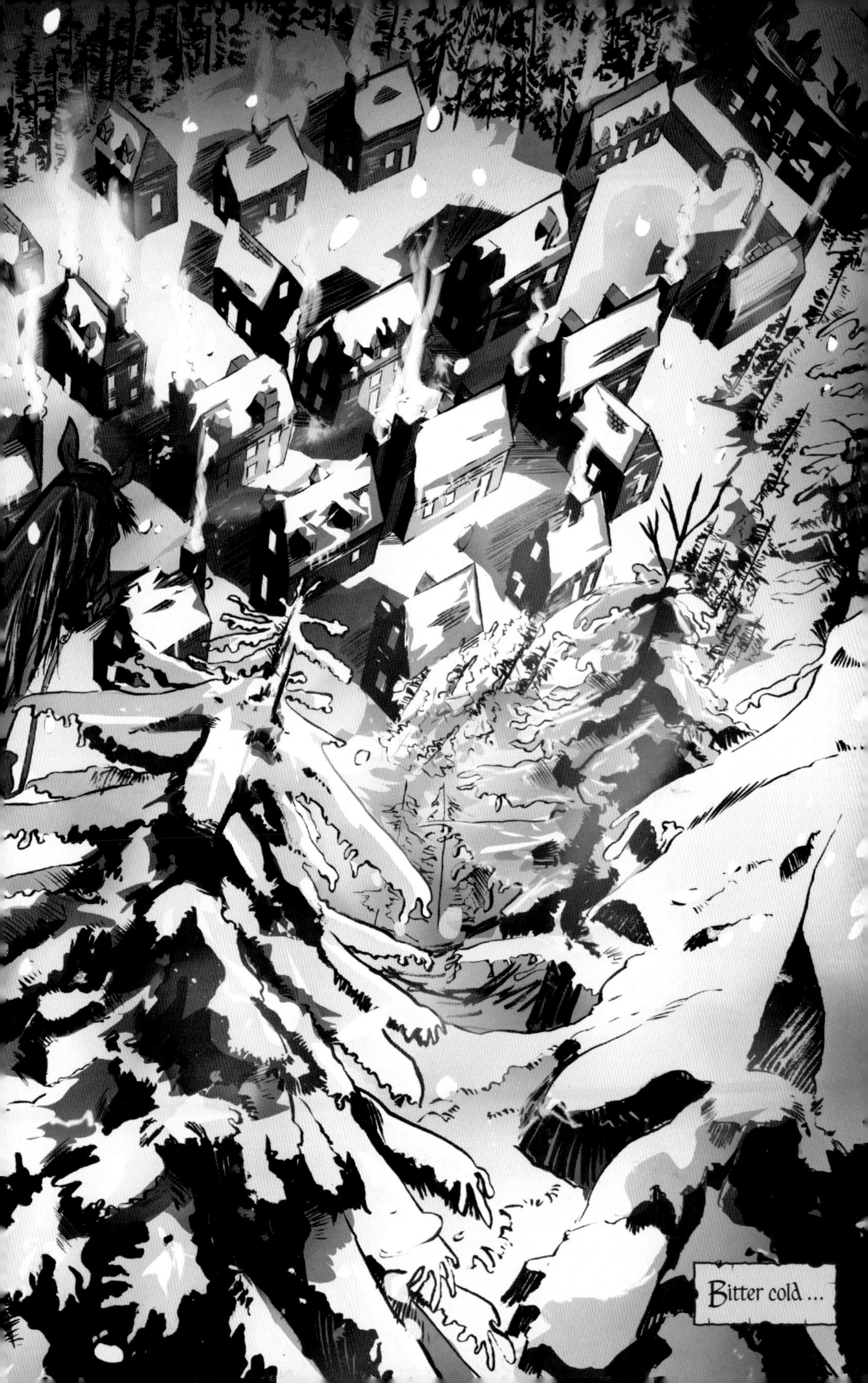
Bitter cold ...

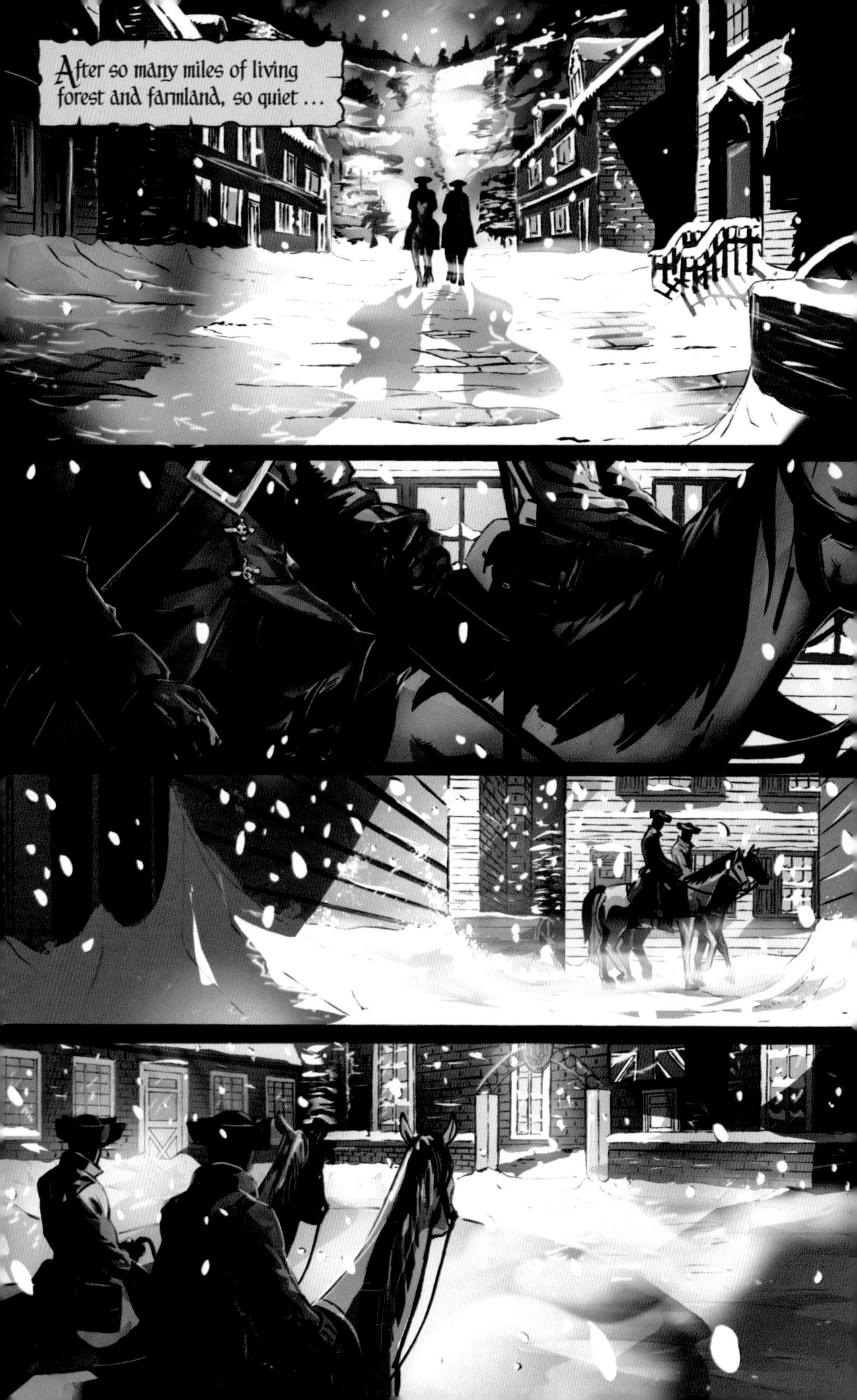
After so many miles of living forest and farmland, so quiet . . .

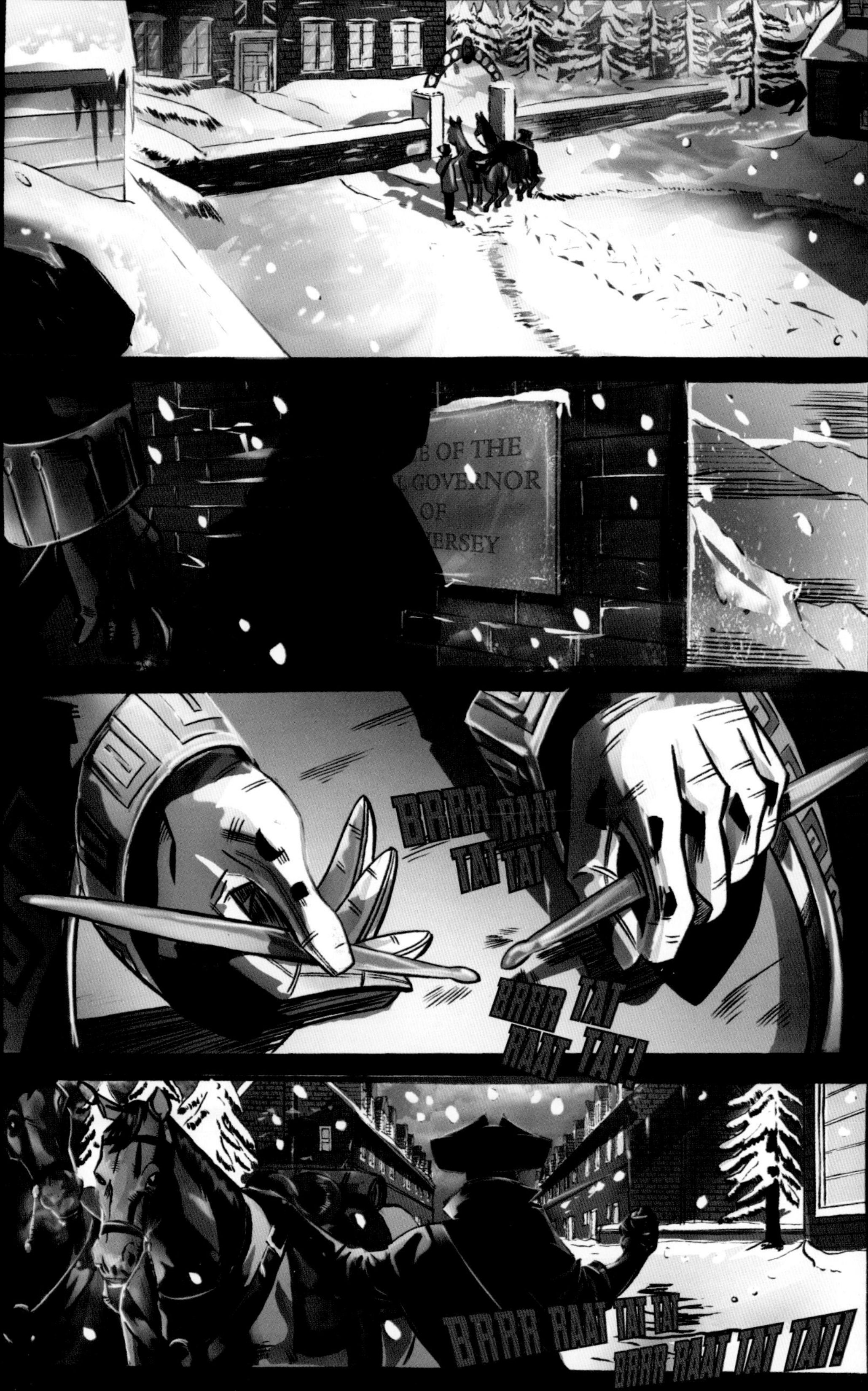
E OF THE
GOVERNOR
OF
ERSEY
BRRR RAAT TAT TAT
BRRR RAAT TAT TAT!
BRRR RAAT TAT TAT
BRRR RAAT TAT TAT!

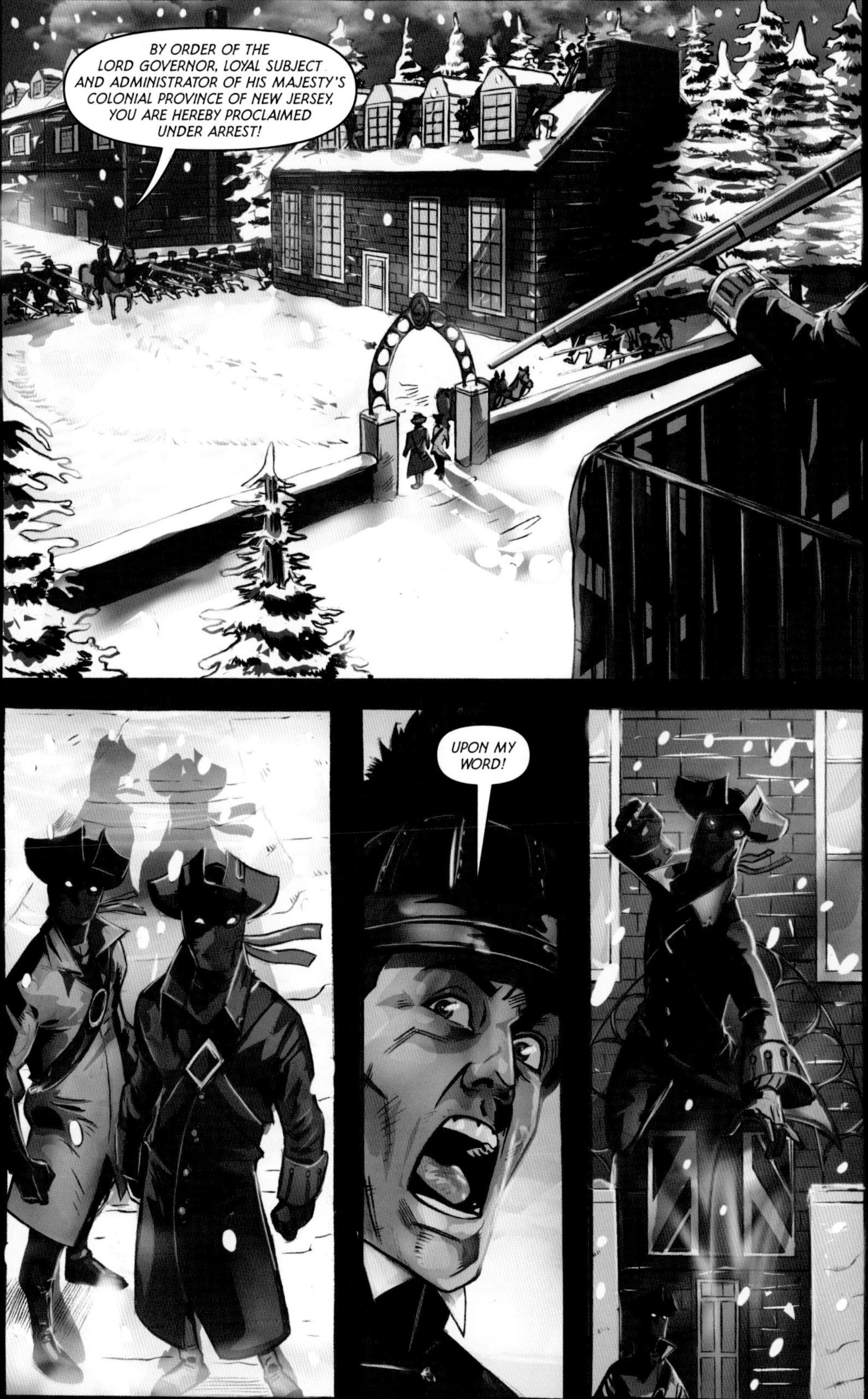
BY ORDER OF THE LORD GOVERNOR, LOYAL SUBJECT AND ADMINISTRATOR OF HIS MAJESTY'S COLONIAL PROVINCE OF NEW JERSEY, YOU ARE HEREBY PROCLAIMED UNDER ARREST!
UPON MY WORD!

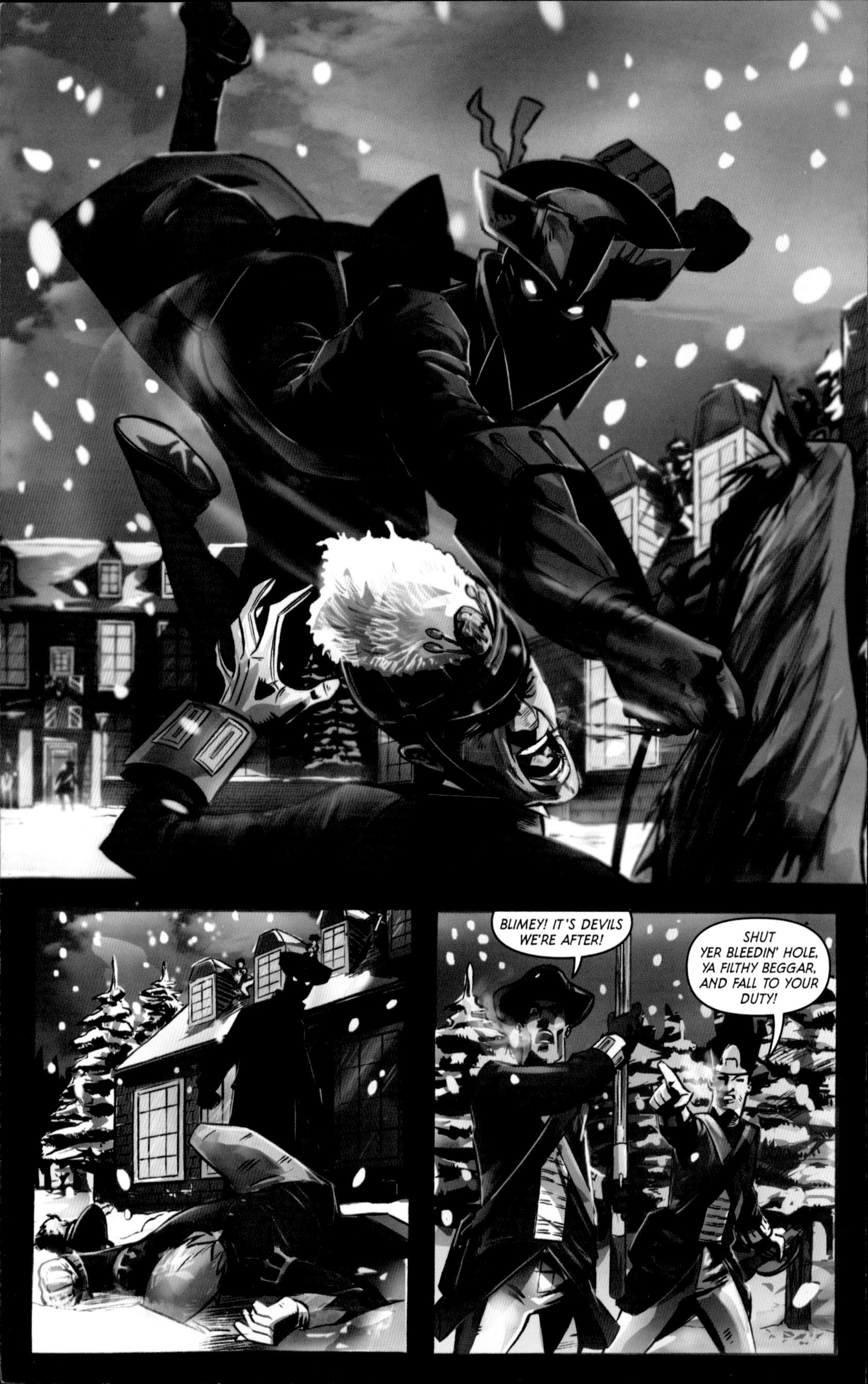
BLIMEY! IT'S DEVILS WE'RE AFTER!
SHUT YER BLEEDIN' HOLE, YA FILTHY BEGGAR, AND FALL TO YOUR DUTY!

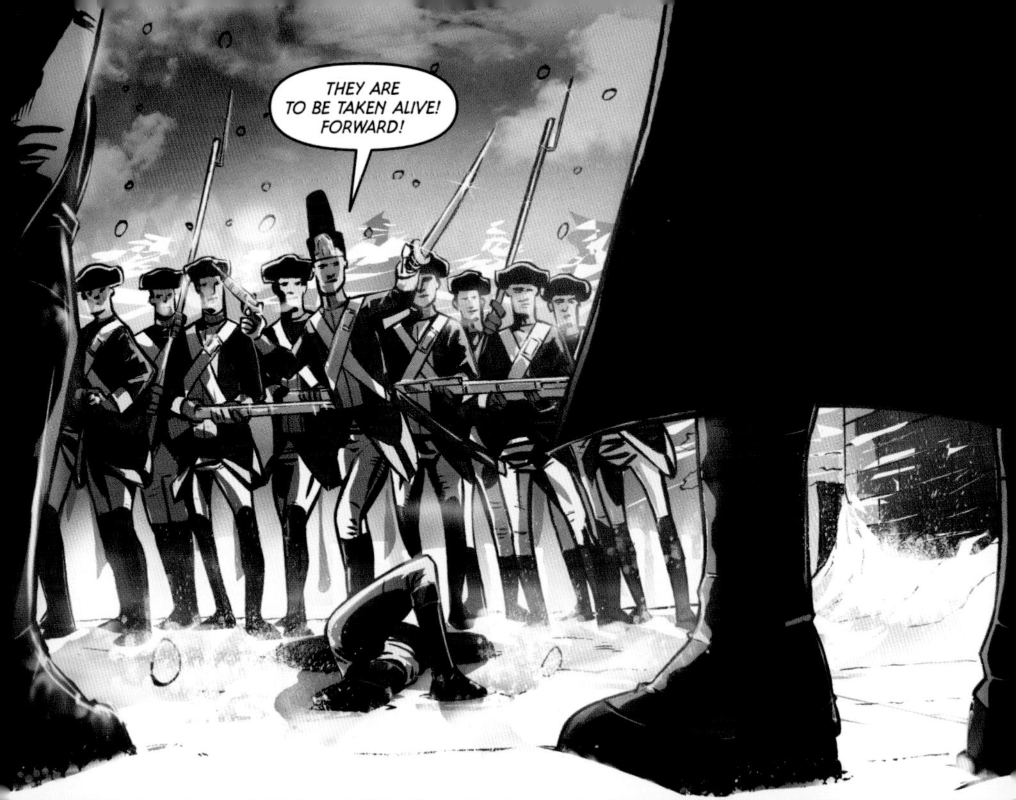
THEY ARE TO BE TAKEN ALIVE! FORWARD!

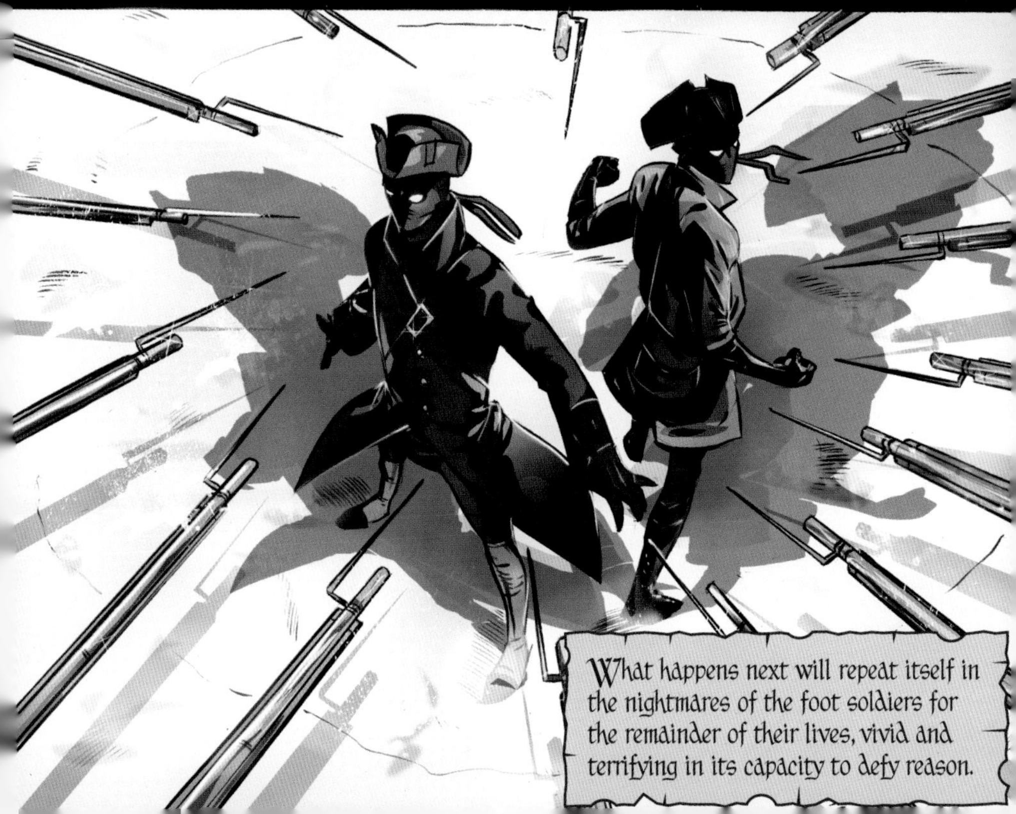
What happens next will repeat itself in the nightmares of the foot soldiers for the remainder of their lives, vivid and terrifying in its capacity to defy reason.

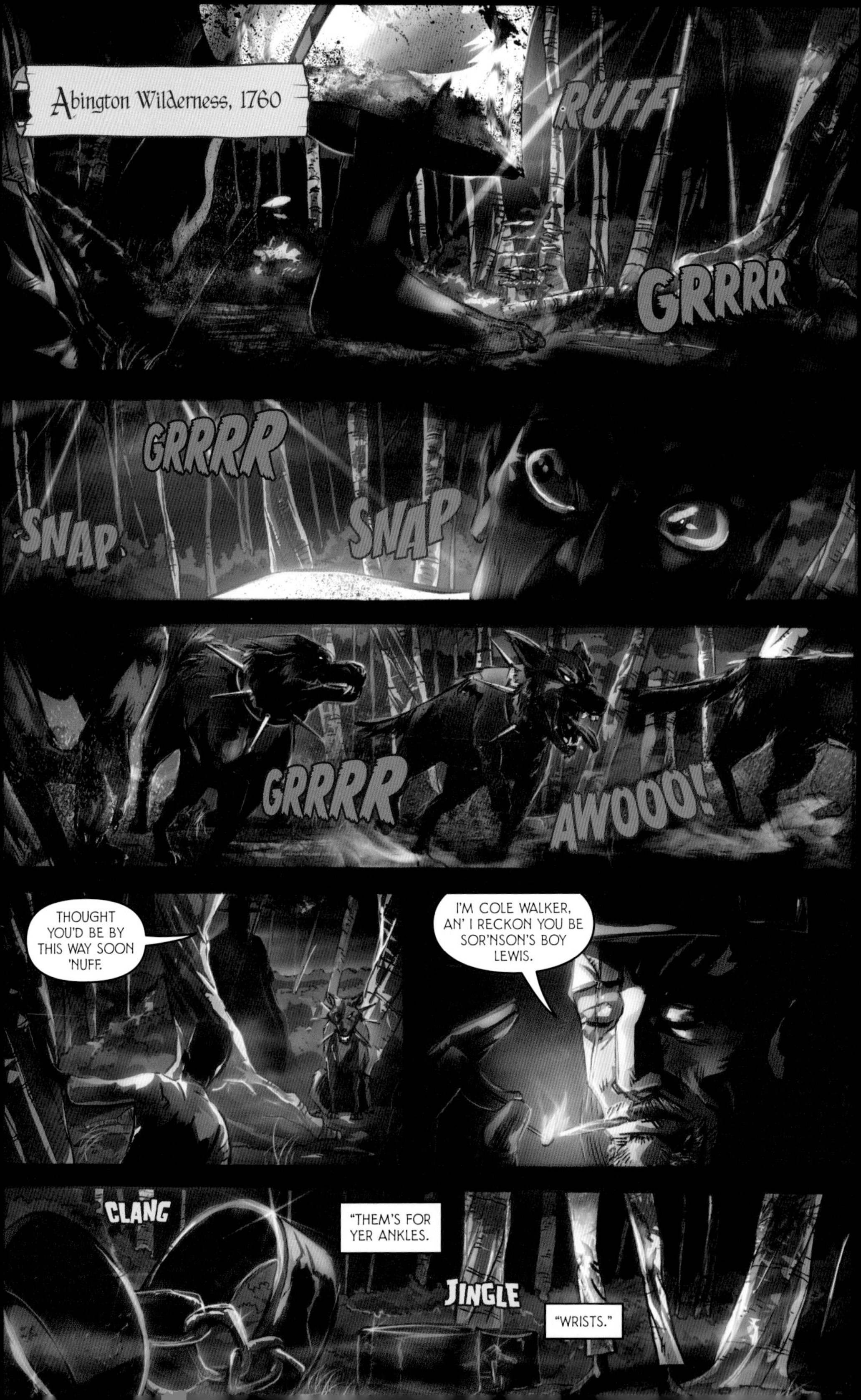
Abington Wilderness, 1760
RUFF
GRRRR
GRRRR
SNAP
SNAP
GRRRR
AWOOO!
THOUGHT YOU'D BE BY THIS WAY SOON 'NUFF.
I'M COLE WALKER, AN' I RECKON YOU BE SOR'NSON'S BOY LEWIS.
CLANG
"THEM'S FOR YER ANKLES.
JINGLE
"WRISTS."

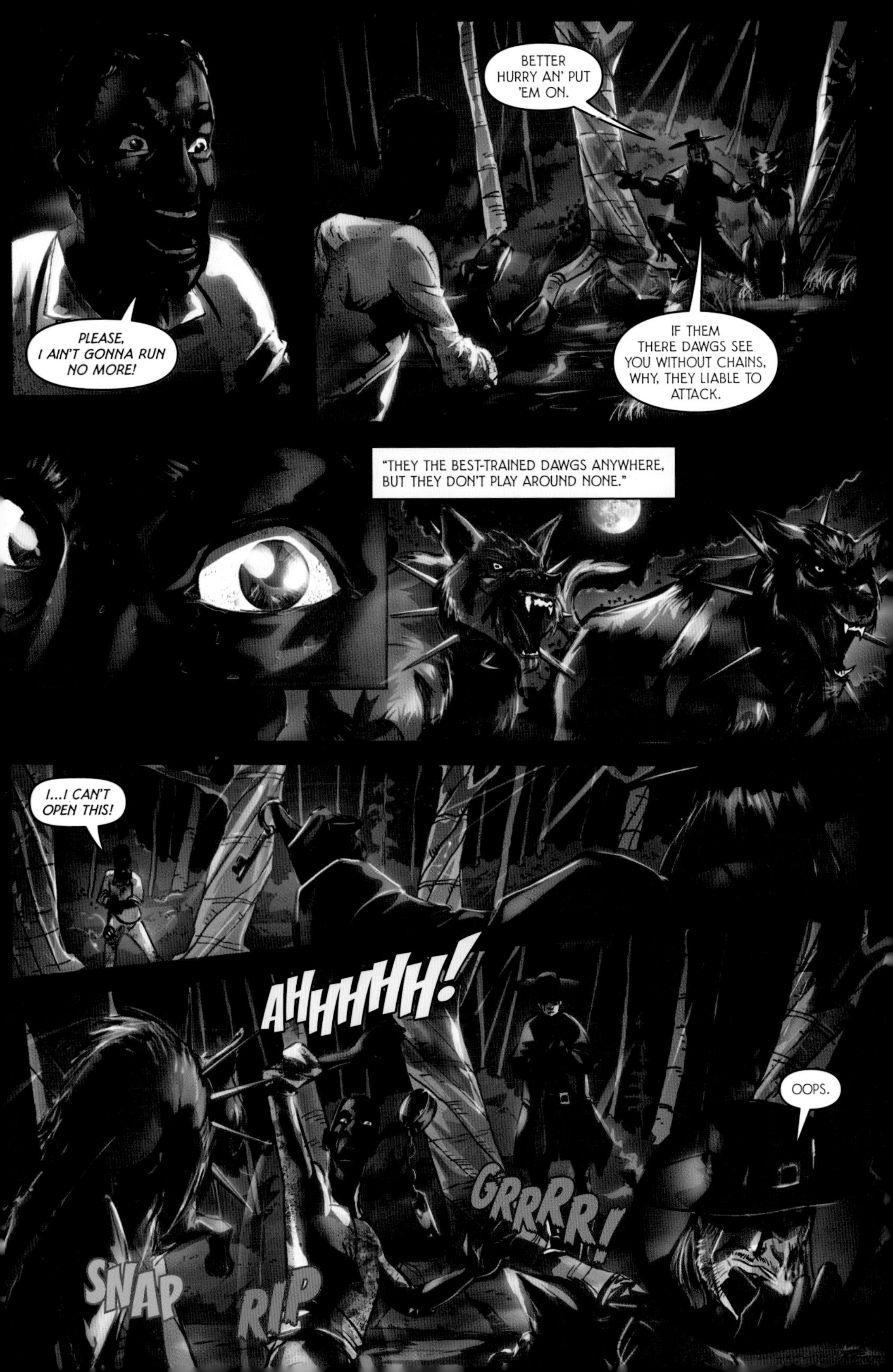
PLEASE, I AIN'T GONNA RUN NO MORE!
BETTER HURRY AN' PUT 'EM ON.
IF THEM THERE DAWGS SEE YOU WITHOUT CHAINS, WHY, THEY LIABLE TO ATTACK.
"THEY THE BEST-TRAINED DAWGS ANYWHERE, BUT THEY DON'T PLAY AROUND NONE."
I...I CAN'T OPEN THIS!
AHHHHHH!
OOPS.
GRRRR!
SNAP
RIP

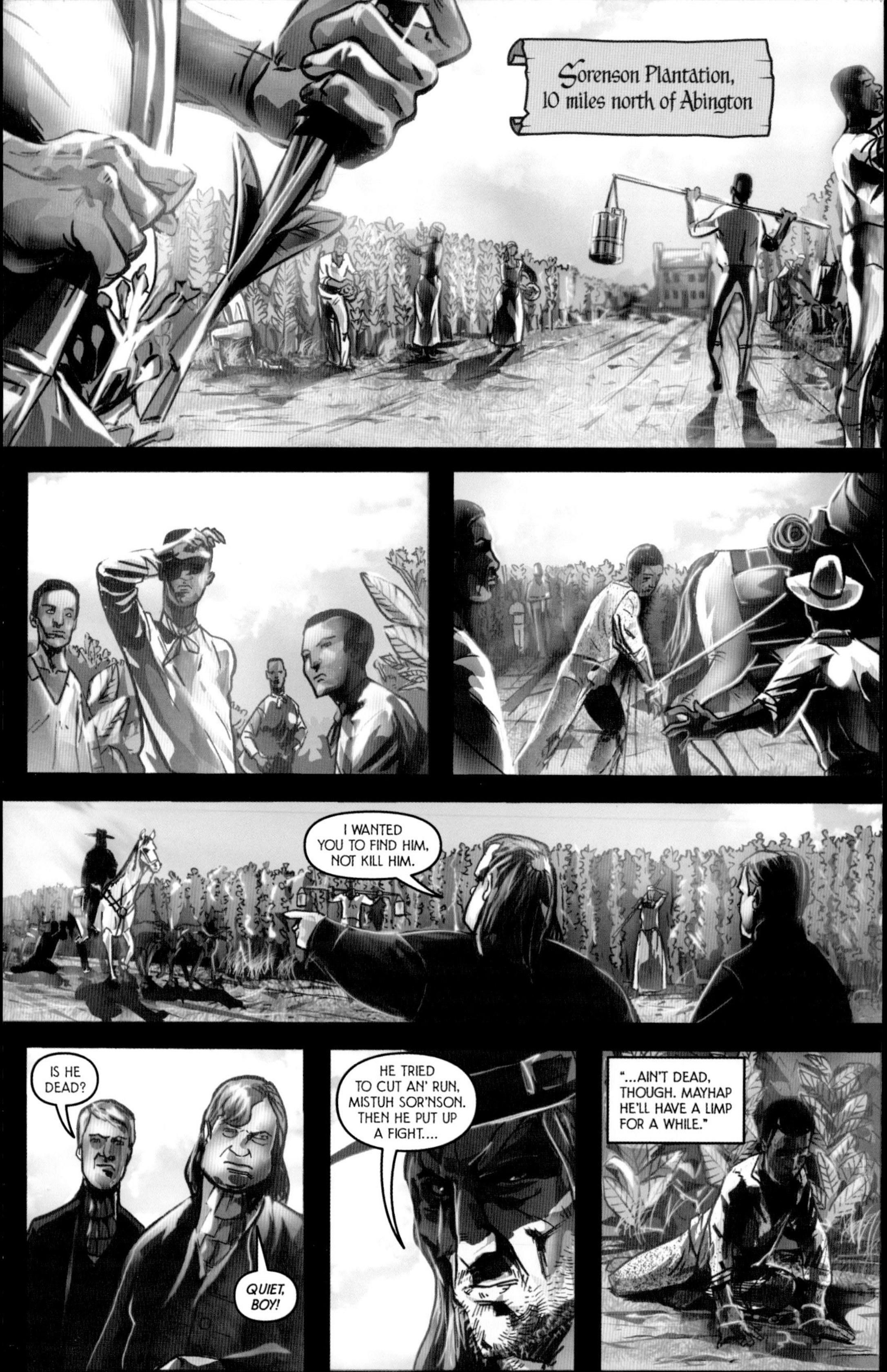
Sorenson Plantation,
10 miles north of Abington
I WANTED YOU TO FIND HIM, NOT KILL HIM.
IS HE DEAD?
QUIET, BOY!
HE TRIED TO CUT AN' RUN, MISTUH SOR'NSON. THEN HE PUT UP A FIGHT....
"...AIN'T DEAD, THOUGH. MAYHAP HE'LL HAVE A LIMP FOR A WHILE."

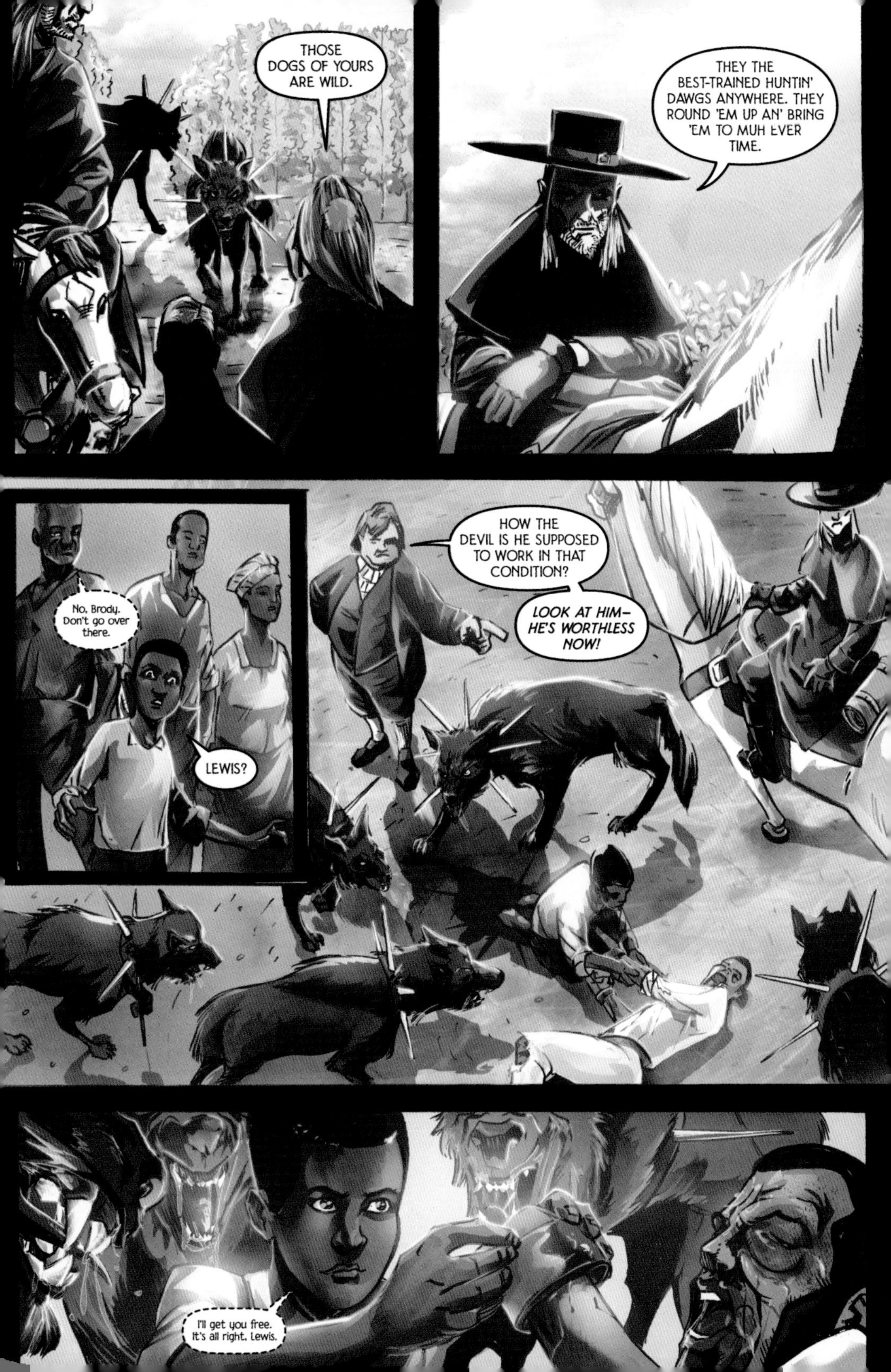
THOSE DOGS OF YOURS ARE WILD.
THEY THE BEST-TRAINED HUNTIN' DAWGS ANYWHERE. THEY ROUND 'EM UP AN' BRING 'EM TO MUH EVER TIME.
No, Brody. Don't go over there.
LEWIS?
HOW THE DEVIL IS HE SUPPOSED TO WORK IN THAT CONDITION?
LOOK AT HIM— HE'S WORTHLESS NOW!
I'll get you free. It's all right, Lewis.

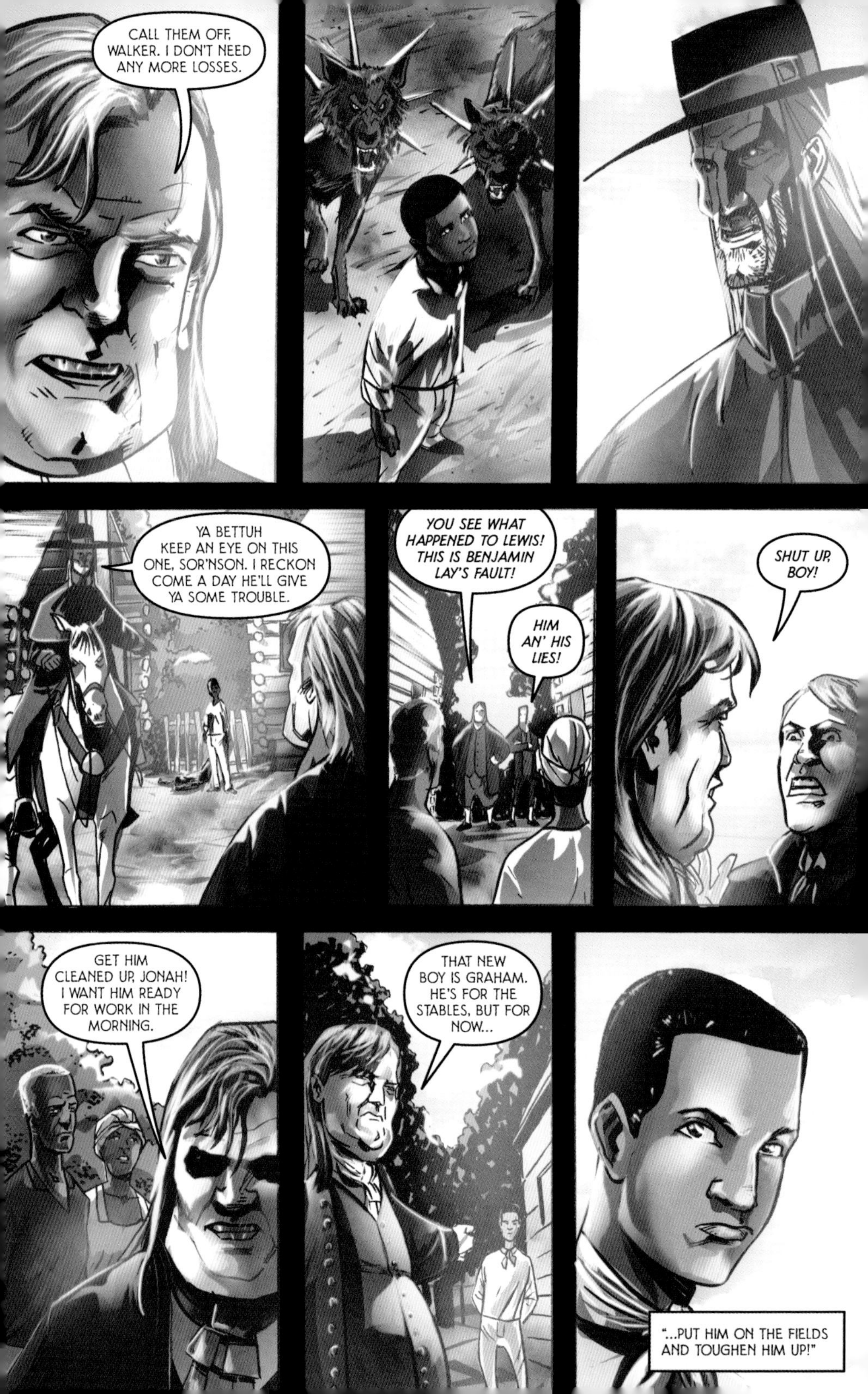
CALL THEM OFF, WALKER. I DON'T NEED ANY MORE LOSSES.
YA BETTUH KEEP AN EYE ON THIS ONE, SOR'NSON. I RECKON COME A DAY HE'LL GIVE YA SOME TROUBLE.
YOU SEE WHAT HAPPENED TO LEWIS! THIS IS BENJAMIN LAY'S FAULT!
HIM AN' HIS LIES!
SHUT UP, BOY!
GET HIM CLEANED UP, JONAH! I WANT HIM READY FOR WORK IN THE MORNING.
THAT NEW BOY IS GRAHAM. HE'S FOR THE STABLES, BUT FOR NOW...
"...PUT HIM ON THE FIELDS AND TOUGHEN HIM UP!"

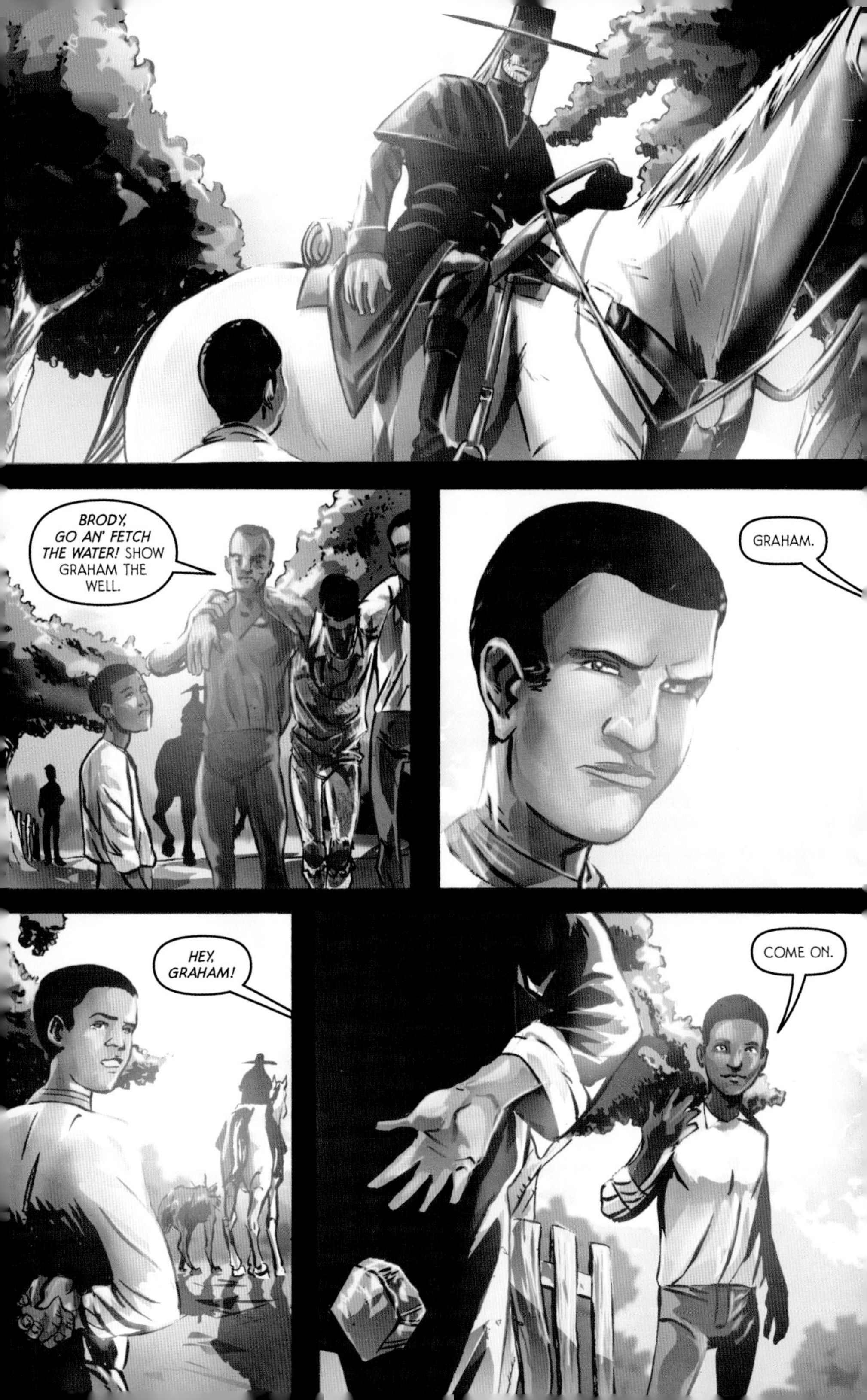
BRODY, GO AN' FETCH THE WATER! SHOW GRAHAM THE WELL.
GRAHAM.
HEY, GRAHAM!
COME ON.

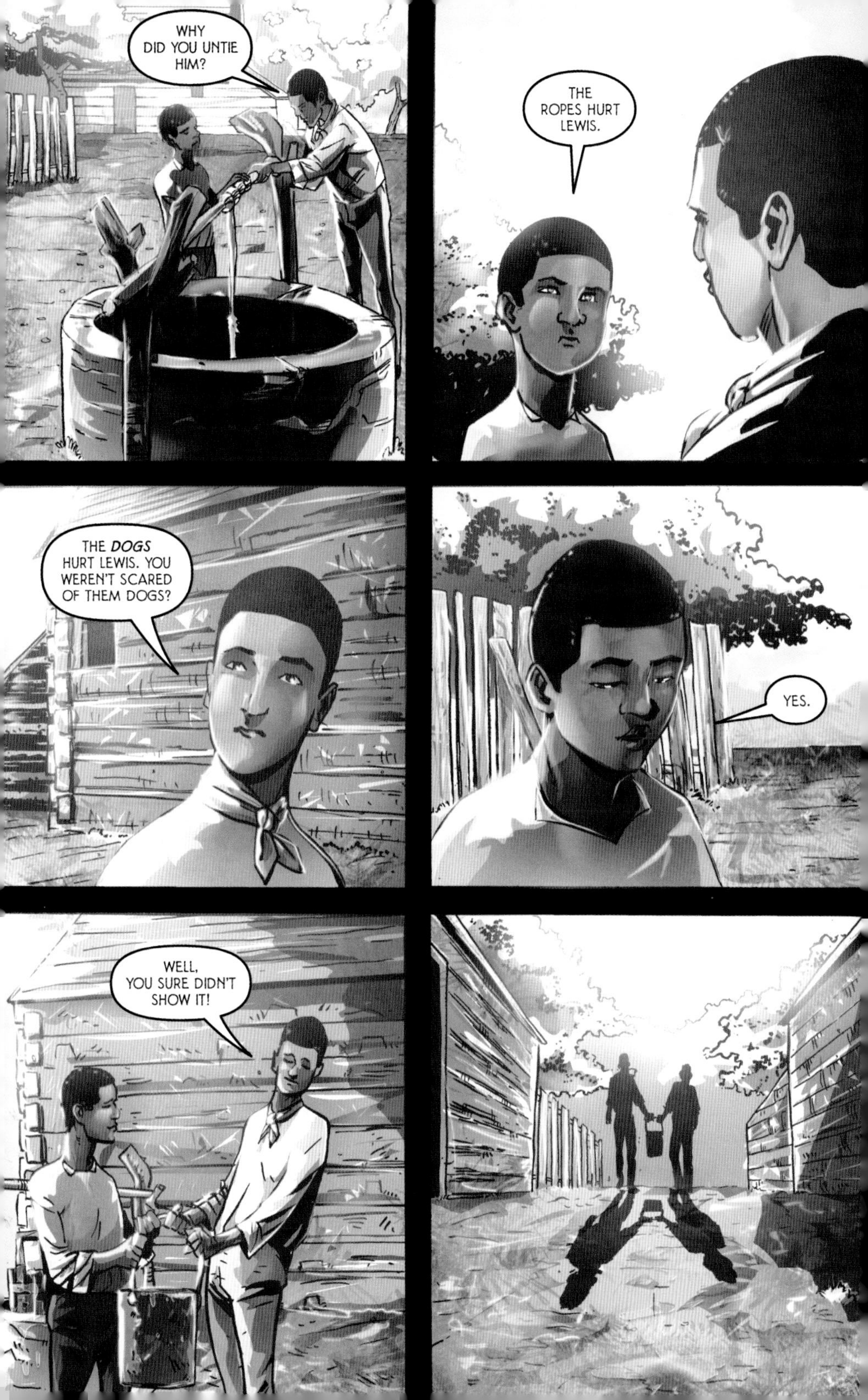
WHY DID YOU UNTIE HIM?
THE ROPES HURT LEWIS.
THE *DOGS* HURT LEWIS. YOU WEREN'T SCARED OF THEM DOGS?
YES.
WELL, YOU SURE DIDN'T SHOW IT!

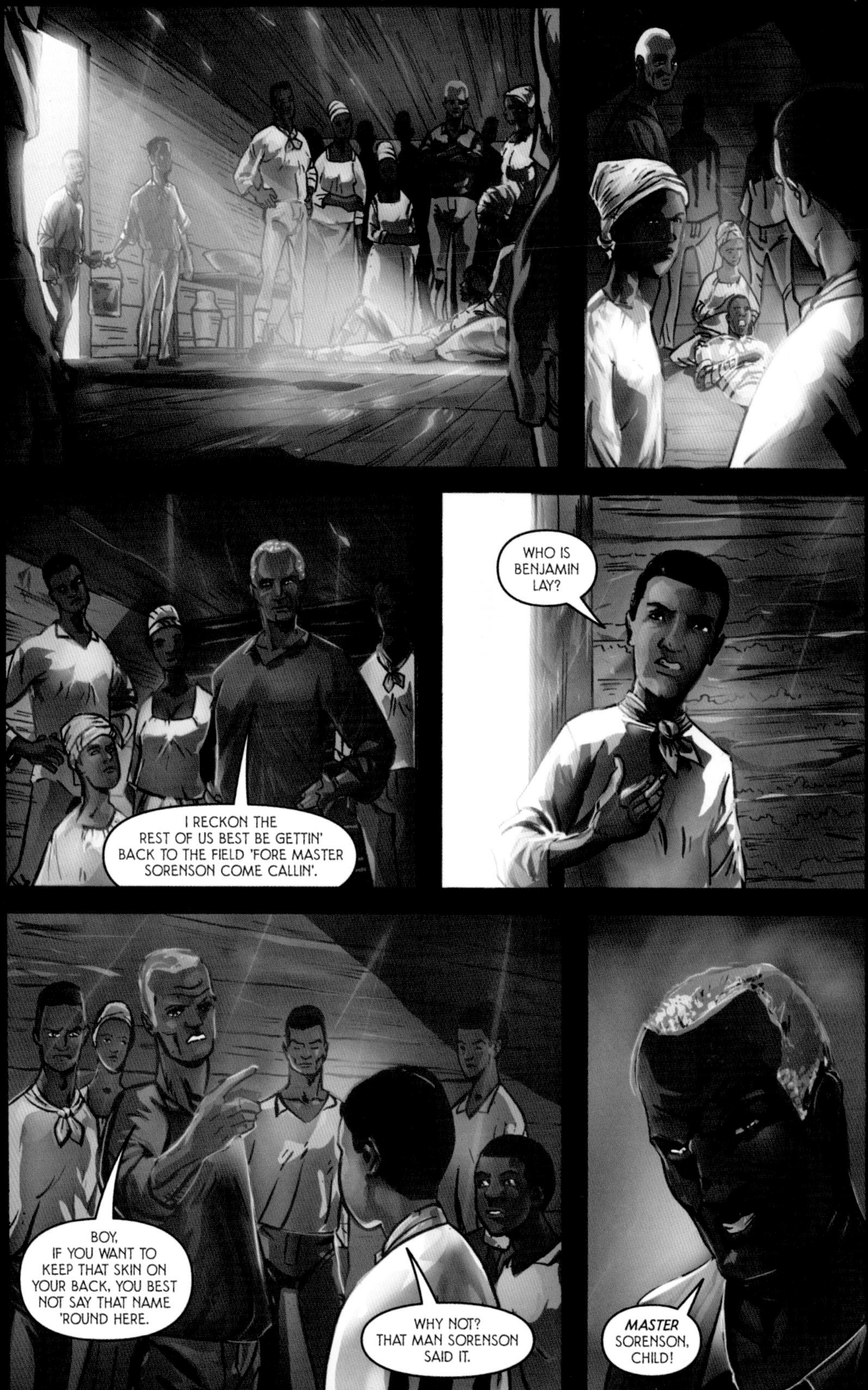
I RECKON THE REST OF US BEST BE GETTIN' BACK TO THE FIELD 'FORE MASTER SORENSON COME CALLIN'.
WHO IS BENJAMIN LAY?
BOY, IF YOU WANT TO KEEP THAT SKIN ON YOUR BACK, YOU BEST NOT SAY THAT NAME 'ROUND HERE.
WHY NOT? THAT MAN SORENSON SAID IT.
MASTER SORENSON, CHILD!

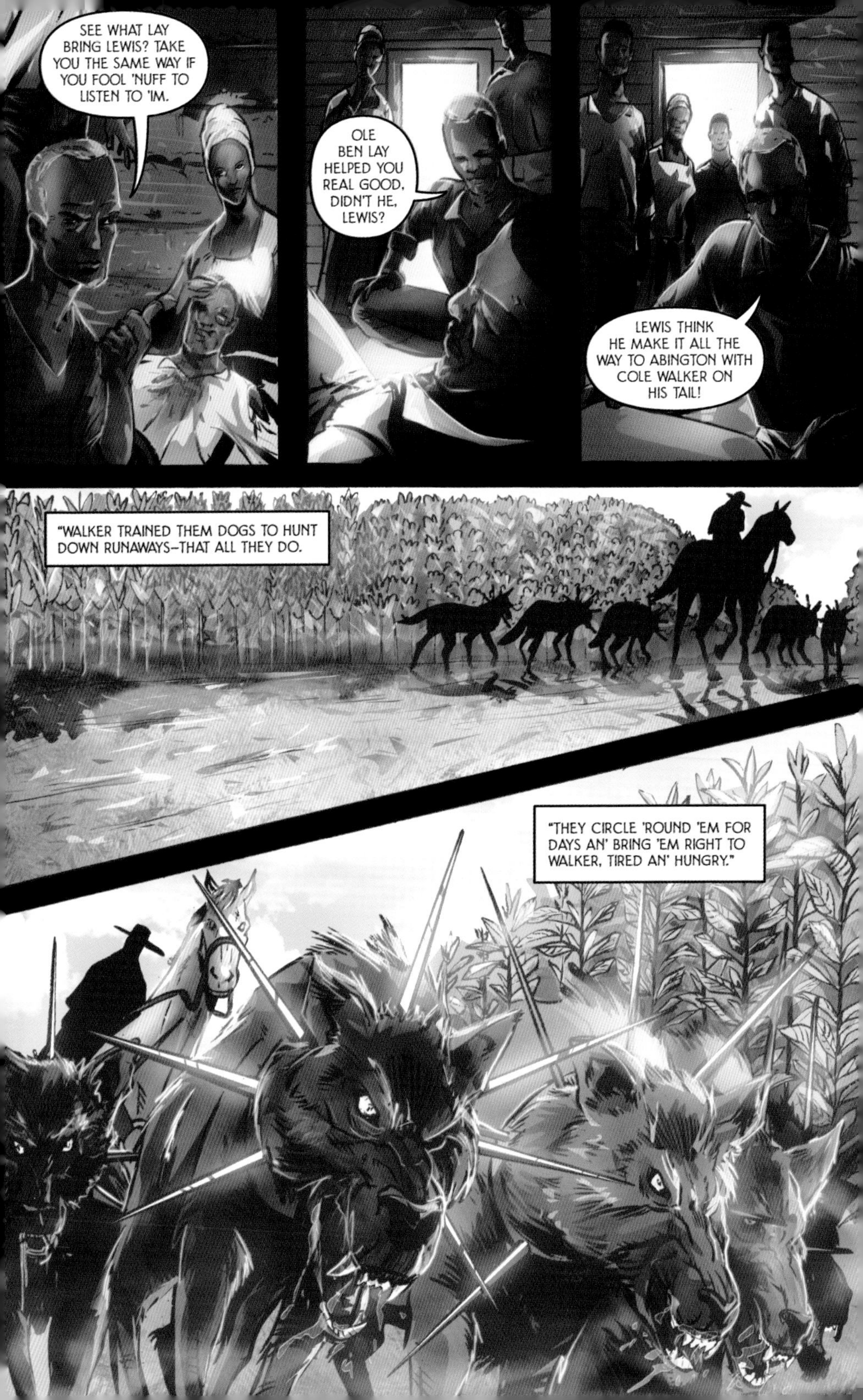
SEE WHAT LAY BRING LEWIS? TAKE YOU THE SAME WAY IF YOU FOOL 'NUFF TO LISTEN TO 'IM.
OLE BEN LAY HELPED YOU REAL GOOD, DIDN'T HE, LEWIS?
LEWIS THINK HE MAKE IT ALL THE WAY TO ABINGTON WITH COLE WALKER ON HIS TAIL!
"WALKER TRAINED THEM DOGS TO HUNT DOWN RUNAWAYS–THAT ALL THEY DO.
"THEY CIRCLE 'ROUND 'EM FOR DAYS AN' BRING 'EM RIGHT TO WALKER, TIRED AN' HUNGRY."

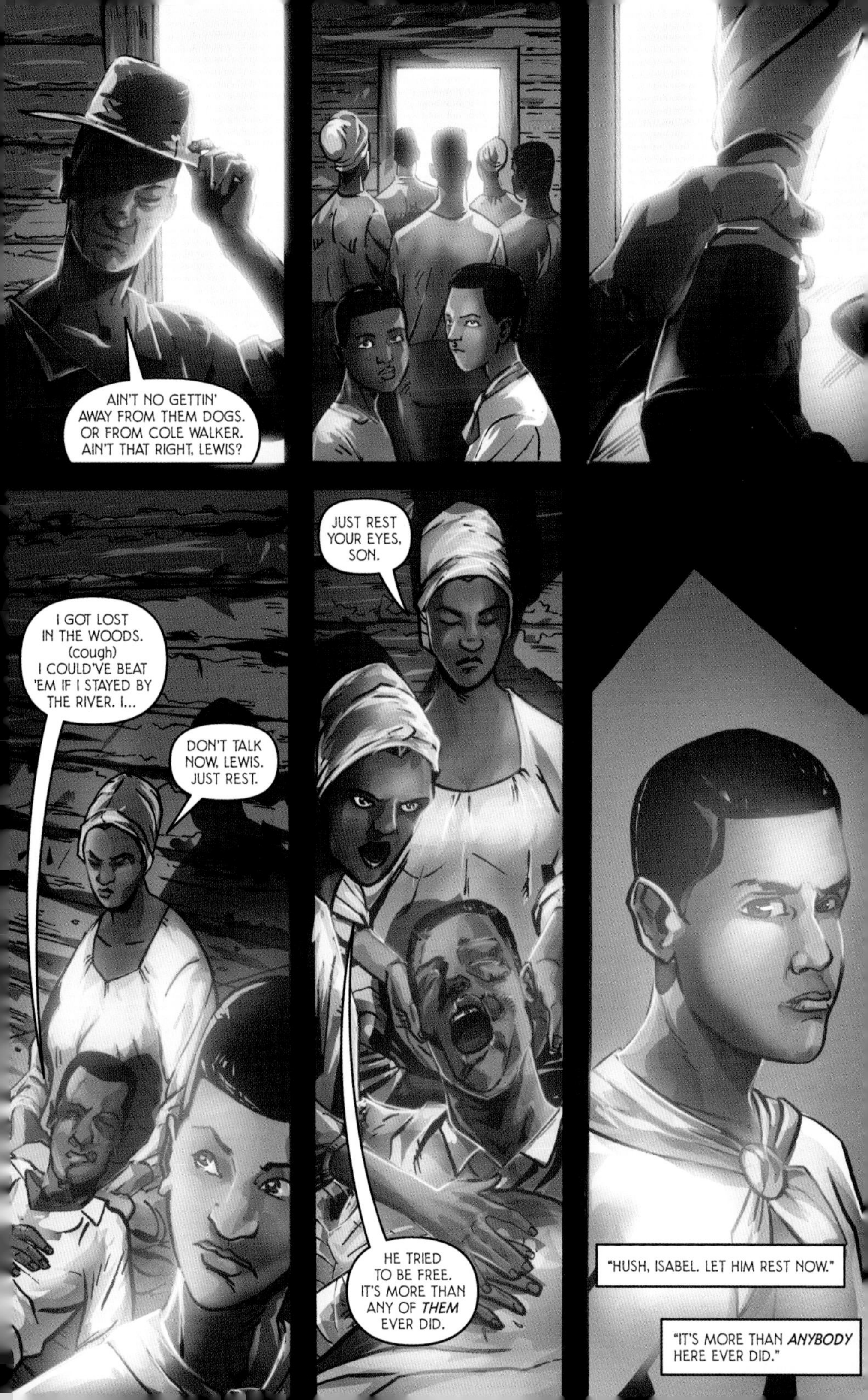
AIN'T NO GETTIN' AWAY FROM THEM DOGS. OR FROM COLE WALKER. AIN'T THAT RIGHT, LEWIS?
I GOT LOST IN THE WOODS. (cough) I COULD'VE BEAT 'EM IF I STAYED BY THE RIVER. I...
DON'T TALK NOW, LEWIS. JUST REST.
JUST REST YOUR EYES, SON.
HE TRIED TO BE FREE. IT'S MORE THAN ANY OF *THEM* EVER DID.
"HUSH, ISABEL. LET HIM REST NOW."
"IT'S MORE THAN *ANYBODY* HERE EVER DID."

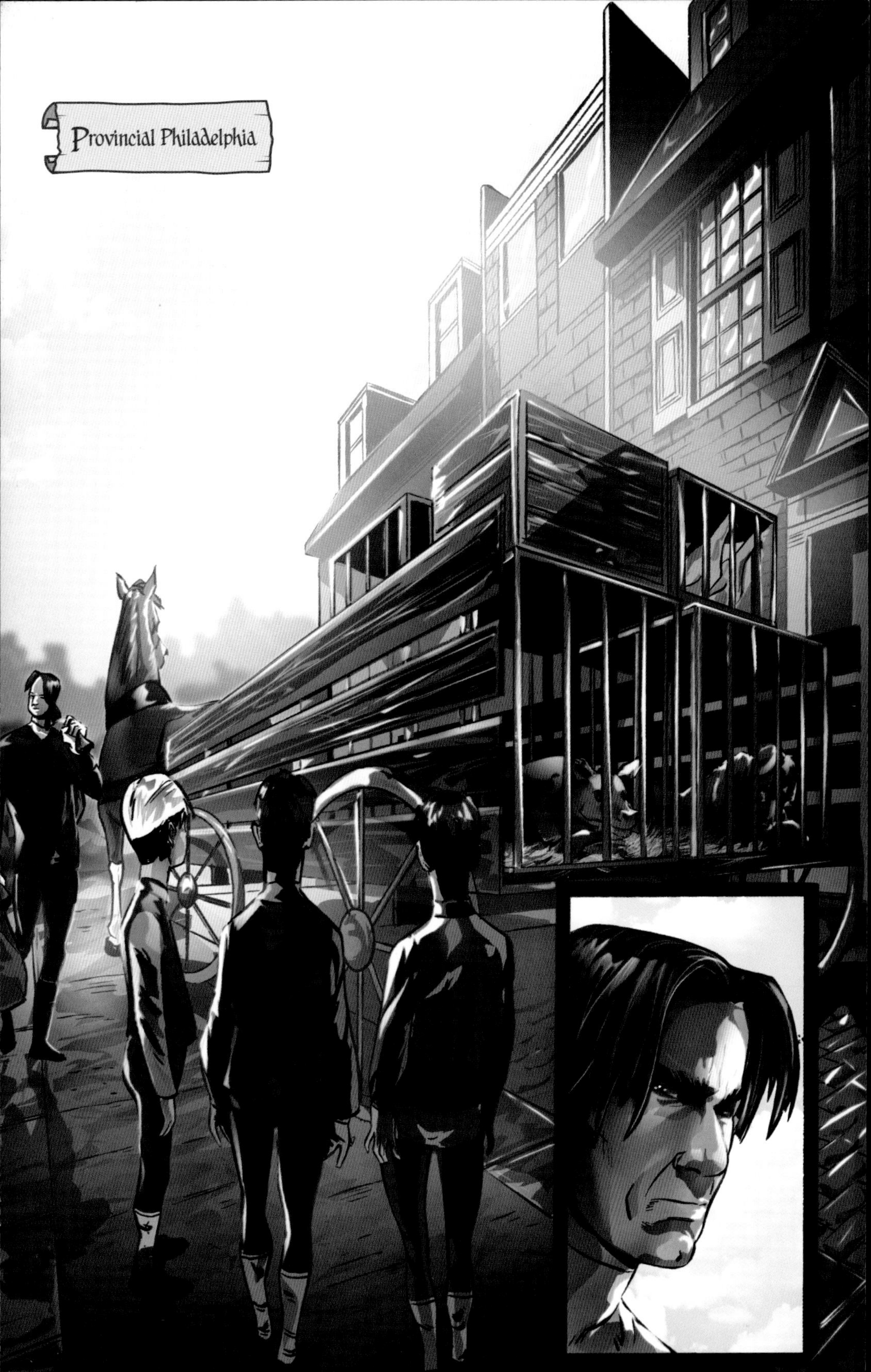
Provincial Philadelphia

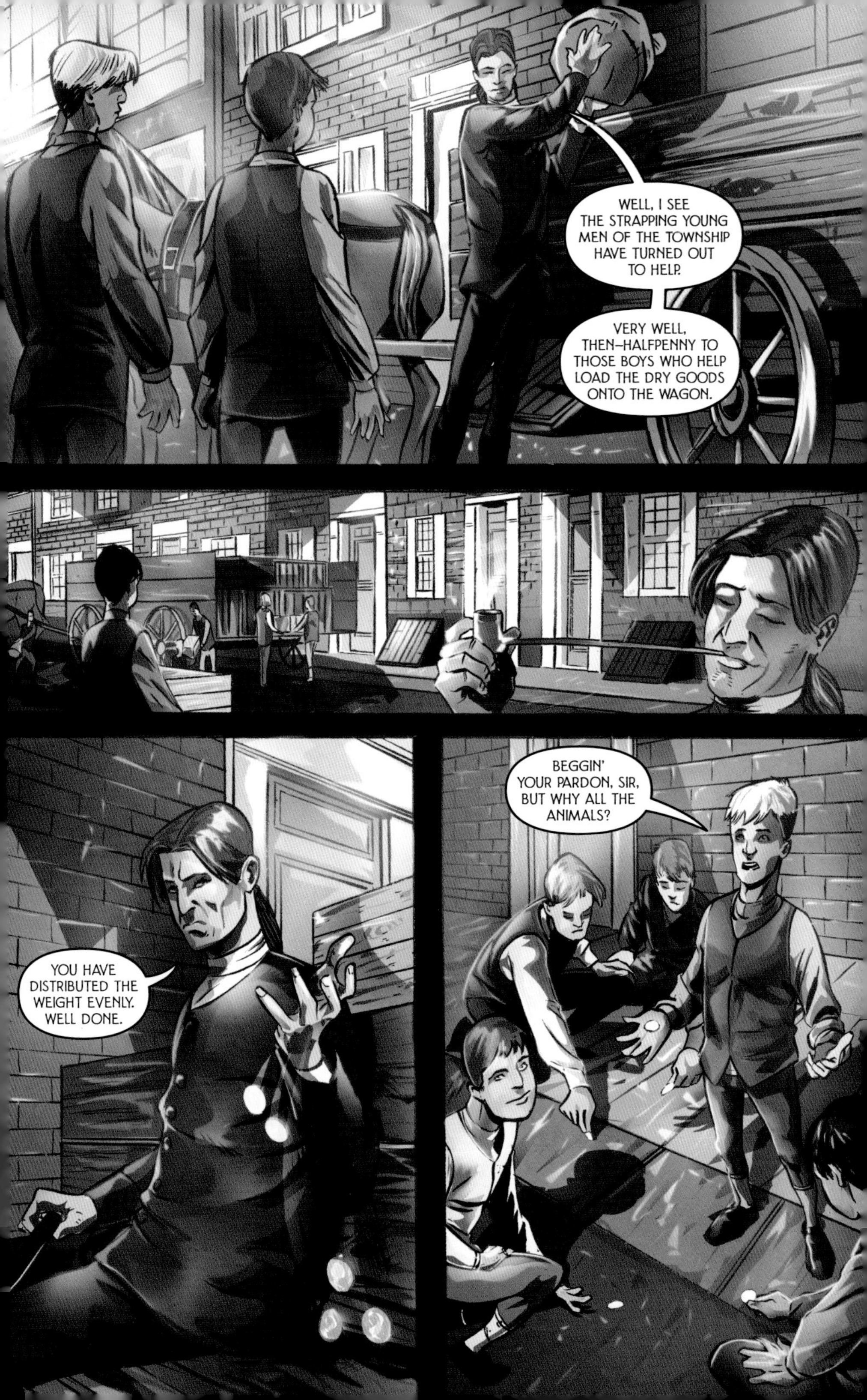
WELL, I SEE THE STRAPPING YOUNG MEN OF THE TOWNSHIP HAVE TURNED OUT TO HELP.
VERY WELL, THEN—HALFPENNY TO THOSE BOYS WHO HELP LOAD THE DRY GOODS ONTO THE WAGON.
YOU HAVE DISTRIBUTED THE WEIGHT EVENLY. WELL DONE.
BEGGIN' YOUR PARDON, SIR, BUT WHY ALL THE ANIMALS?

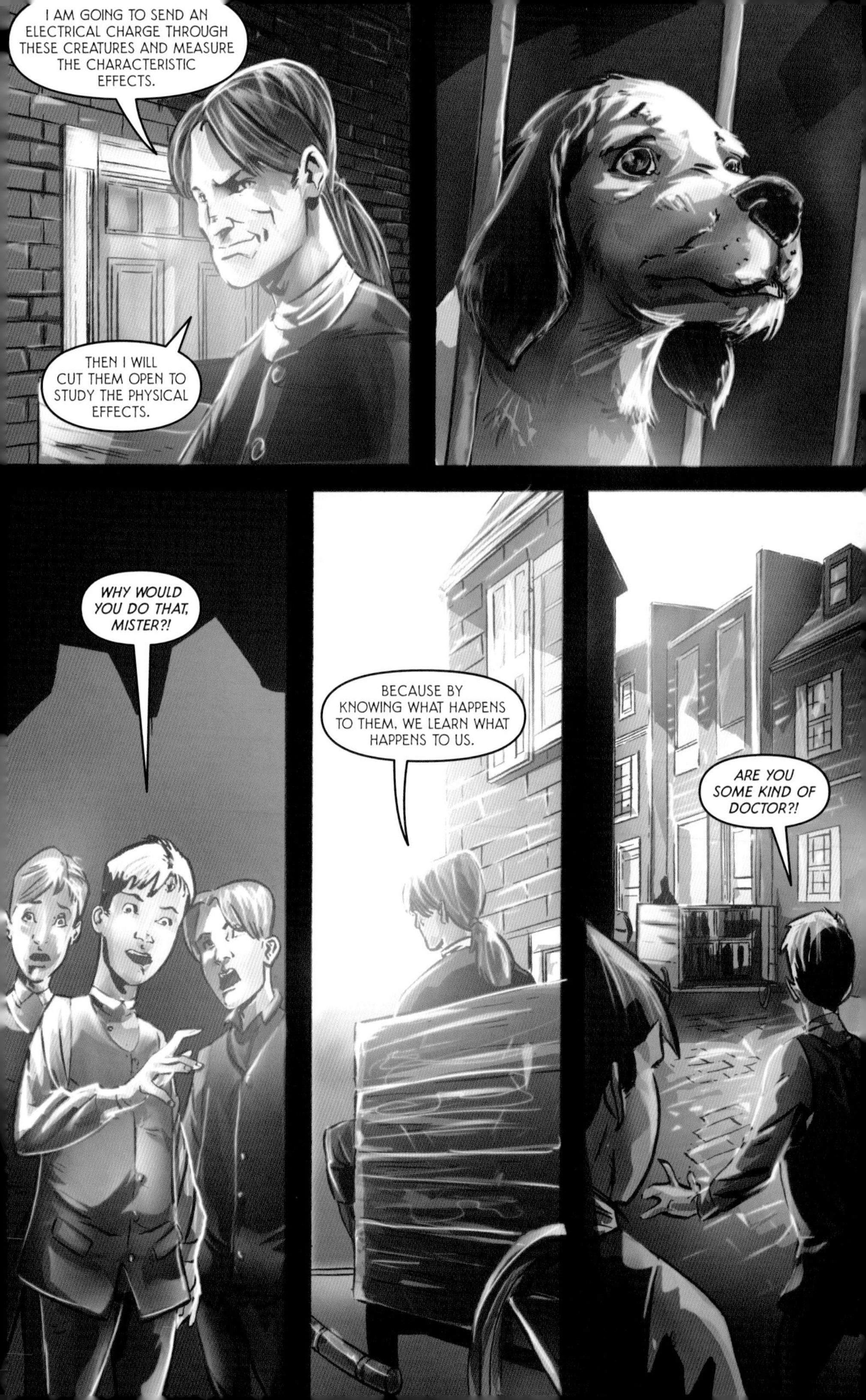

I AM GOING TO SEND AN ELECTRICAL CHARGE THROUGH THESE CREATURES AND MEASURE THE CHARACTERISTIC EFFECTS.
THEN I WILL CUT THEM OPEN TO STUDY THE PHYSICAL EFFECTS.
WHY WOULD YOU DO THAT, MISTER?!
BECAUSE BY KNOWING WHAT HAPPENS TO THEM, WE LEARN WHAT HAPPENS TO US.
ARE YOU SOME KIND OF DOCTOR?!

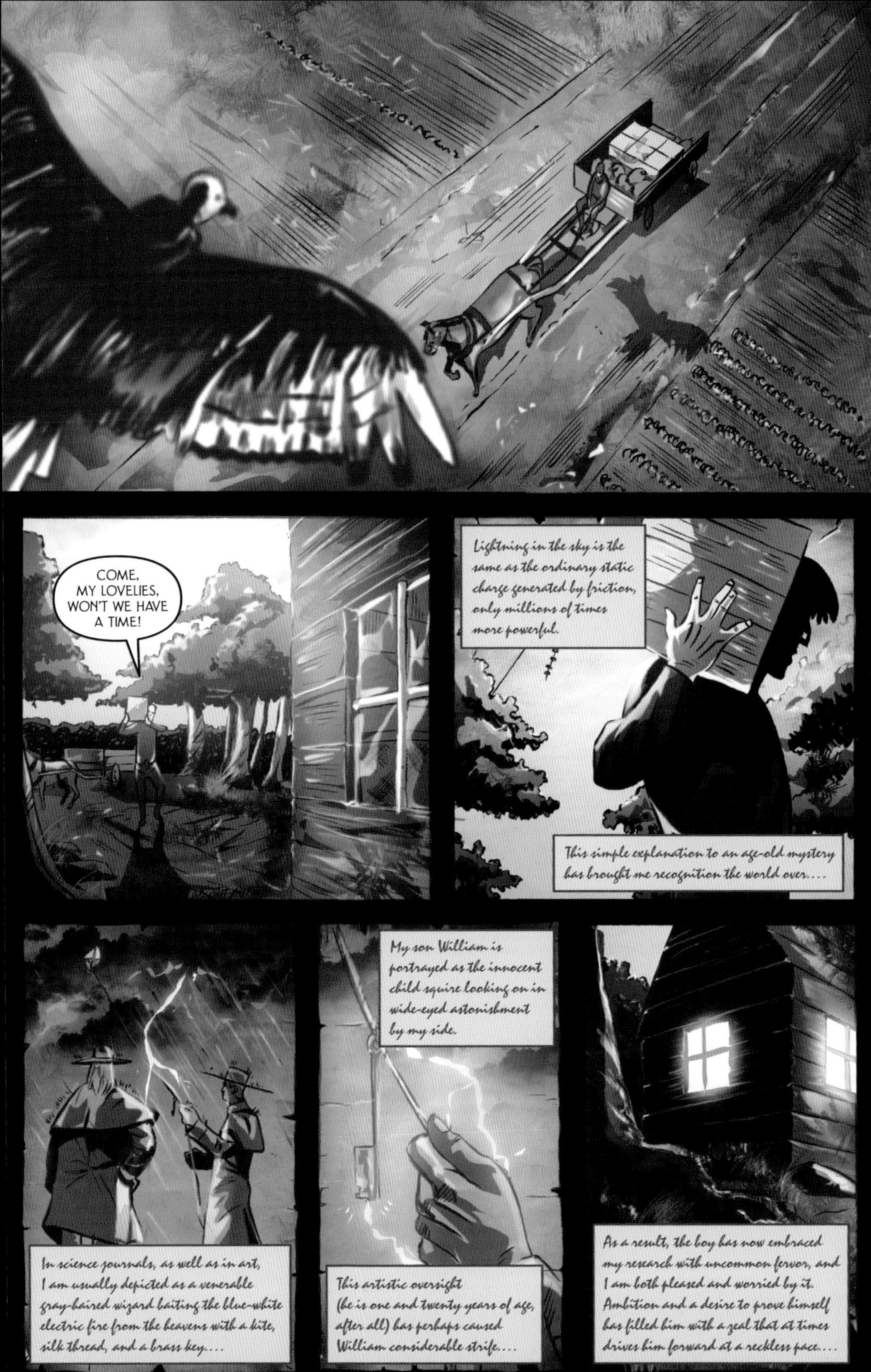
COME, MY LOVELIES, WON'T WE HAVE A TIME!
Lightning in the sky is the same as the ordinary static charge generated by friction, only millions of times more powerful.
This simple explanation to an age-old mystery has brought me recognition the world over. . . .
In science journals, as well as in art, I am usually depicted as a venerable gray-haired wizard baiting the blue-white electric fire from the heavens with a kite, silk thread, and a brass key. . .
My son William is portrayed as the innocent child squire looking on in wide-eyed astonishment by my side.
This artistic oversight (he is one and twenty years of age, after all) has perhaps caused William considerable strife. . .
As a result, the boy has now embraced my research with uncommon fervor, and I am both pleased and worried by it. Ambition and a desire to prove himself has filled him with a zeal that at times drives him forward at a reckless pace. . . .

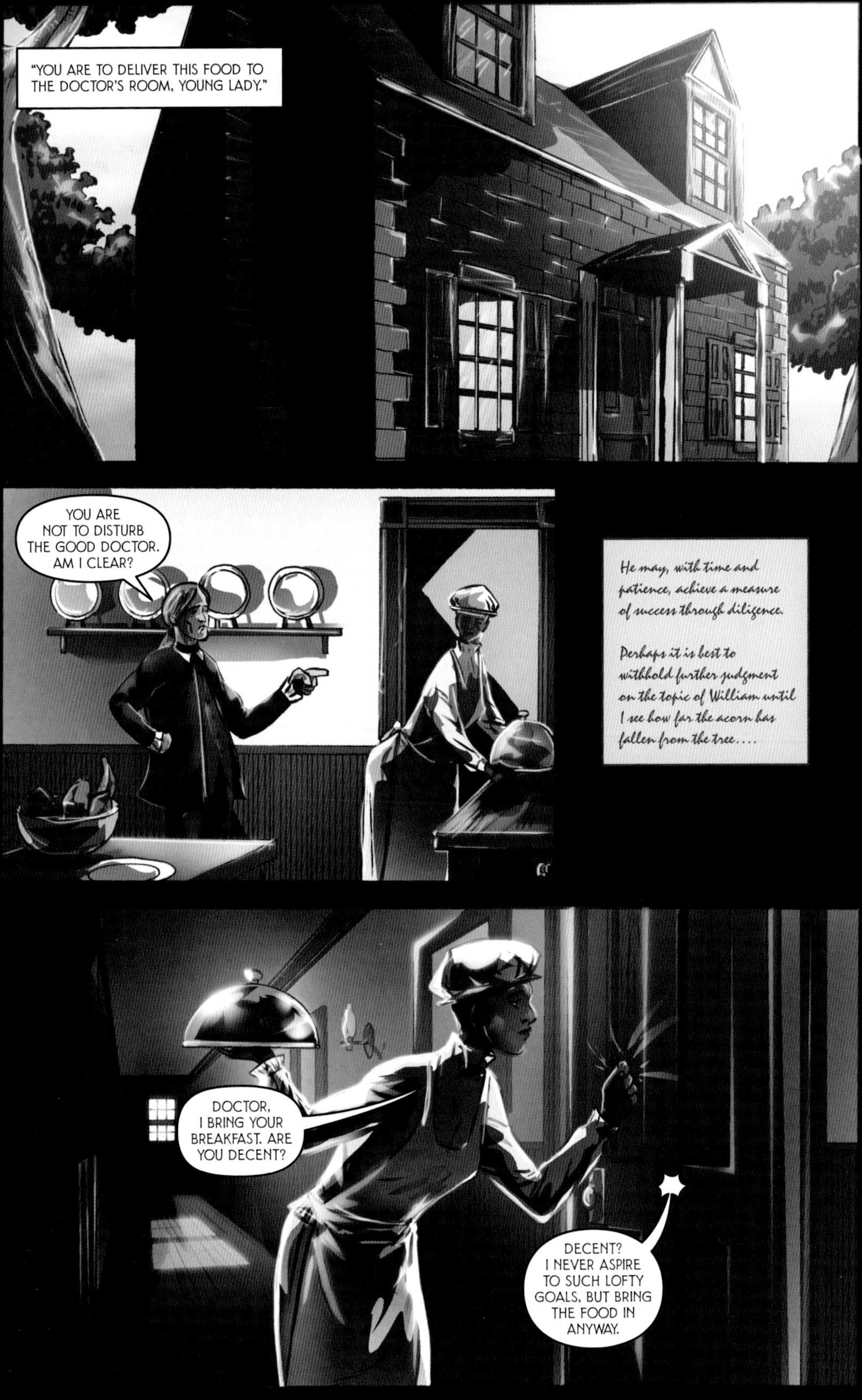
"YOU ARE TO DELIVER THIS FOOD TO THE DOCTOR'S ROOM, YOUNG LADY."
YOU ARE NOT TO DISTURB THE GOOD DOCTOR. AM I CLEAR?
He may, with time and patience, achieve a measure of success through diligence.
Perhaps it is best to withhold further judgment on the topic of William until I see how far the acorn has fallen from the tree....
DOCTOR, I BRING YOUR BREAKFAST. ARE YOU DECENT?
DECENT? I NEVER ASPIRE TO SUCH LOFTY GOALS, BUT BRING THE FOOD IN ANYWAY.

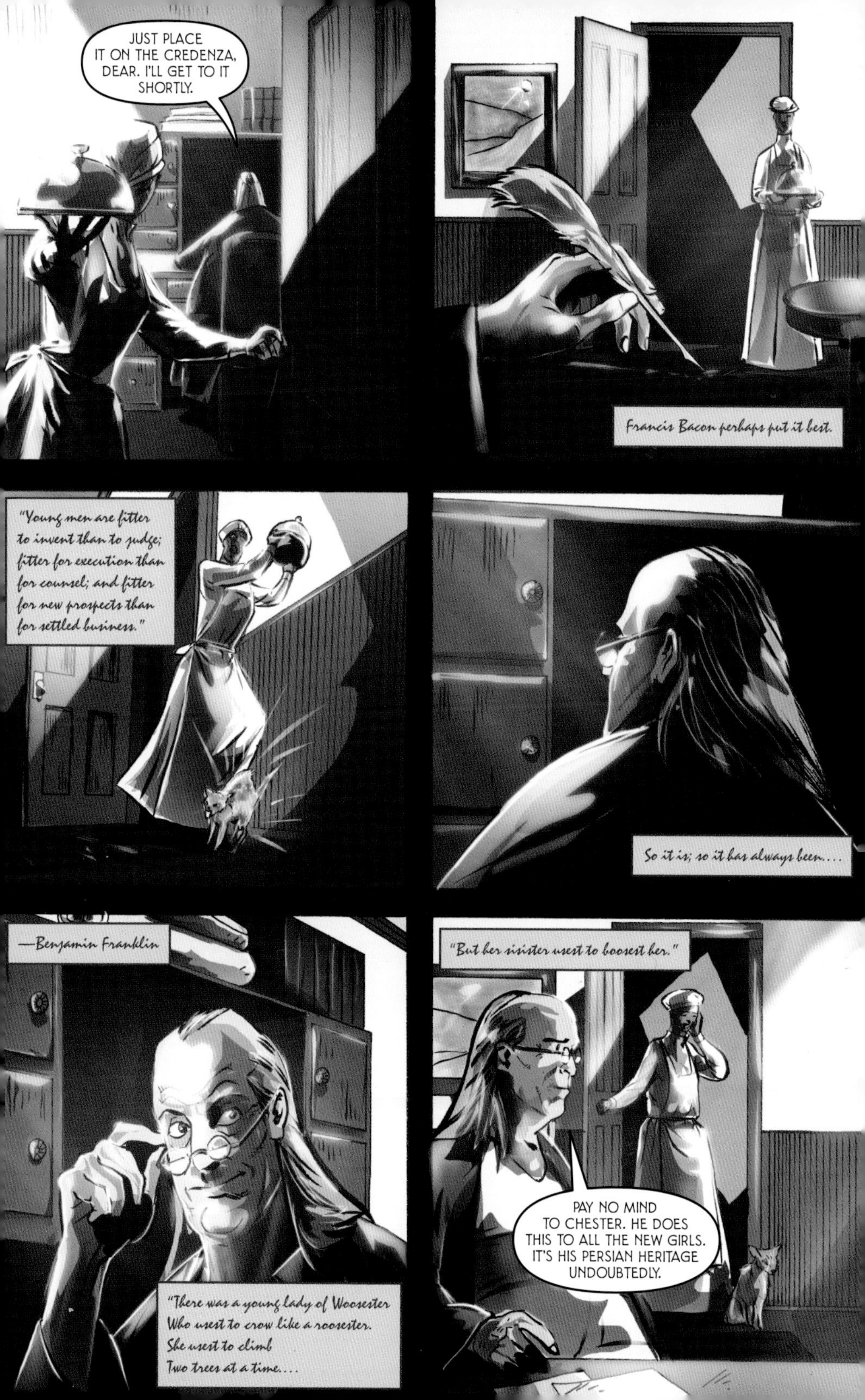
JUST PLACE IT ON THE CREDENZA, DEAR. I'LL GET TO IT SHORTLY.
Francis Bacon perhaps put it best.
"Young men are fitter to invent than to judge; fitter for execution than for counsel; and fitter for new prospects than for settled business."
So it is; so it has always been....
—Benjamin Franklin
"There was a young lady of Woosester
Who usest to crow like a roosester.
She usest to climb
Two trees at a time....
"But her sisister usest to boosest her."
PAY NO MIND TO CHESTER. HE DOES THIS TO ALL THE NEW GIRLS. IT'S HIS PERSIAN HERITAGE UNDOUBTEDLY.

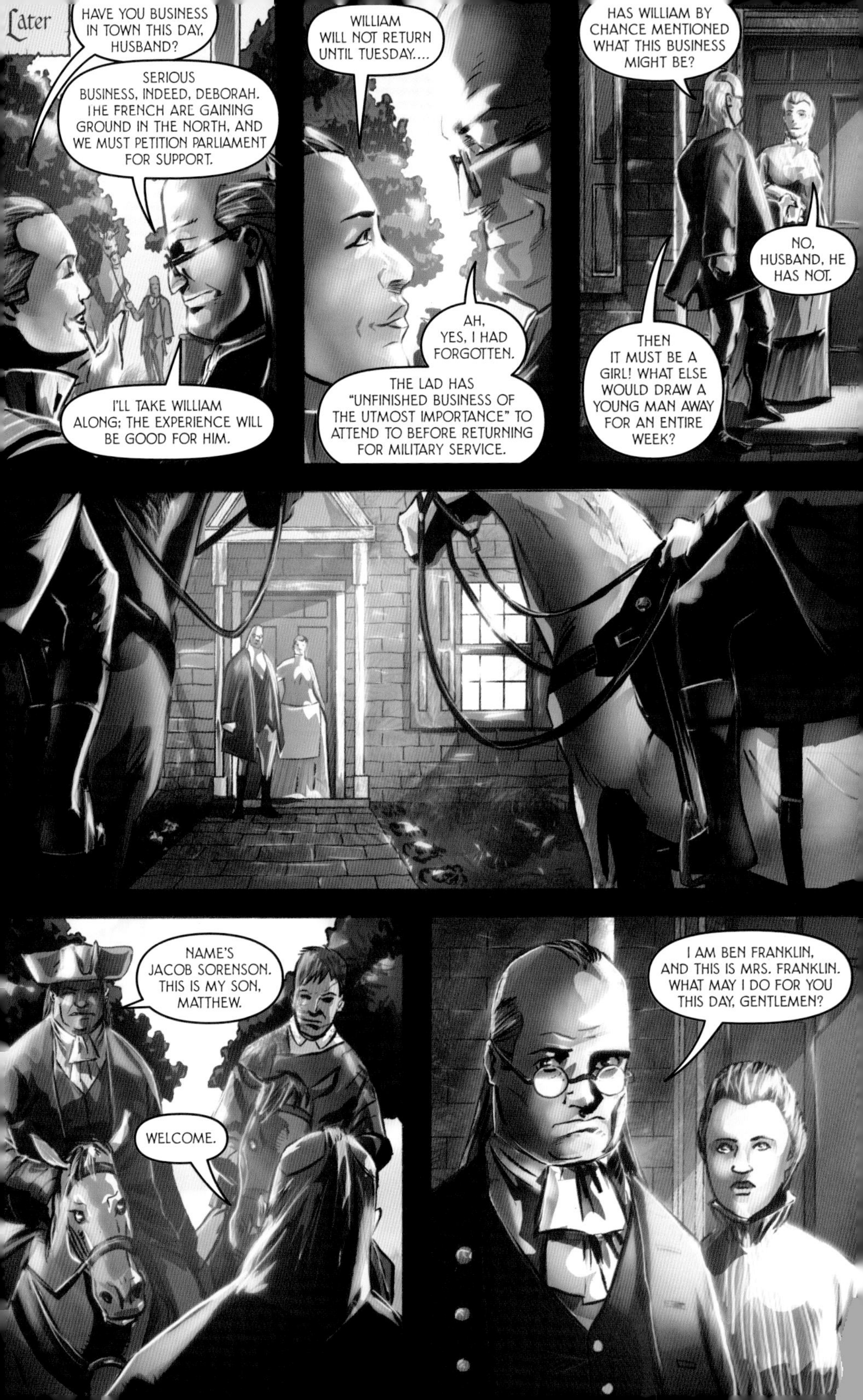
Later
HAVE YOU BUSINESS IN TOWN THIS DAY, HUSBAND?
SERIOUS BUSINESS, INDEED, DEBORAH. THE FRENCH ARE GAINING GROUND IN THE NORTH, AND WE MUST PETITION PARLIAMENT FOR SUPPORT.
I'LL TAKE WILLIAM ALONG; THE EXPERIENCE WILL BE GOOD FOR HIM.
WILLIAM WILL NOT RETURN UNTIL TUESDAY....
AH, YES, I HAD FORGOTTEN.
THE LAD HAS "UNFINISHED BUSINESS OF THE UTMOST IMPORTANCE" TO ATTEND TO BEFORE RETURNING FOR MILITARY SERVICE.
HAS WILLIAM BY CHANCE MENTIONED WHAT THIS BUSINESS MIGHT BE?
NO, HUSBAND, HE HAS NOT.
THEN IT MUST BE A GIRL! WHAT ELSE WOULD DRAW A YOUNG MAN AWAY FOR AN ENTIRE WEEK?
NAME'S JACOB SORENSON. THIS IS MY SON, MATTHEW.
WELCOME.
I AM BEN FRANKLIN, AND THIS IS MRS. FRANKLIN. WHAT MAY I DO FOR YOU THIS DAY, GENTLEMEN?

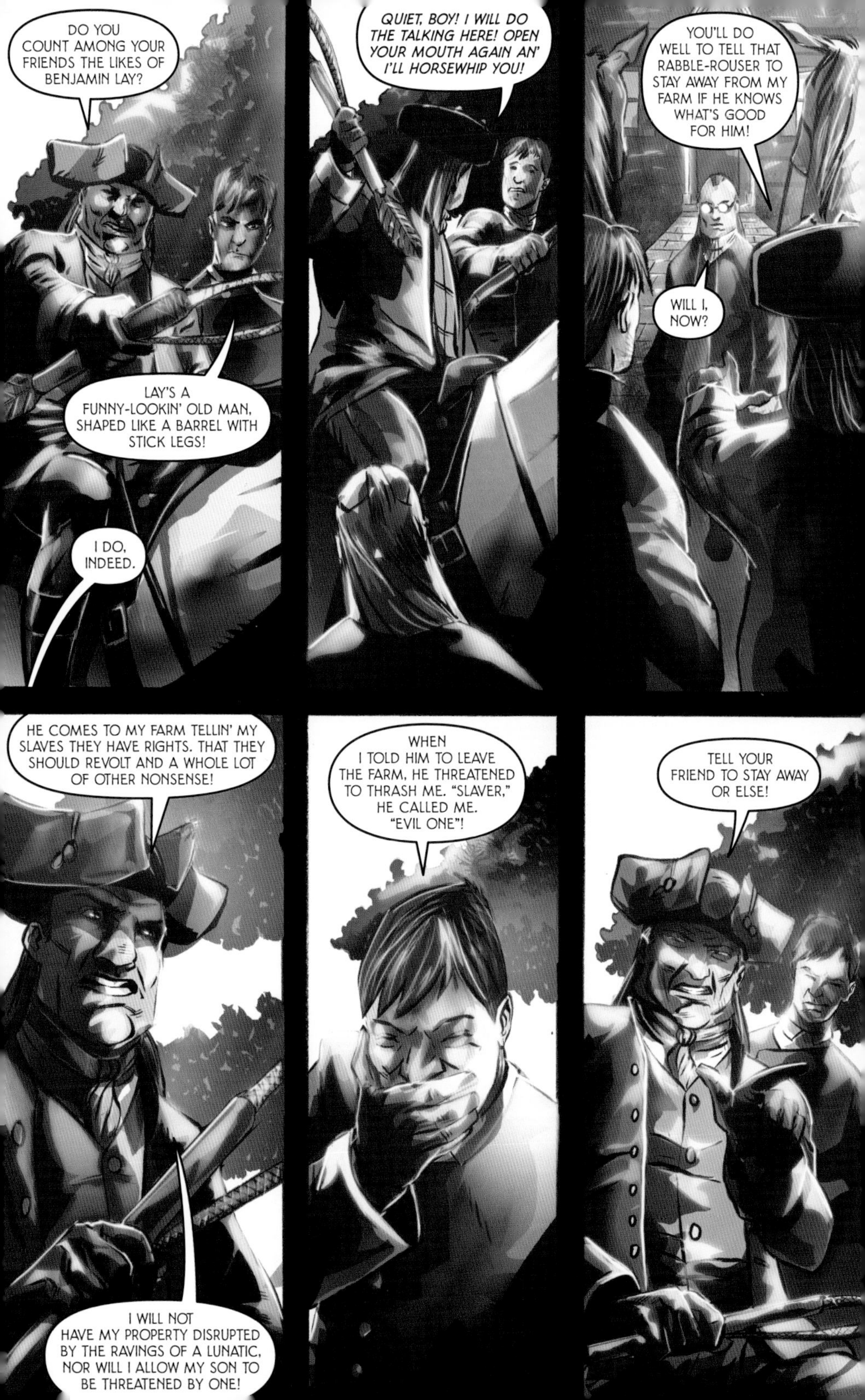
DO YOU COUNT AMONG YOUR FRIENDS THE LIKES OF BENJAMIN LAY?
LAY'S A FUNNY-LOOKIN' OLD MAN, SHAPED LIKE A BARREL WITH STICK LEGS!
I DO, INDEED.
QUIET, BOY! I WILL DO THE TALKING HERE! OPEN YOUR MOUTH AGAIN AN' I'LL HORSEWHIP YOU!
YOU'LL DO WELL TO TELL THAT RABBLE-ROUSER TO STAY AWAY FROM MY FARM IF HE KNOWS WHAT'S GOOD FOR HIM!
WILL I, NOW?
HE COMES TO MY FARM TELLIN' MY SLAVES THEY HAVE RIGHTS. THAT THEY SHOULD REVOLT AND A WHOLE LOT OF OTHER NONSENSE!
I WILL NOT HAVE MY PROPERTY DISRUPTED BY THE RAVINGS OF A LUNATIC, NOR WILL I ALLOW MY SON TO BE THREATENED BY ONE!
WHEN I TOLD HIM TO LEAVE THE FARM, HE THREATENED TO THRASH ME. "SLAVER," HE CALLED ME. "EVIL ONE"!
TELL YOUR FRIEND TO STAY AWAY OR ELSE!

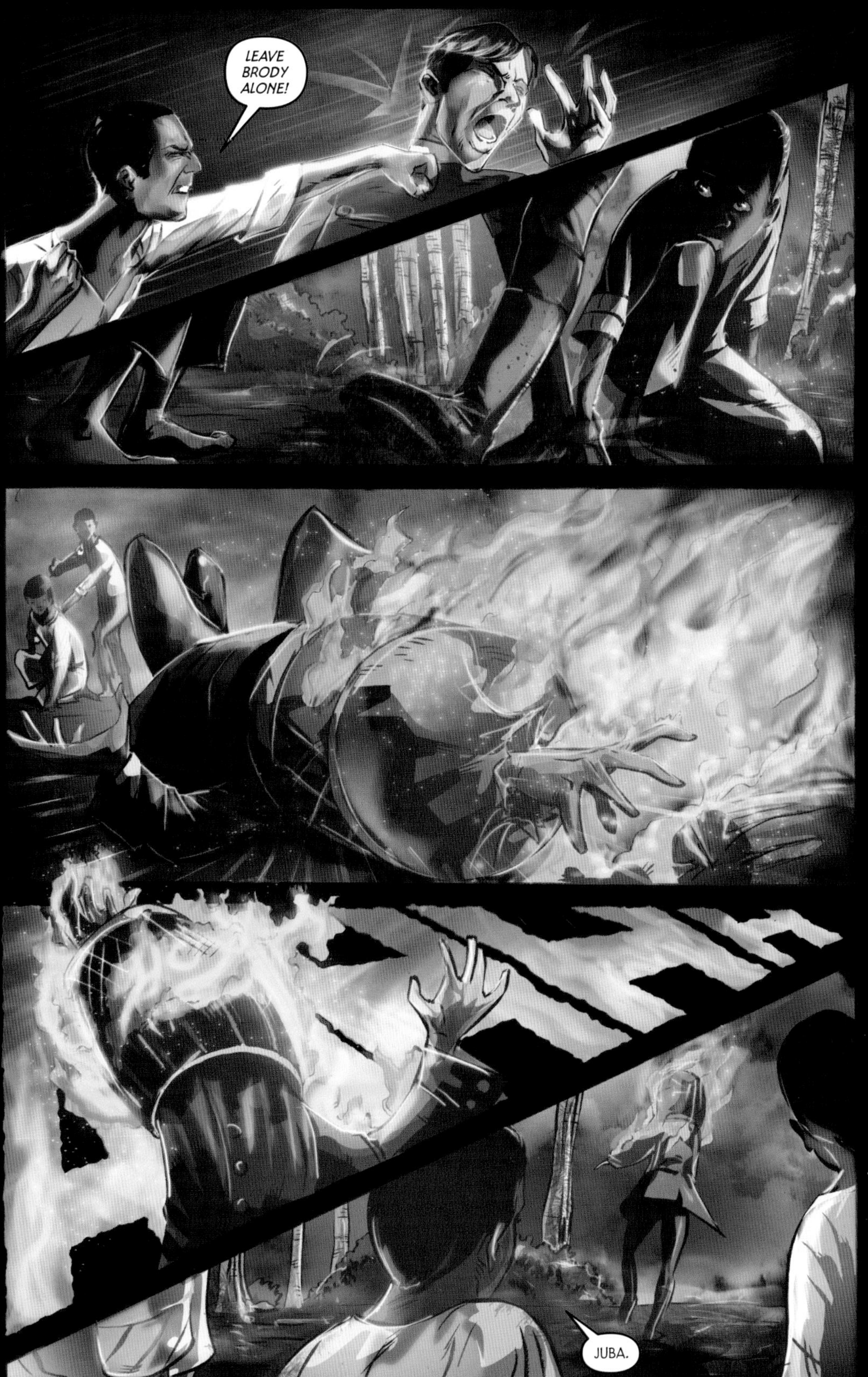
LEAVE BRODY ALONE!
JUBA.

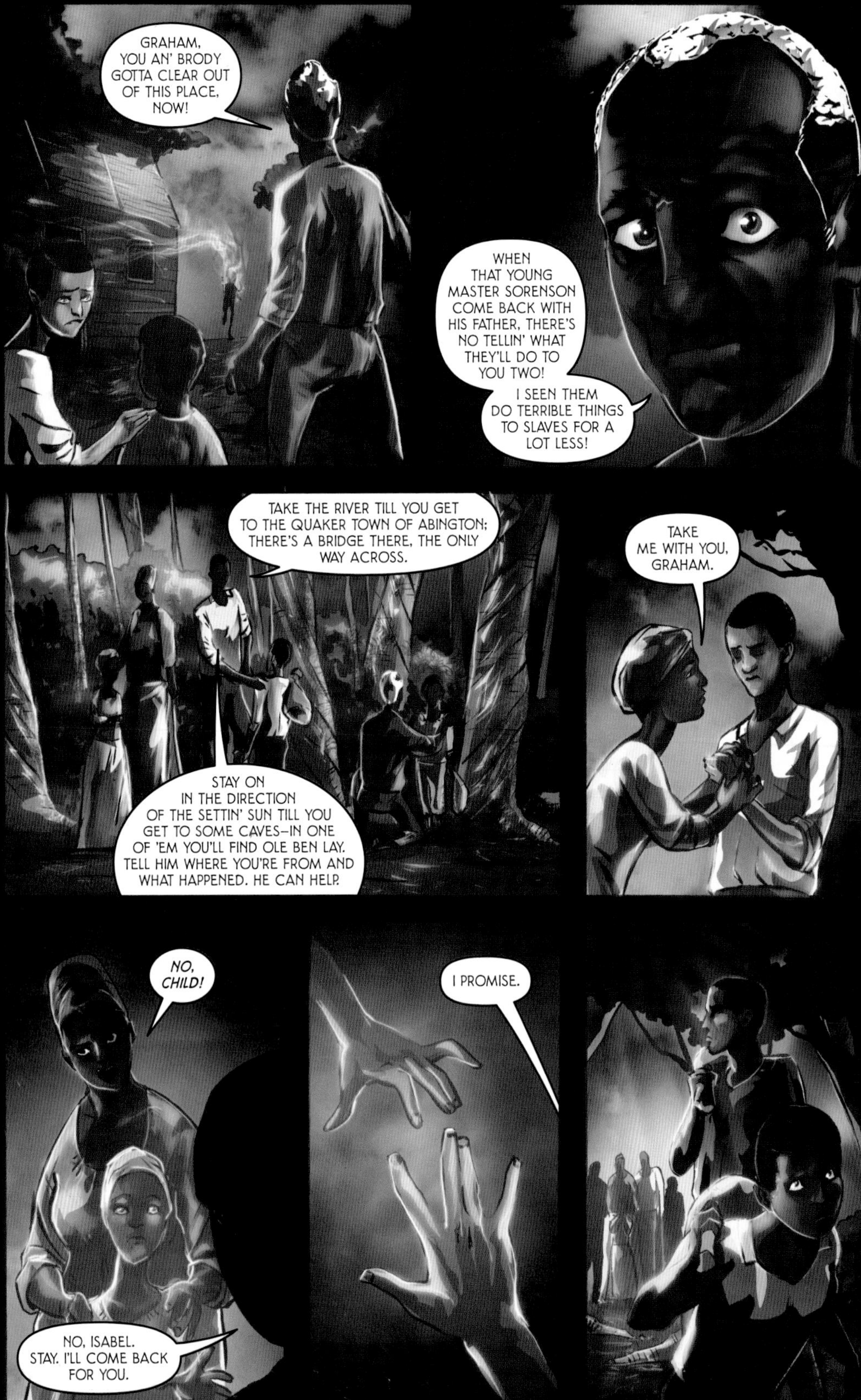
GRAHAM, YOU AN' BRODY GOTTA CLEAR OUT OF THIS PLACE, NOW!
WHEN THAT YOUNG MASTER SORENSON COME BACK WITH HIS FATHER, THERE'S NO TELLIN' WHAT THEY'LL DO TO YOU TWO!
I SEEN THEM DO TERRIBLE THINGS TO SLAVES FOR A LOT LESS!
TAKE THE RIVER TILL YOU GET TO THE QUAKER TOWN OF ABINGTON; THERE'S A BRIDGE THERE, THE ONLY WAY ACROSS.
STAY ON IN THE DIRECTION OF THE SETTIN' SUN TILL YOU GET TO SOME CAVES—IN ONE OF 'EM YOU'LL FIND OLE BEN LAY. TELL HIM WHERE YOU'RE FROM AND WHAT HAPPENED. HE CAN HELP.
TAKE ME WITH YOU, GRAHAM.
NO, CHILD!
NO, ISABEL. STAY. I'LL COME BACK FOR YOU.
I PROMISE.

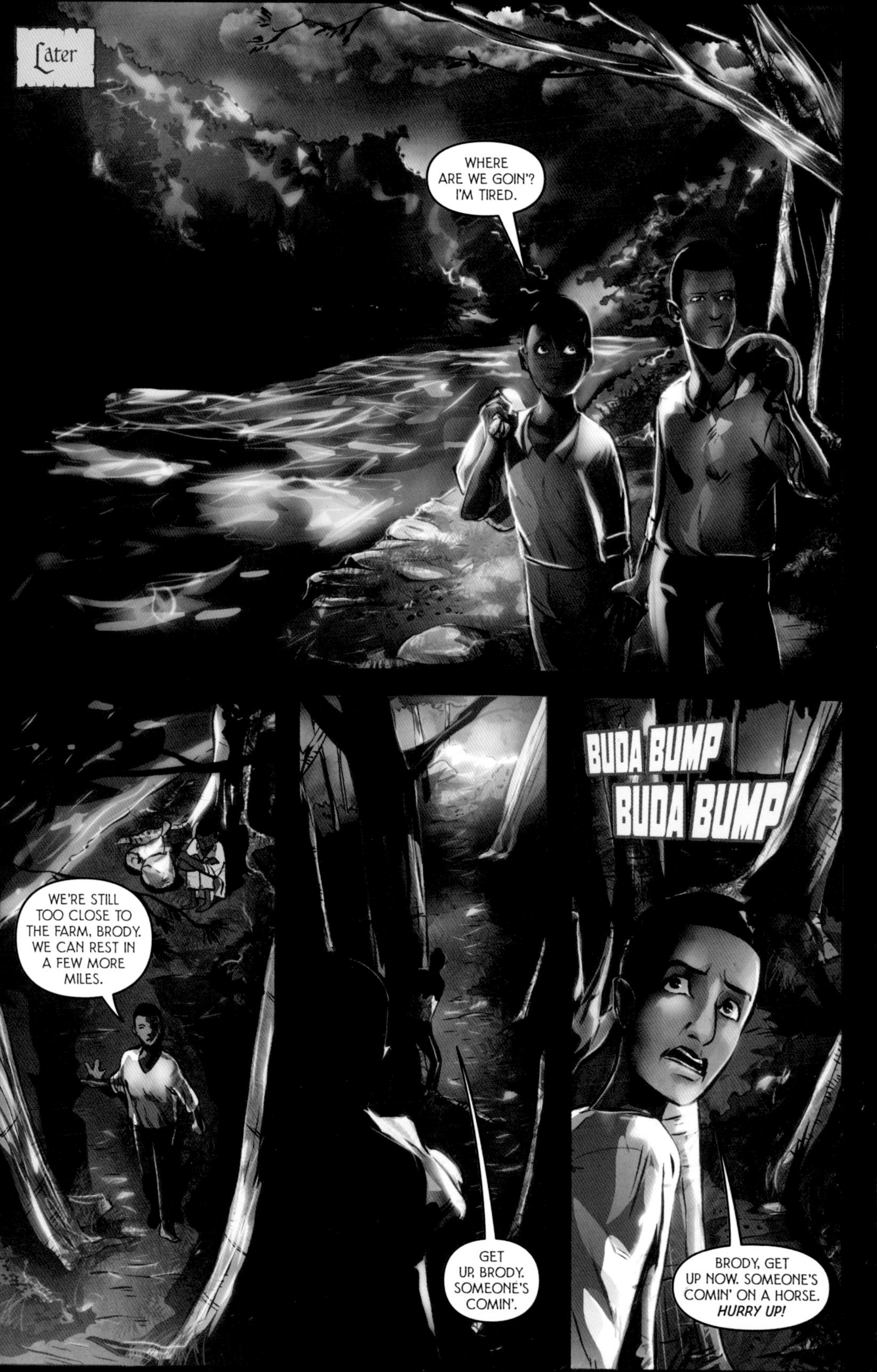
Later
WHERE ARE WE GOIN'? I'M TIRED.
WE'RE STILL TOO CLOSE TO THE FARM, BRODY. WE CAN REST IN A FEW MORE MILES.
GET UP, BRODY. SOMEONE'S COMIN'.
BUDA BUMP
BUDA BUMP
BRODY, GET UP NOW. SOMEONE'S COMIN' ON A HORSE. *HURRY UP!*

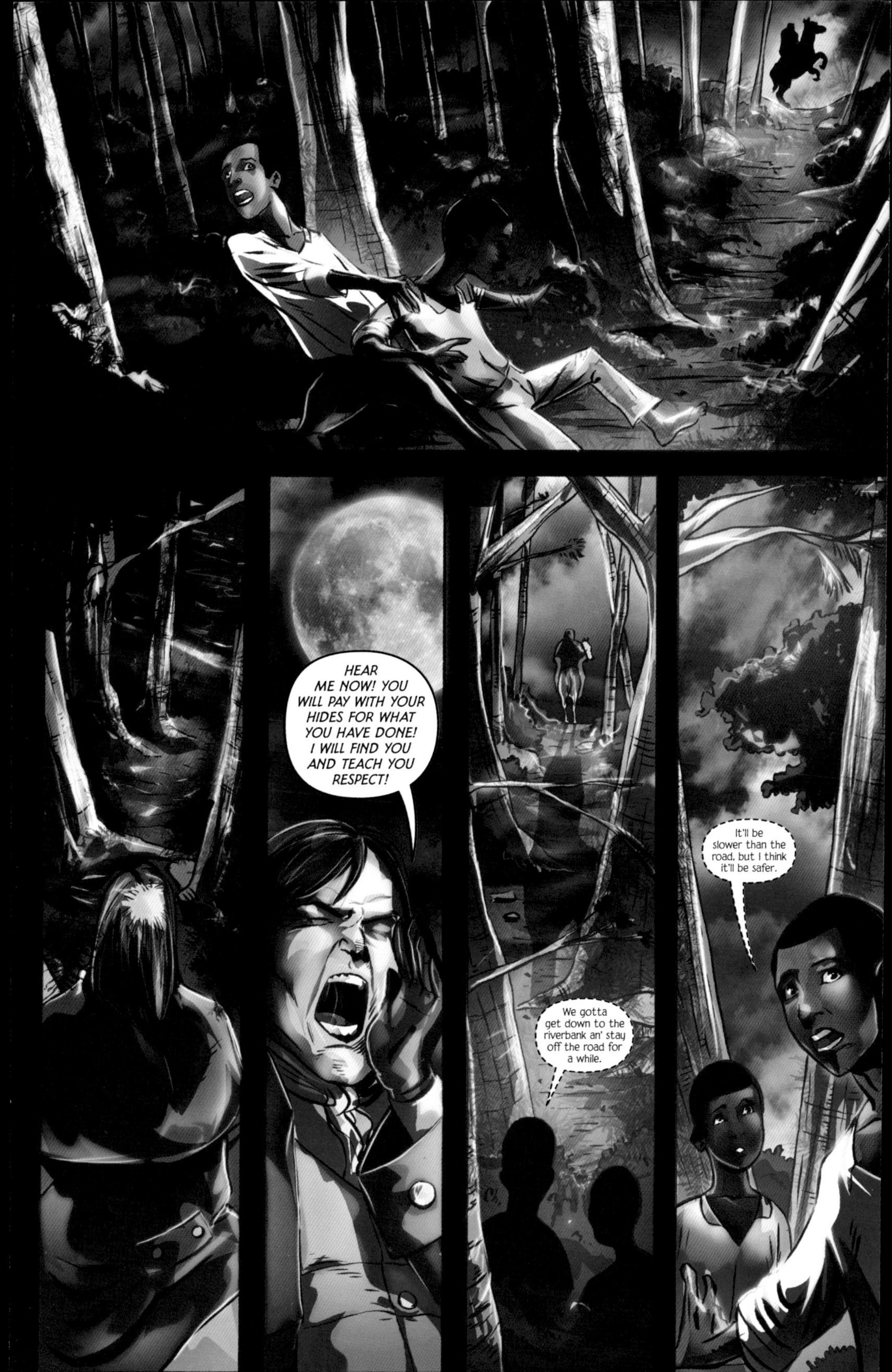
HEAR ME NOW! YOU WILL PAY WITH YOUR HIDES FOR WHAT YOU HAVE DONE! I WILL FIND YOU AND TEACH YOU RESPECT!
We gotta get down to the riverbank an' stay off the road for a while.
It'll be slower than the road, but I think it'll be safer.

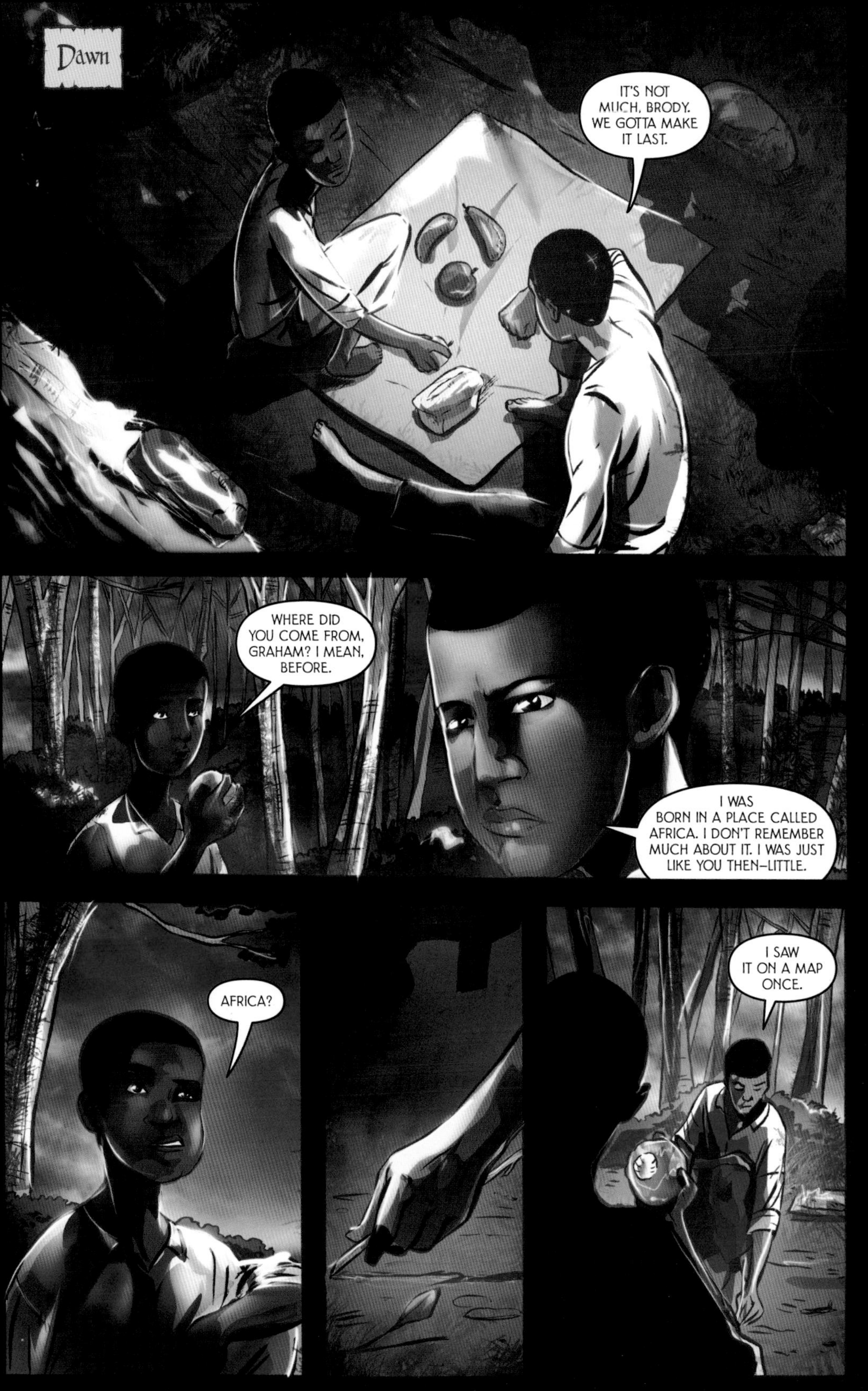
Dawn
IT'S NOT MUCH, BRODY. WE GOTTA MAKE IT LAST.
WHERE DID YOU COME FROM, GRAHAM? I MEAN, BEFORE.
I WAS BORN IN A PLACE CALLED AFRICA. I DON'T REMEMBER MUCH ABOUT IT. I WAS JUST LIKE YOU THEN–LITTLE.
AFRICA?
I SAW IT ON A MAP ONCE.

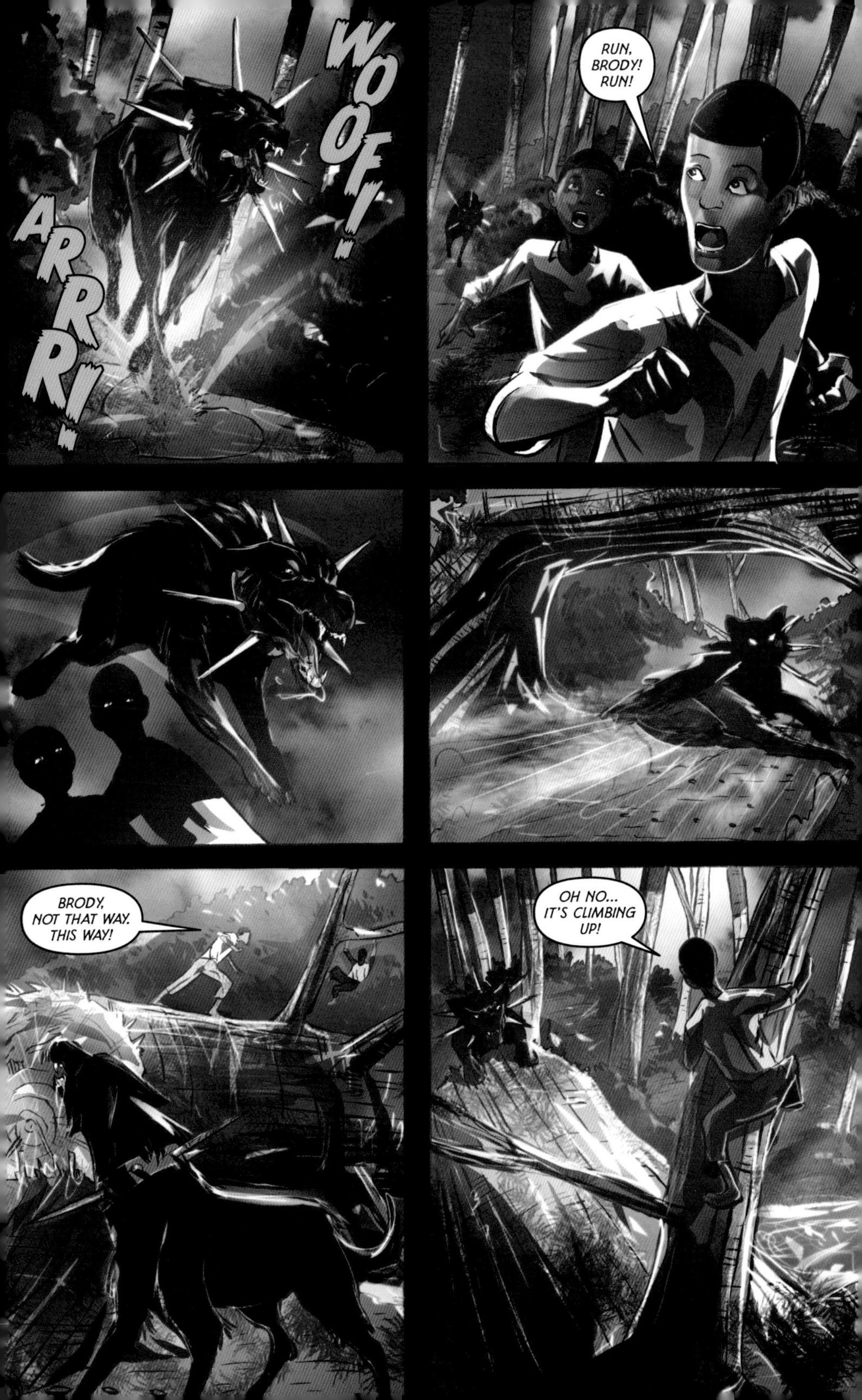
WOOF!!
ARRR!!
RUN, BRODY! RUN!
BRODY, NOT THAT WAY. THIS WAY!
OH NO... IT'S CLIMBING UP!

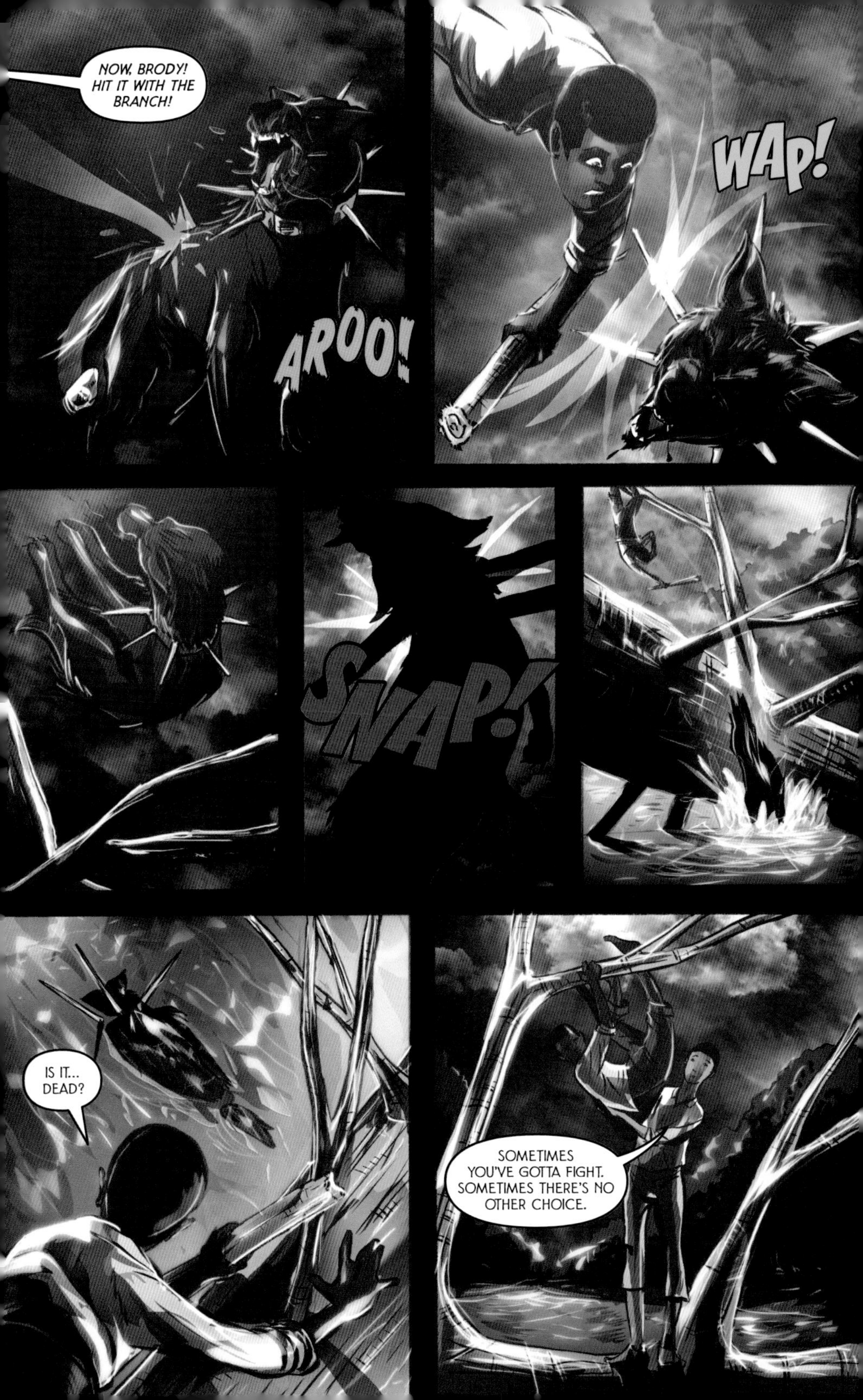
NOW, BRODY! HIT IT WITH THE BRANCH!
AROO!
WAP!
SNAP!
IS IT... DEAD?
SOMETIMES YOU'VE GOTTA FIGHT. SOMETIMES THERE'S NO OTHER CHOICE.

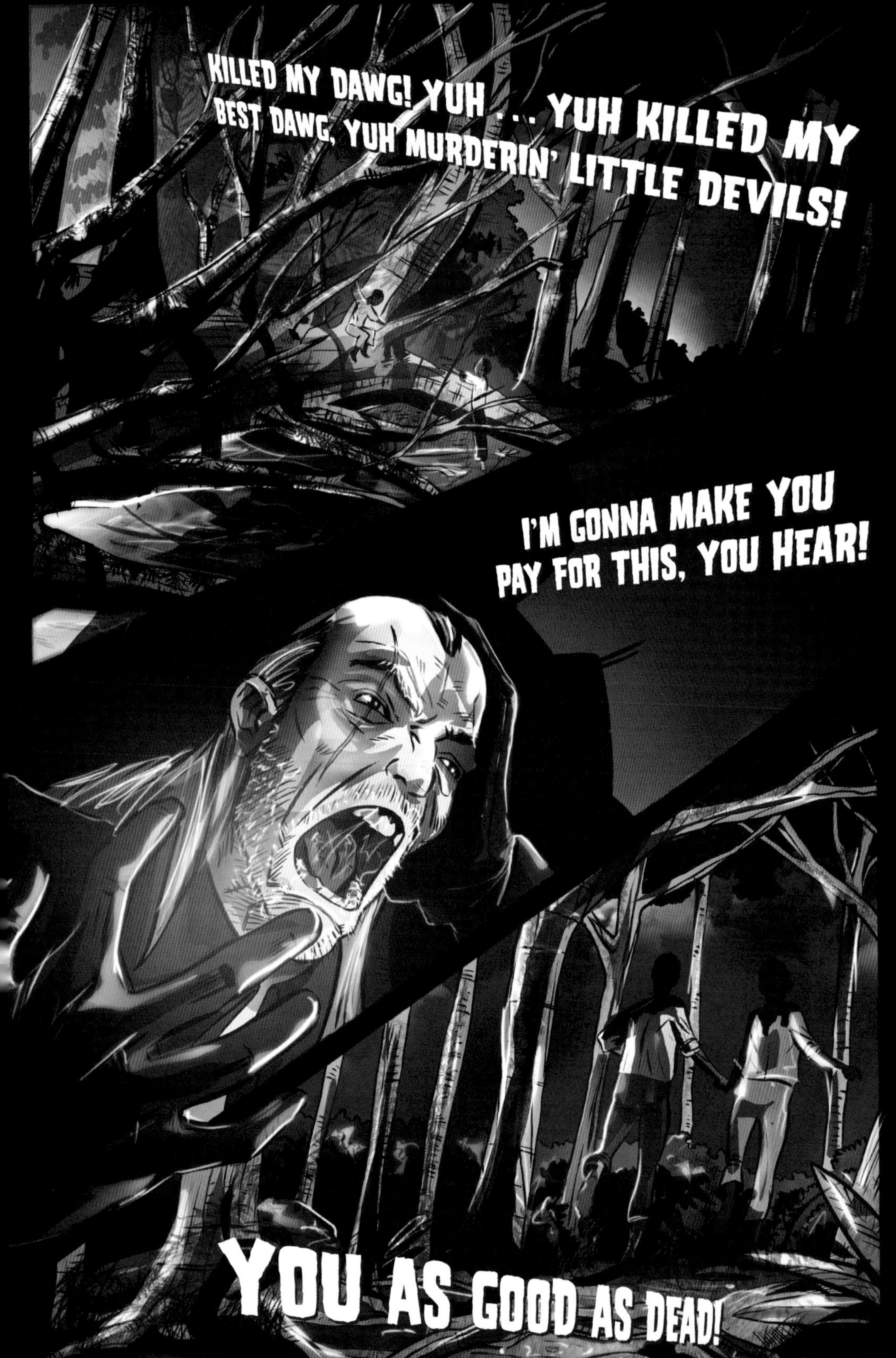
KILLED MY DAWG! YUH . . . YUH KILLED MY BEST DAWG, YUH MURDERIN' LITTLE DEVILS!
I'M GONNA MAKE YOU PAY FOR THIS, YOU HEAR!
YOU AS GOOD AS DEAD!

HEH...HEH...
I SHALL REPLY TO THIS
LETTER WITH A THANK-YOU,
FOR THE KIND ATTENTION
IT SHOWS.

IT IS, HOWEVER,
UNNECESSARY FOR THE
GOOD DR. FRANKLIN TO
CONCERN HIMSELF WITH
MY WELFARE.

ALTHOUGH
MY PERSON IS
DISAGREEABLE
TO SOME, I AM
KNOWN AND
TOLERATED, IF NOT
RESPECTED, BY
MANY MORE.

INJURY CAUSED
TO ME WOULD REAP RUIN FOR
SORENSON'S BUSINESS INTERESTS
IN ABINGTON, AND I DO NOT
BELIEVE HIM TO BE THAT
MUCH A FOOL.

I SHALL
COMPOSE A REPLY IN WRITING
TO DR. FRANKLIN. WOULD YE BE
SO KIND TO DELIVER IT TO HIM
FOR ME? HERE IS PAYMENT
FOR YE TROUBLE.

HONEST PAY
FOR HONEST WORK:
THE RIGHT OF ALL
FREE MEN.

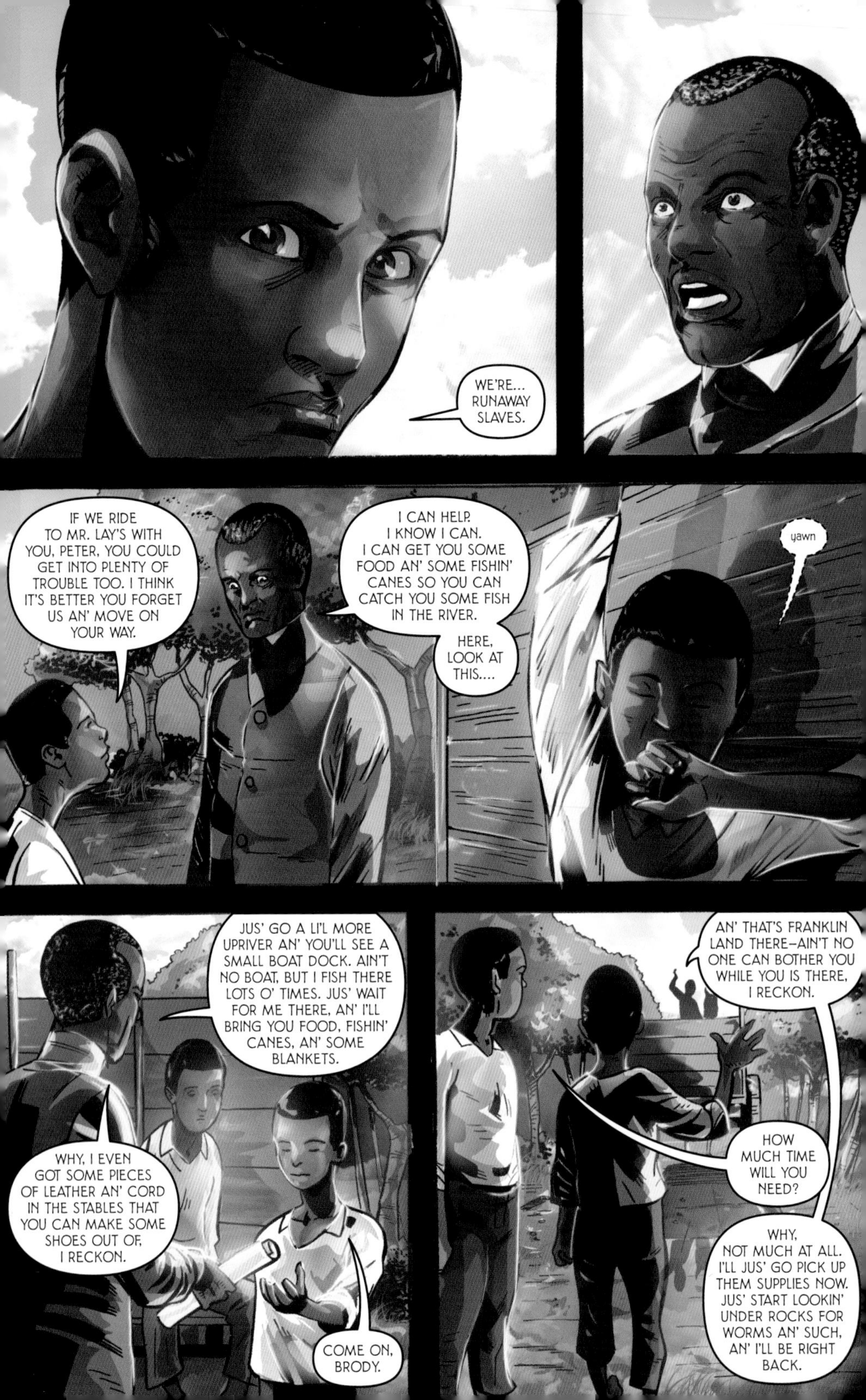
WE'RE... RUNAWAY SLAVES.
IF WE RIDE TO MR. LAY'S WITH YOU, PETER, YOU COULD GET INTO PLENTY OF TROUBLE TOO. I THINK IT'S BETTER YOU FORGET US AN' MOVE ON YOUR WAY.
I CAN HELP. I KNOW I CAN. I CAN GET YOU SOME FOOD AN' SOME FISHIN' CANES SO YOU CAN CATCH YOU SOME FISH IN THE RIVER.
HERE, LOOK AT THIS....
yawn
JUS' GO A LI'L MORE UPRIVER AN' YOU'LL SEE A SMALL BOAT DOCK. AIN'T NO BOAT, BUT I FISH THERE LOTS O' TIMES. JUS' WAIT FOR ME THERE, AN' I'LL BRING YOU FOOD, FISHIN' CANES, AN' SOME BLANKETS.
WHY, I EVEN GOT SOME PIECES OF LEATHER AN' CORD IN THE STABLES THAT YOU CAN MAKE SOME SHOES OUT OF, I RECKON.
COME ON, BRODY.
AN' THAT'S FRANKLIN LAND THERE—AIN'T NO ONE CAN BOTHER YOU WHILE YOU IS THERE, I RECKON.
HOW MUCH TIME WILL YOU NEED?
WHY, NOT MUCH AT ALL. I'LL JUS' GO PICK UP THEM SUPPLIES NOW. JUS' START LOOKIN' UNDER ROCKS FOR WORMS AN' SUCH, AN' I'LL BE RIGHT BACK.

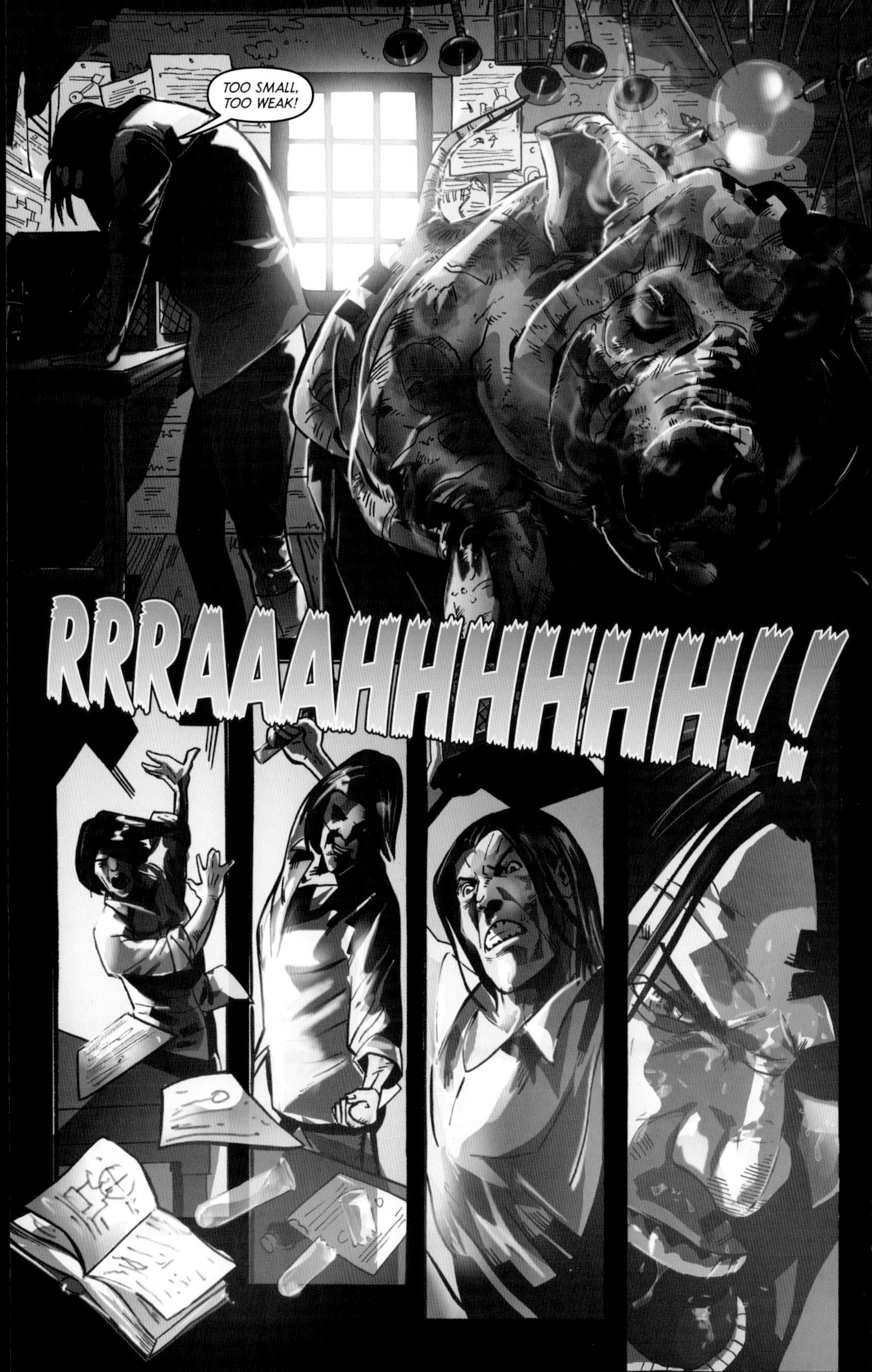
TOO SMALL, TOO WEAK!
RRRAAAHHHHHHH!!

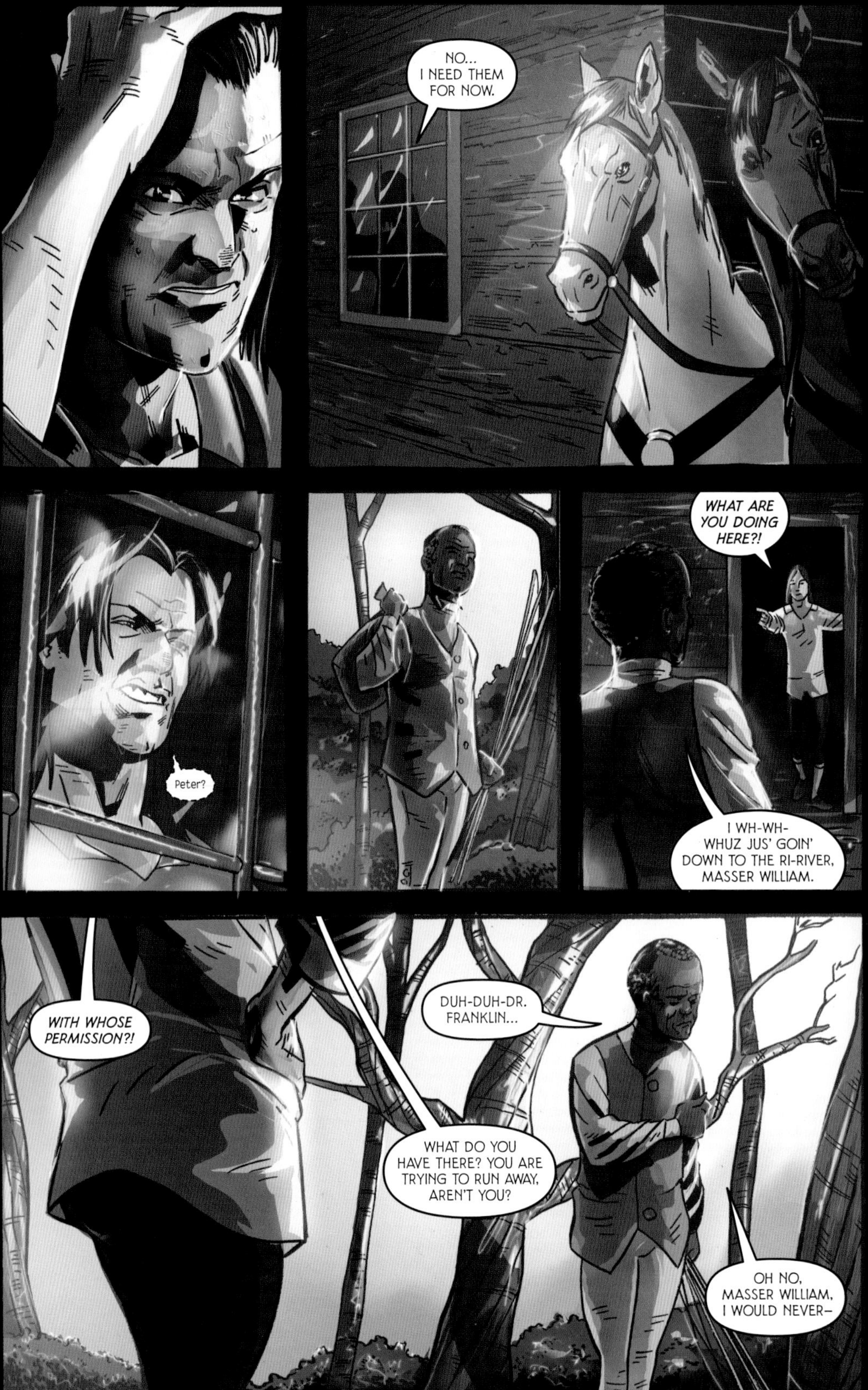
NO... I NEED THEM FOR NOW.
Peter?
WHAT ARE YOU DOING HERE?!
I WH-WH-WHUZ JUS' GOIN' DOWN TO THE RI-RIVER, MASSER WILLIAM.
WITH WHOSE PERMISSION?!
DUH-DUH-DR. FRANKLIN...
WHAT DO YOU HAVE THERE? YOU ARE TRYING TO RUN AWAY, AREN'T YOU?
OH NO, MASSER WILLIAM, I WOULD NEVER—

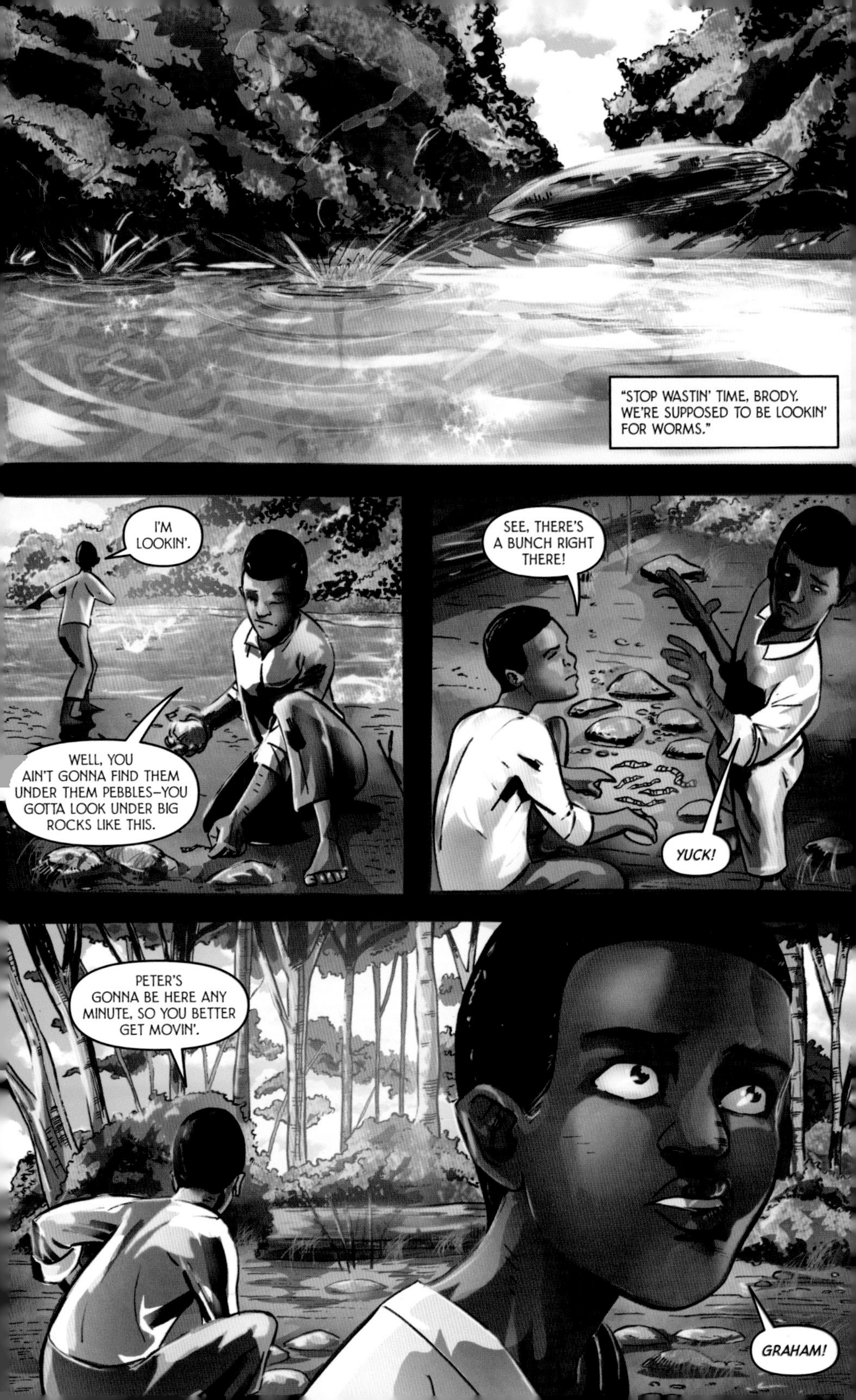
"STOP WASTIN' TIME, BRODY. WE'RE SUPPOSED TO BE LOOKIN' FOR WORMS."
I'M LOOKIN'.
WELL, YOU AIN'T GONNA FIND THEM UNDER THEM PEBBLES—YOU GOTTA LOOK UNDER BIG ROCKS LIKE THIS.
SEE, THERE'S A BUNCH RIGHT THERE!
YUCK!
PETER'S GONNA BE HERE ANY MINUTE, SO YOU BETTER GET MOVIN'.
GRAHAM!

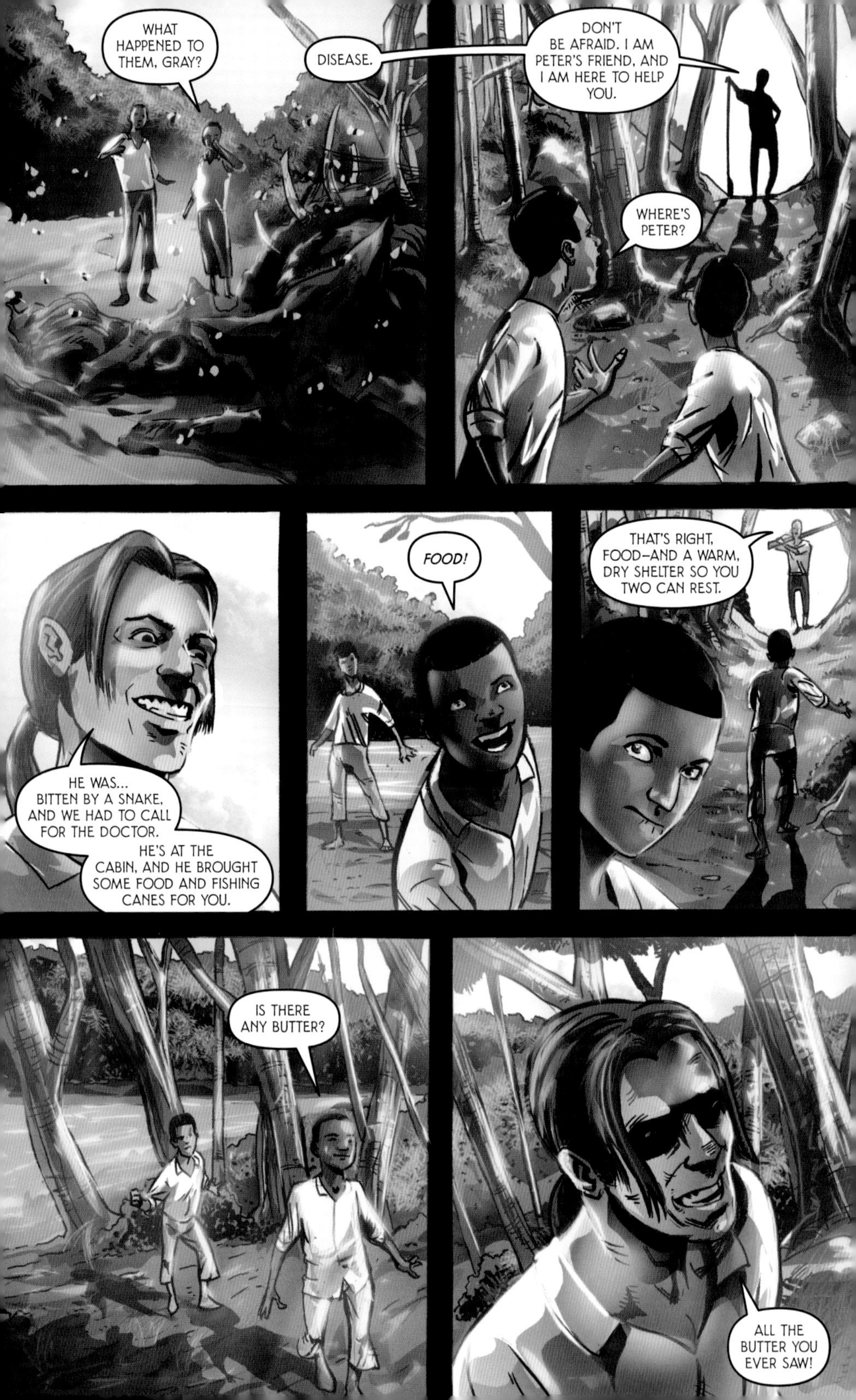
WHAT HAPPENED TO THEM, GRAY?
DISEASE.
DON'T BE AFRAID. I AM PETER'S FRIEND, AND I AM HERE TO HELP YOU.
WHERE'S PETER?
HE WAS... BITTEN BY A SNAKE, AND WE HAD TO CALL FOR THE DOCTOR.
HE'S AT THE CABIN, AND HE BROUGHT SOME FOOD AND FISHING CANES FOR YOU.
FOOD!
THAT'S RIGHT, FOOD—AND A WARM, DRY SHELTER SO YOU TWO CAN REST.
IS THERE ANY BUTTER?
ALL THE BUTTER YOU EVER SAW!

NOW, WHAT IS SO IMPORTANT THAT IT CANNOT WAIT AWHILE?

I FOUND THESE LI'L BOYS OUT THERE BY THE RIVER, DOCTOR. THEY IS TIRED AN' HUNGRY, AN' THEY WAITIN' FOR ME.

MUH LI'L FRIENDS GRAHAM AN' BRODY. I WAS FIXIN' TO TAKE THEM SOME FISHIN' CANES AN' FOOD, AN' NOW I CAN'T.

WHO ARE THESE BOYS?

WHERE DID THESE BOYS COME FROM?

They runaway slaves. They lookin' for ole Ben Lay. They ain't done nothin' wrong, Dr. Franklin.

Masser William say I was tryin' to run, too, but that ain't so....

OUT YON CABIN BY THE RIVER. MASSER WILLIAM SAY THAT I CAN'T SAY NOTHIN' 'BOUT SEEIN' HIM THERE, BUT MUH LI'L FRIENDS NEED ME.

BE AT EASE, PETER, AND RETURN TO THE HOUSE.

WILLIAM? HERE?

THIS IS ALL VERY STRANGE BUSINESS. JUST AS SOON AS I FINISH HERE, I WILL SEE TO GRAHAM AND BRODY MYSELF.

What are you doing in the cabin, William?

DR. FRANKLIN, YOU HAVE MISSED MY ENTIRE PRESENTATION!

LIGHTNING STRIKES THE ROD ON THE BARREL, WHICH INSTANTLY HEATS THE WATER INSIDE.

ALTHOUGH I FIND WARM BATHS ENJOYABLE, TO WAIT FOR AN ELECTRICAL STORM TO BATHE WOULD RESULT IN MY BEING THE FOULEST-SMELLING CREATURE IN PHILADELPHIA.

HAHAHA HAHA!!!

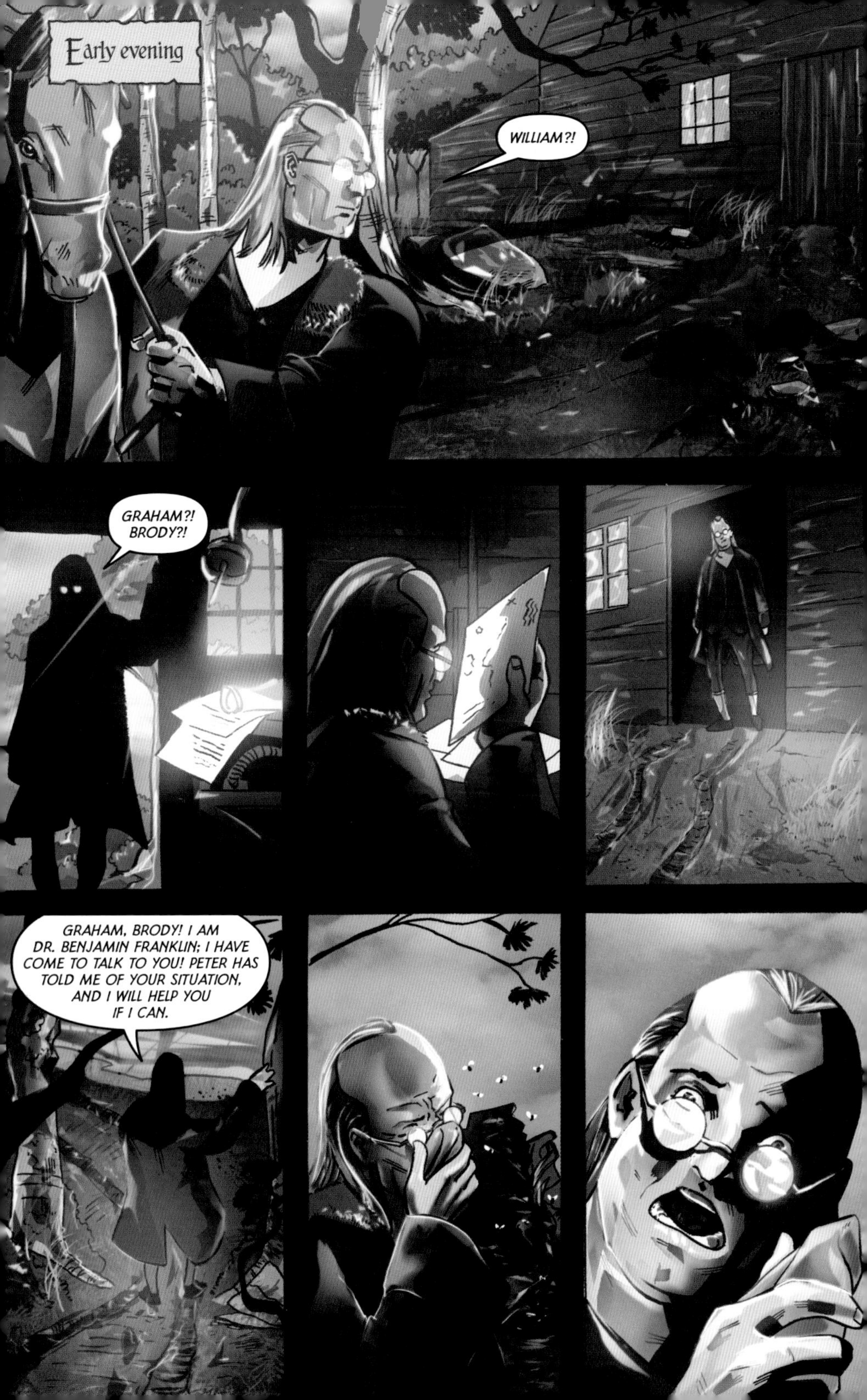
Early evening
WILLIAM?!
GRAHAM?! BRODY?!
GRAHAM, BRODY! I AM DR. BENJAMIN FRANKLIN; I HAVE COME TO TALK TO YOU! PETER HAS TOLD ME OF YOUR SITUATION, AND I WILL HELP YOU IF I CAN.

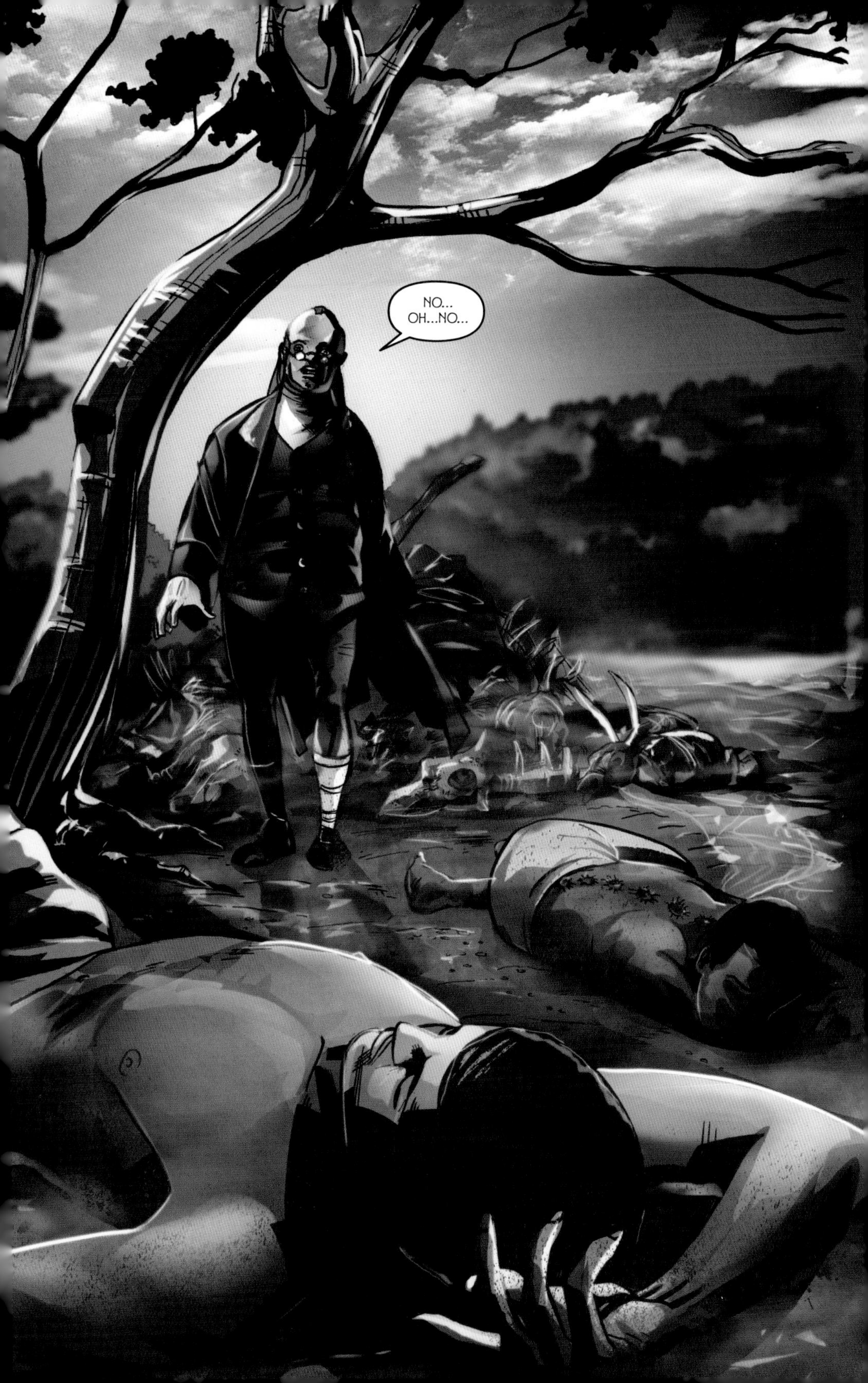
NO...
OH...NO...

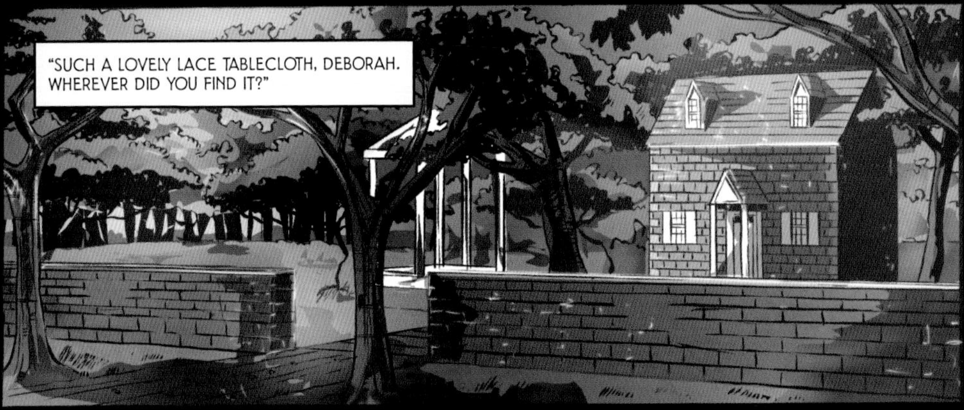
"SUCH A LOVELY LACE TABLECLOTH, DEBORAH. WHEREVER DID YOU FIND IT?"

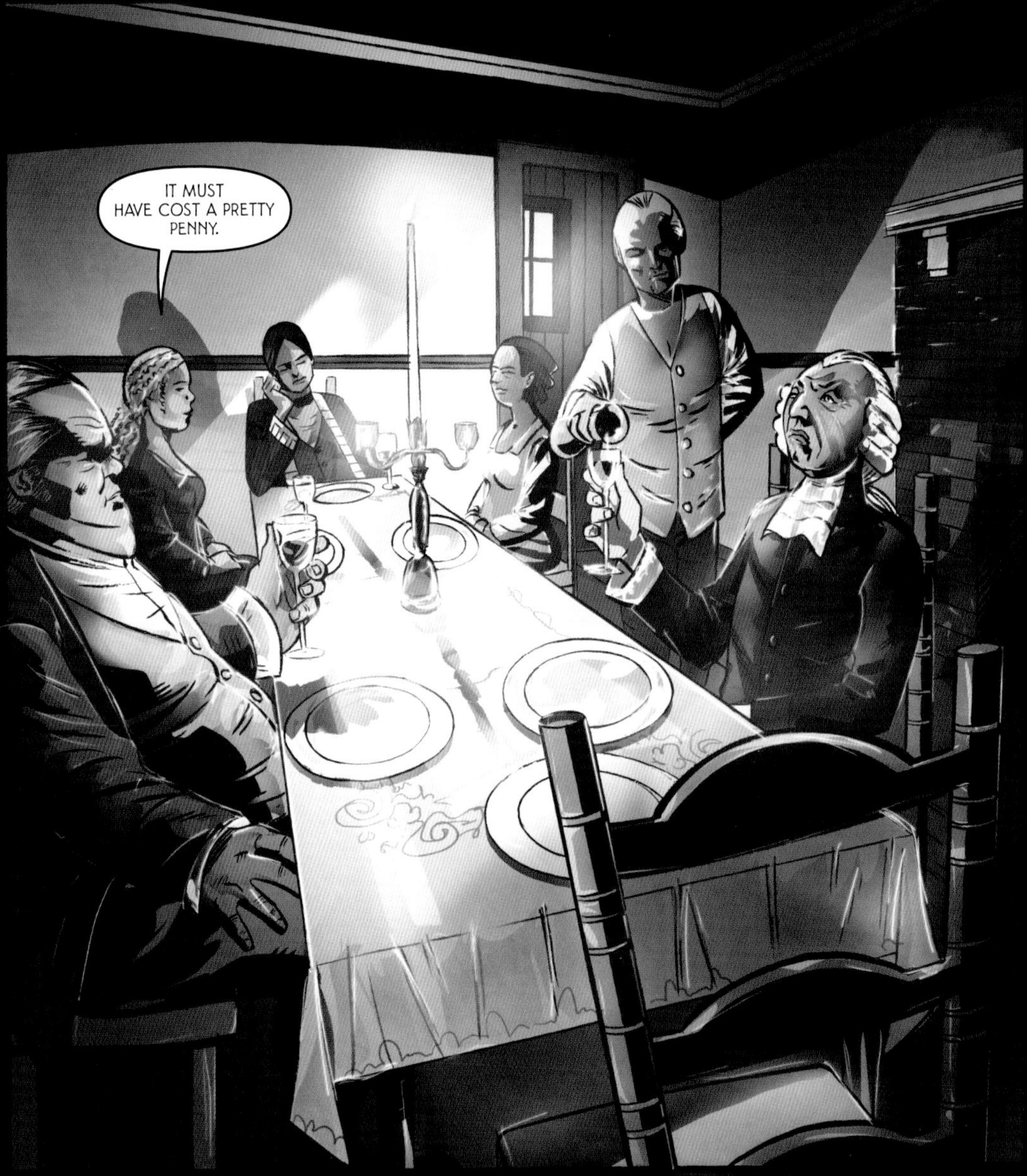
IT MUST HAVE COST A PRETTY PENNY.

TELL ME, JENNINGS, HOW IS THE PORK TRADE THESE DAYS? TREATING YOU FANCY, I'LL WAGER?

WHAT I NEED IS A WELL-KNOWN PERSON OF MEANS TO HELP ME GET A HEARING—SOMEONE LIKE BEN FRANKLIN.

FINE, IN SUPPLYING THE KING'S MEN AT WAR, BUT SLOW IN COLLECTIN' WHAT'S OWED. THEY CLAIM THE MEAT IS OLD. IMAGINE THAT!

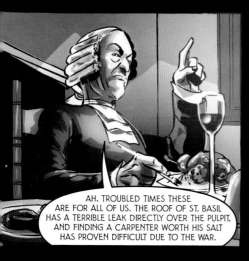
AH, TROUBLED TIMES THESE ARE FOR ALL OF US. THE ROOF OF ST. BASIL HAS A TERRIBLE LEAK DIRECTLY OVER THE PULPIT, AND FINDING A CARPENTER WORTH HIS SALT HAS PROVEN DIFFICULT DUE TO THE WAR.

SHOULD BEN FRANKLIN INTERVENE ON OUR BEHALF, HOWEVER, I AM SURE SOMETHING WILL BE DONE FOR US.

DEAR DEBORAH, IT WOULD SEEM EACH OF US HAS BUSINESS TO DISCUSS WITH YOUR HUSBAND. DO YOU EXPECT HIM SOON?

IT IS POSSIBLE BEN HAS SIMPLY OVERLOOKED THE TIME; THOSE JUNTO MEETINGS ARE QUITE ABSORBING, I UNDERSTAND.

OH, A JUNTO MEETING, IS IT? WELL, I BEEN TO ONE OR TWO OF THOSE MYSELF, AND YOU ARE RIGHT— THEY ARE ABSORBING.

ESPECIALLY THE ENDLESS TOASTING. HA, HA, HA, SUWEEEE, SUWEEE!

PERHAPS YOU COULD DISCUSS YOUR BUSINESS WITH ME?

I'M SORRY, LAD. I KNOW YE MEAN WELL, AN' I DUNNA MEAN TO LAUGH AT YE, BUT THIS SORT OF BUSINESS NEEDS YER FATHER'S EXPERIENCE BEHIND IT. YE UNDERSTAND THAT, DON'T YE?

IT'S BEEN MY BLESSIN' TO KNOW THE FRANKLIN CLAN FOR THIRTY OR MORE YEARS. I WATCHED LITTLE BILLY HERE GROW UP FROM A WEE LAD. YES, I DID.

HEAR, HEAR!

FEW MEN HAVE DONE GREATER SERVICE FOR THE BRITISH EMPIRE AND FOR HIS FRIENDS THAN BENJAMIN FRANKLIN, AND I SALUTE HIM HERE IN THE PRESENCE OF HIS FRIENDS AND FAMILY.

ARE YOU FORGETTING SOMETHING?

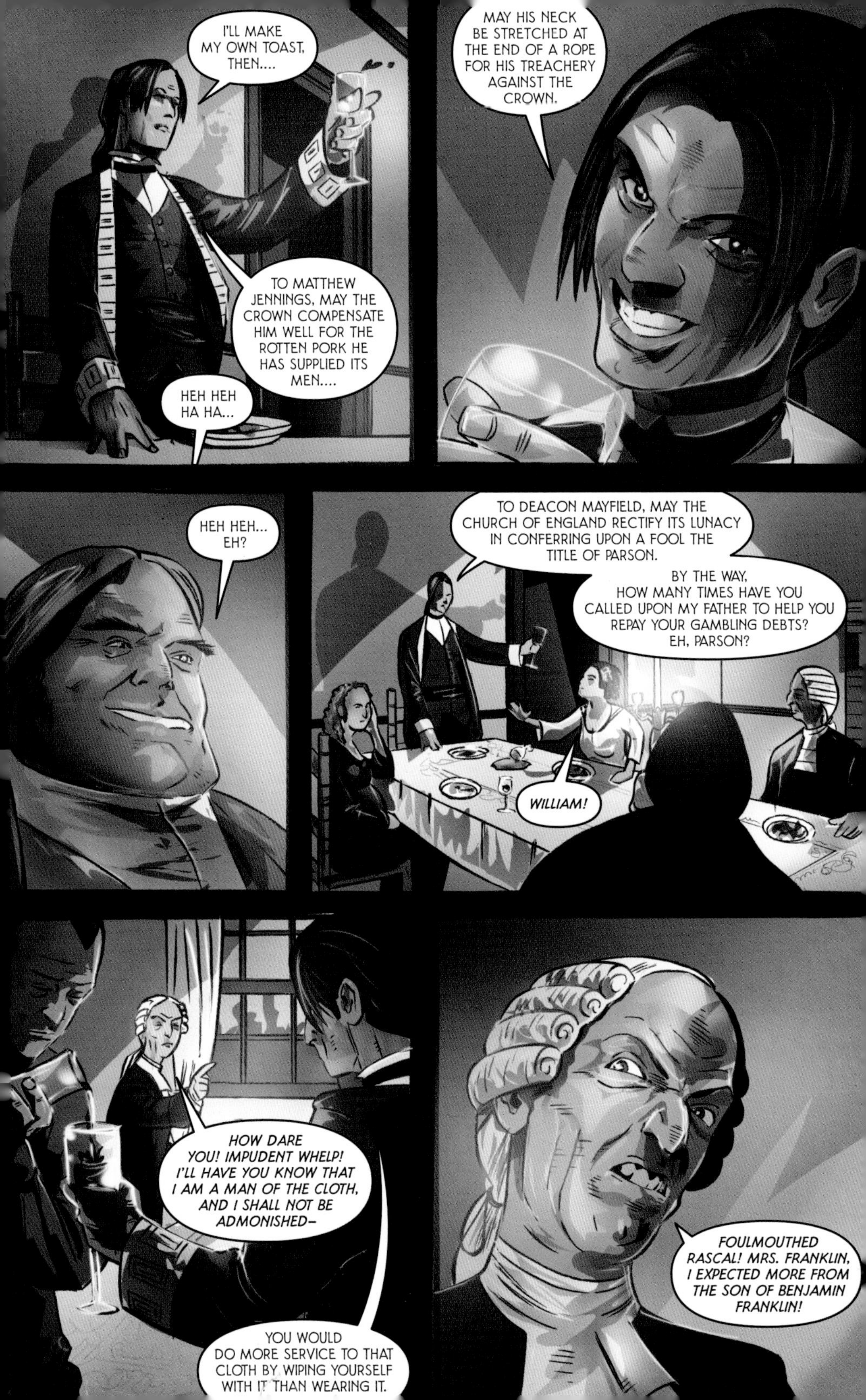
I'LL MAKE MY OWN TOAST, THEN....
TO MATTHEW JENNINGS, MAY THE CROWN COMPENSATE HIM WELL FOR THE ROTTEN PORK HE HAS SUPPLIED ITS MEN....
HEH HEH HA HA...
MAY HIS NECK BE STRETCHED AT THE END OF A ROPE FOR HIS TREACHERY AGAINST THE CROWN.
HEH HEH... EH?
TO DEACON MAYFIELD, MAY THE CHURCH OF ENGLAND RECTIFY ITS LUNACY IN CONFERRING UPON A FOOL THE TITLE OF PARSON.
BY THE WAY, HOW MANY TIMES HAVE YOU CALLED UPON MY FATHER TO HELP YOU REPAY YOUR GAMBLING DEBTS? EH, PARSON?
WILLIAM!
HOW DARE YOU! IMPUDENT WHELP! I'LL HAVE YOU KNOW THAT I AM A MAN OF THE CLOTH, AND I SHALL NOT BE ADMONISHED–
YOU WOULD DO MORE SERVICE TO THAT CLOTH BY WIPING YOURSELF WITH IT THAN WEARING IT.
FOULMOUTHED RASCAL! MRS. FRANKLIN, I EXPECTED MORE FROM THE SON OF BENJAMIN FRANKLIN!

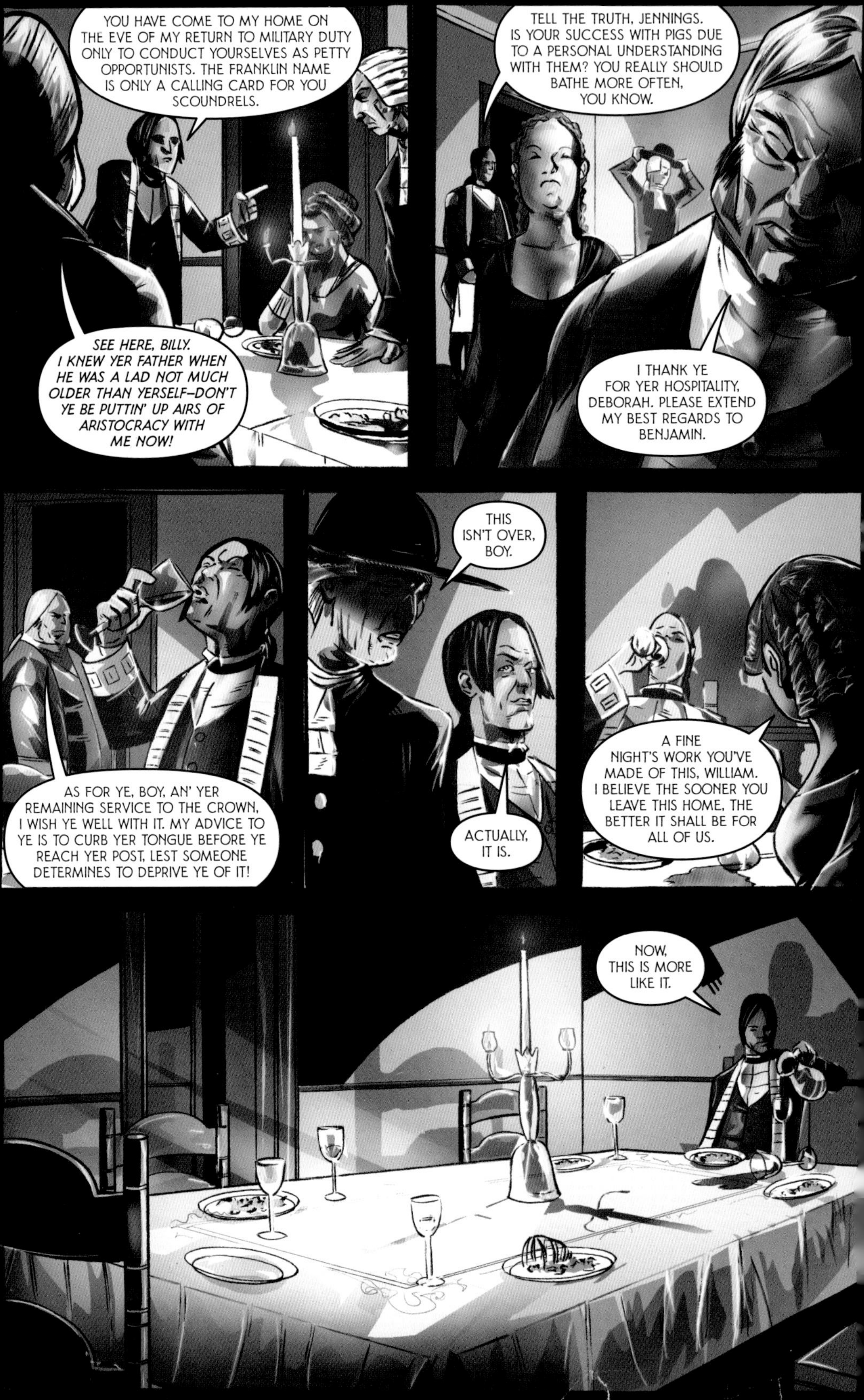

YOU HAVE COME TO MY HOME ON THE EVE OF MY RETURN TO MILITARY DUTY ONLY TO CONDUCT YOURSELVES AS PETTY OPPORTUNISTS. THE FRANKLIN NAME IS ONLY A CALLING CARD FOR YOU SCOUNDRELS.
SEE HERE, BILLY. I KNEW YER FATHER WHEN HE WAS A LAD NOT MUCH OLDER THAN YERSELF—DON'T YE BE PUTTIN' UP AIRS OF ARISTOCRACY WITH ME NOW!
TELL THE TRUTH, JENNINGS. IS YOUR SUCCESS WITH PIGS DUE TO A PERSONAL UNDERSTANDING WITH THEM? YOU REALLY SHOULD BATHE MORE OFTEN, YOU KNOW.
I THANK YE FOR YER HOSPITALITY, DEBORAH. PLEASE EXTEND MY BEST REGARDS TO BENJAMIN.
AS FOR YE, BOY, AN' YER REMAINING SERVICE TO THE CROWN, I WISH YE WELL WITH IT. MY ADVICE TO YE IS TO CURB YER TONGUE BEFORE YE REACH YER POST, LEST SOMEONE DETERMINES TO DEPRIVE YE OF IT!
THIS ISN'T OVER, BOY.
ACTUALLY, IT IS.
A FINE NIGHT'S WORK YOU'VE MADE OF THIS, WILLIAM. I BELIEVE THE SOONER YOU LEAVE THIS HOME, THE BETTER IT SHALL BE FOR ALL OF US.
NOW, THIS IS MORE LIKE IT.

TSHHH

YOU POOR CHILD.

HUMPH. I KNOW OF ONLY ONE INSTRUMENT CAPABLE OF PRODUCING MARKS SUCH AS THESE.

William...

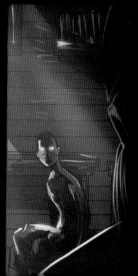

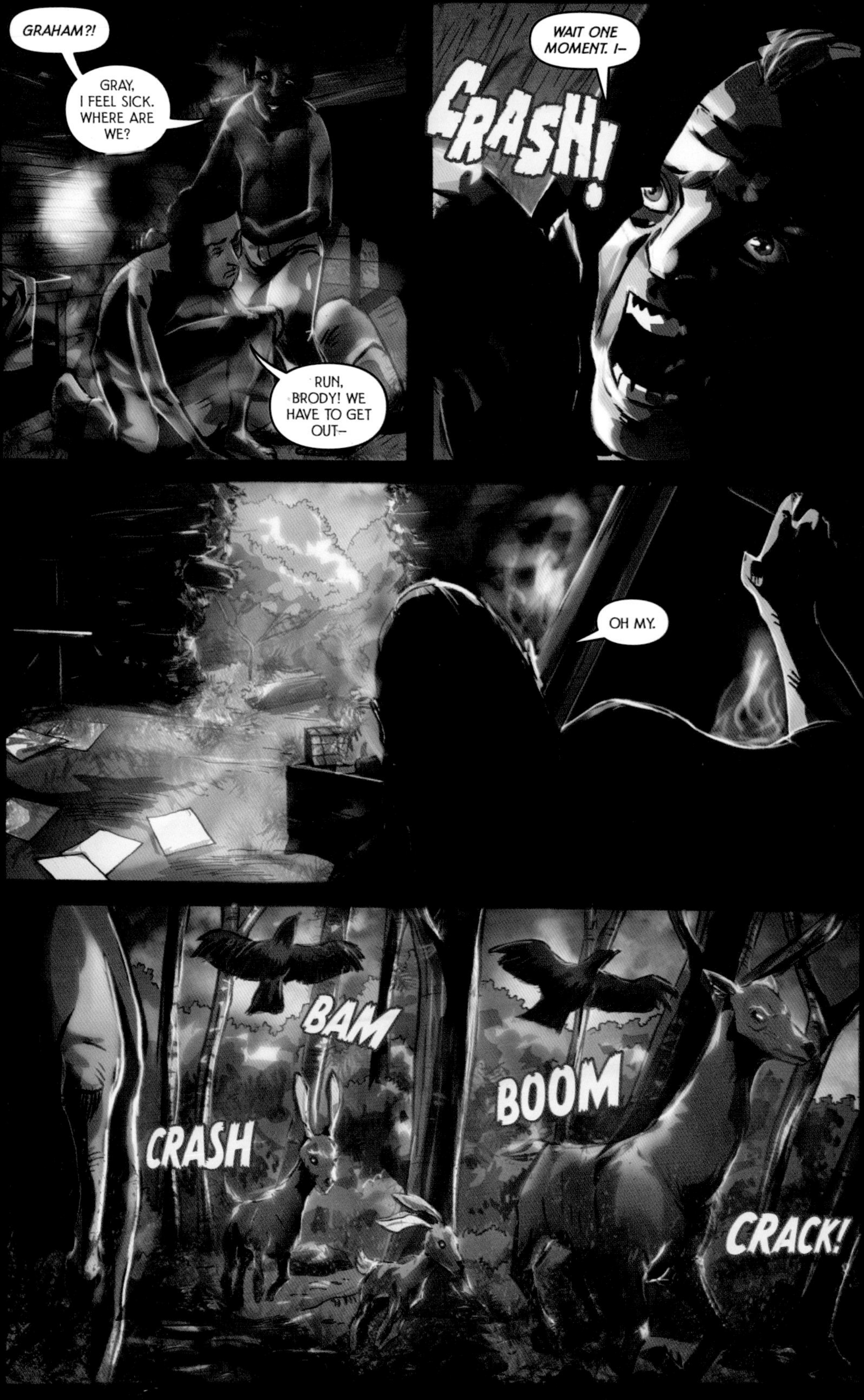
GRAHAM?!
GRAY, I FEEL SICK. WHERE ARE WE?
RUN, BRODY! WE HAVE TO GET OUT–
WAIT ONE MOMENT. I–
CRASH!
OH MY.
CRASH
BAM
BOOM
CRACK!

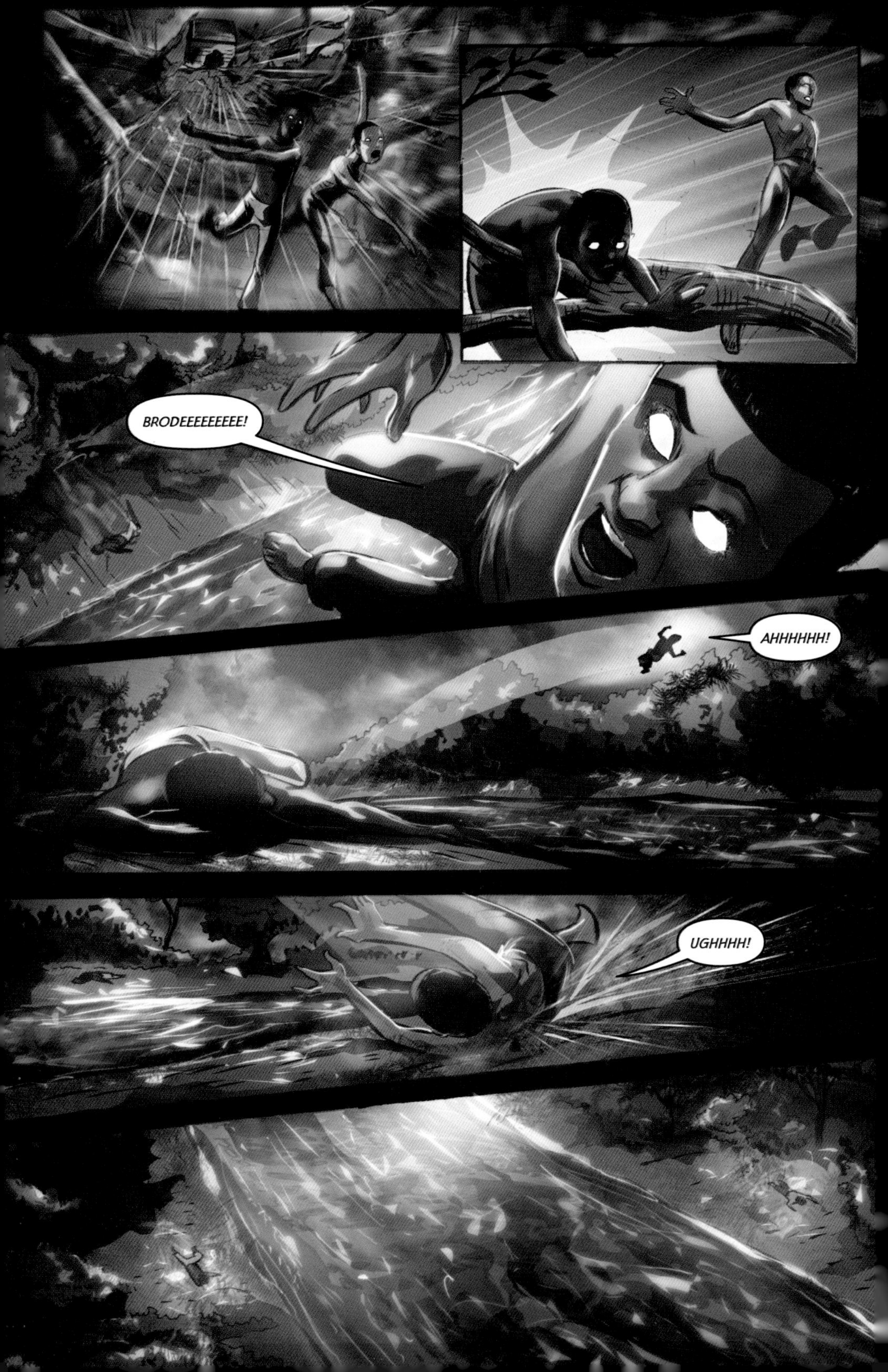
BRODEEEEEEEEE!
AHHHHHH!
UGHHHH!

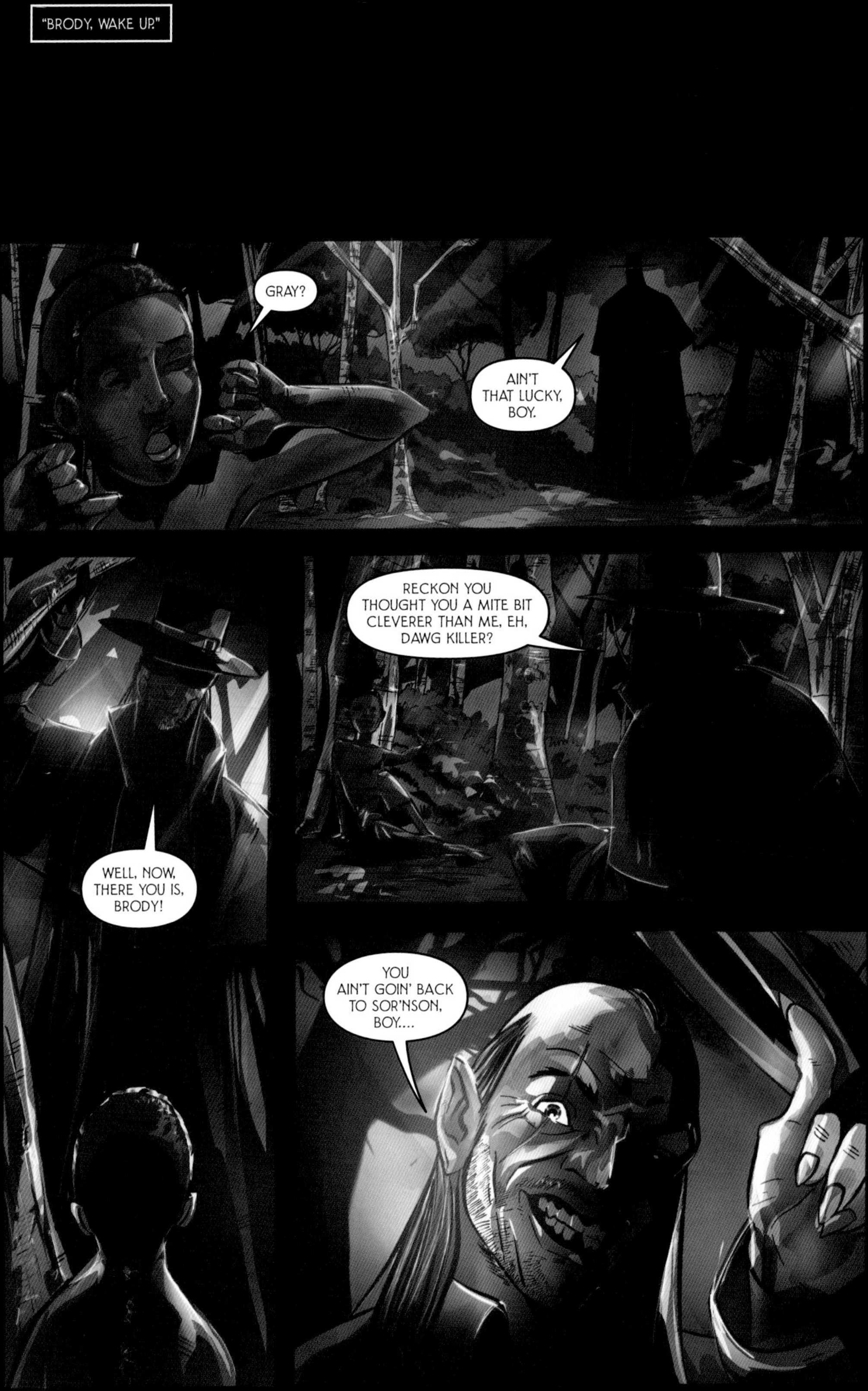
"BRODY, WAKE UP."
GRAY?
AIN'T THAT LUCKY, BOY.
WELL, NOW, THERE YOU IS, BRODY!
RECKON YOU THOUGHT YOU A MITE BIT CLEVERER THAN ME, EH, DAWG KILLER?
YOU AIN'T GOIN' BACK TO SOR'NSON, BOY....

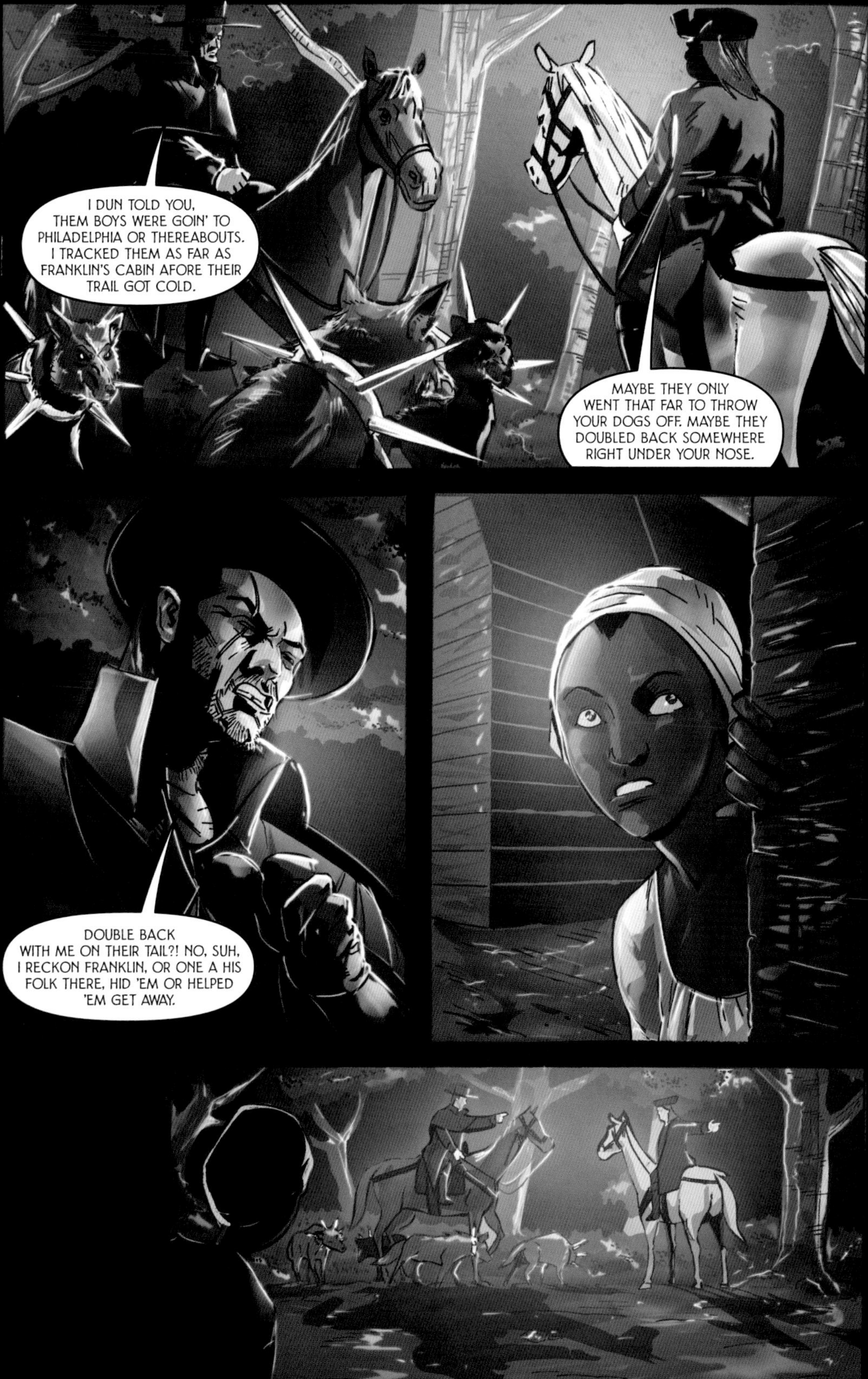
I DUN TOLD YOU, THEM BOYS WERE GOIN' TO PHILADELPHIA OR THEREABOUTS. I TRACKED THEM AS FAR AS FRANKLIN'S CABIN AFORE THEIR TRAIL GOT COLD.
MAYBE THEY ONLY WENT THAT FAR TO THROW YOUR DOGS OFF. MAYBE THEY DOUBLED BACK SOMEWHERE RIGHT UNDER YOUR NOSE.
DOUBLE BACK WITH ME ON THEIR TAIL?! NO, SUH, I RECKON FRANKLIN, OR ONE A HIS FOLK THERE, HID 'EM OR HELPED 'EM GET AWAY.

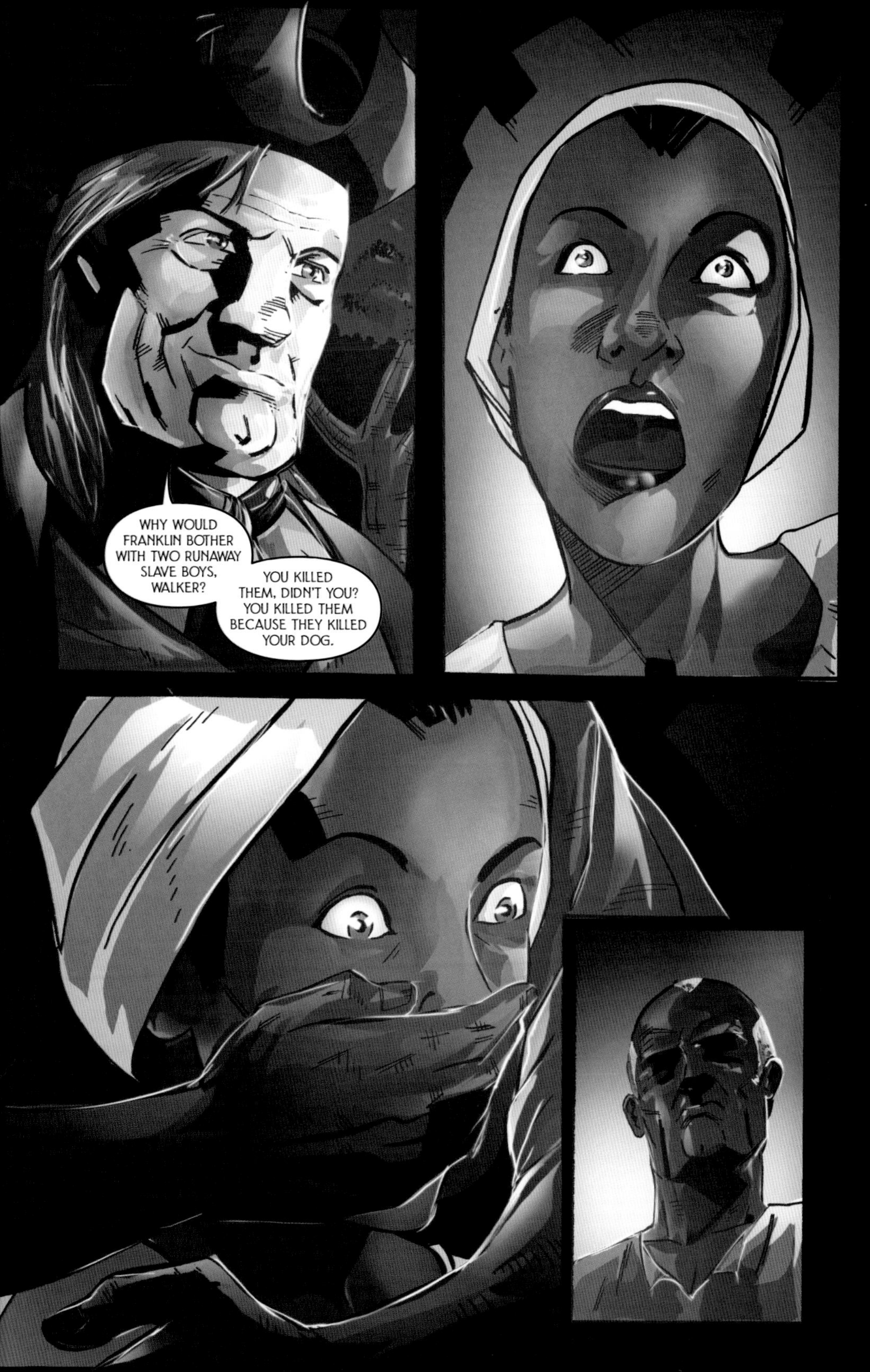
WHY WOULD FRANKLIN BOTHER WITH TWO RUNAWAY SLAVE BOYS, WALKER?
YOU KILLED THEM, DIDN'T YOU? YOU KILLED THEM BECAUSE THEY KILLED YOUR DOG.

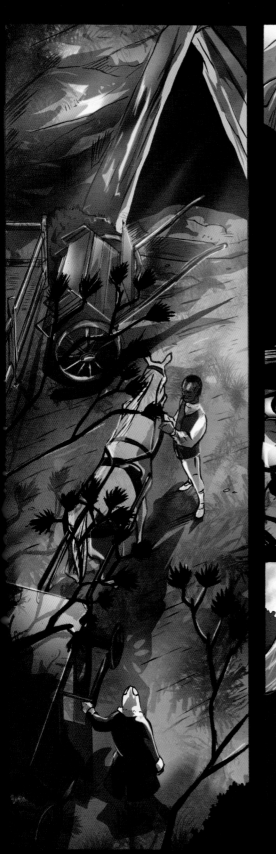

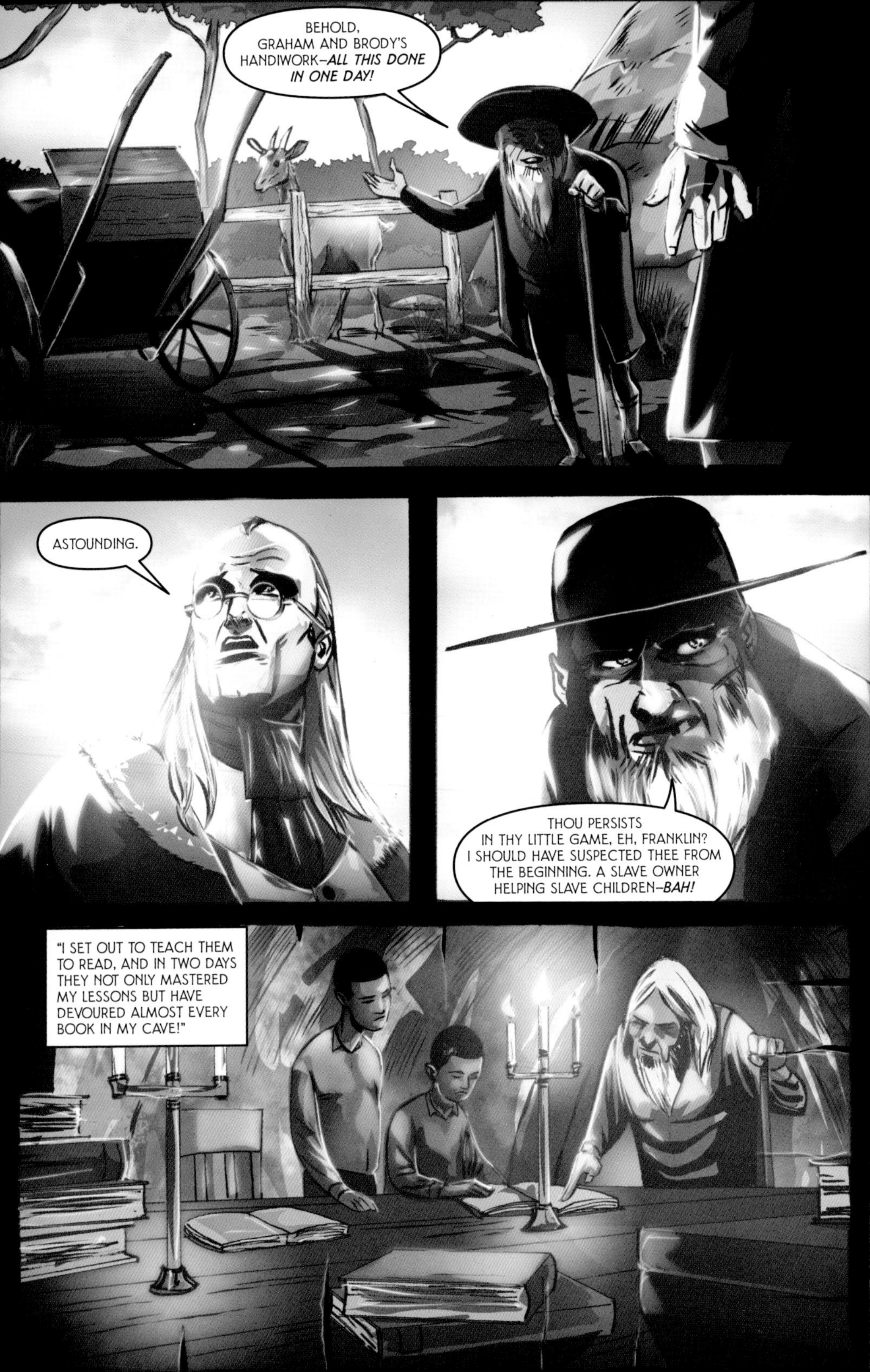
BEHOLD, GRAHAM AND BRODY'S HANDIWORK–*ALL THIS DONE IN ONE DAY!*
ASTOUNDING.
THOU PERSISTS IN THY LITTLE GAME, EH, FRANKLIN? I SHOULD HAVE SUSPECTED THEE FROM THE BEGINNING. A SLAVE OWNER HELPING SLAVE CHILDREN–*BAH!*
"I SET OUT TO TEACH THEM TO READ, AND IN TWO DAYS THEY NOT ONLY MASTERED MY LESSONS BUT HAVE DEVOURED ALMOST EVERY BOOK IN MY CAVE!"

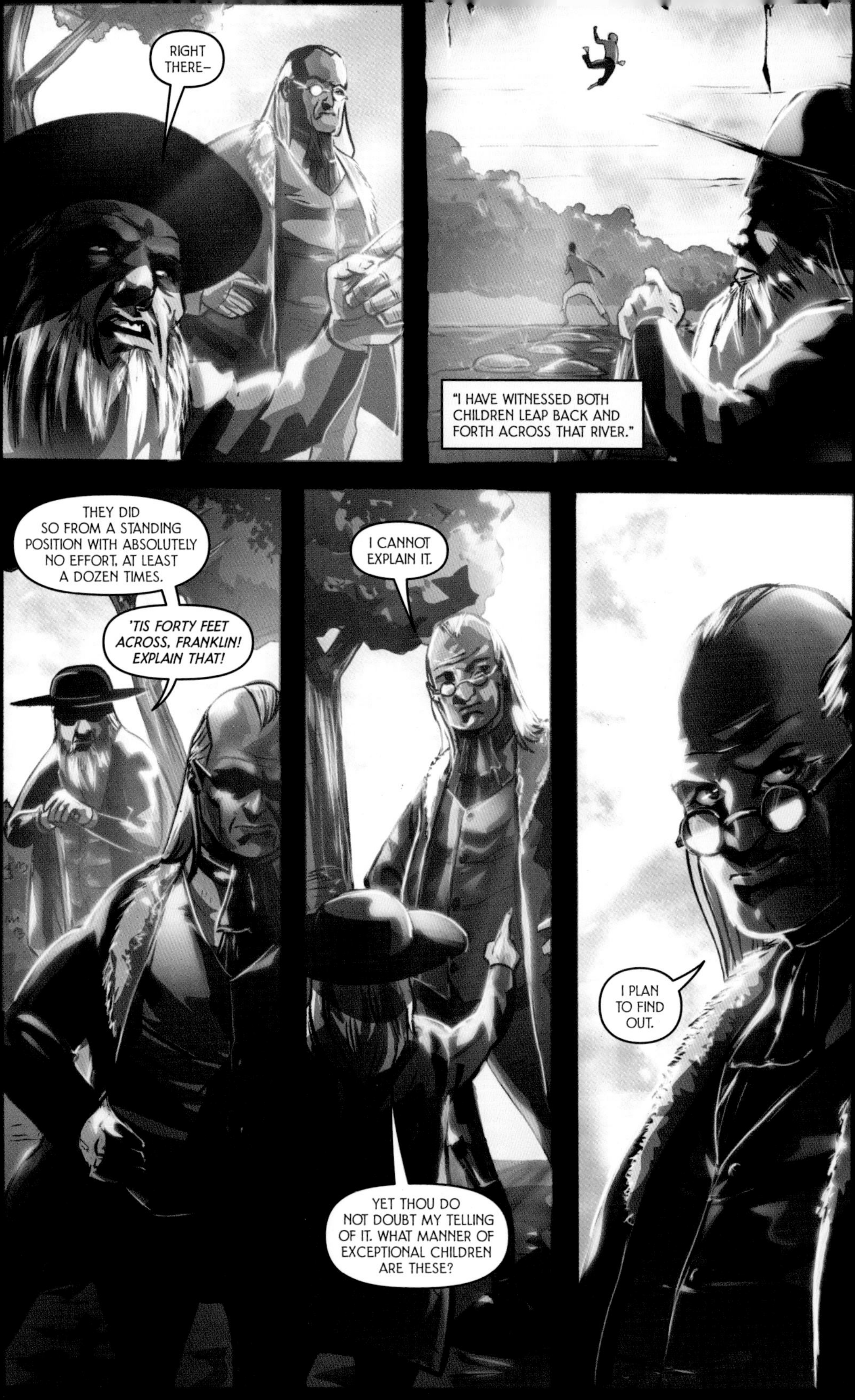
RIGHT THERE–
"I HAVE WITNESSED BOTH CHILDREN LEAP BACK AND FORTH ACROSS THAT RIVER."
THEY DID SO FROM A STANDING POSITION WITH ABSOLUTELY NO EFFORT, AT LEAST A DOZEN TIMES.
'TIS FORTY FEET ACROSS, FRANKLIN! EXPLAIN THAT!
I CANNOT EXPLAIN IT.
YET THOU DO NOT DOUBT MY TELLING OF IT. WHAT MANNER OF EXCEPTIONAL CHILDREN ARE THESE?
I PLAN TO FIND OUT.

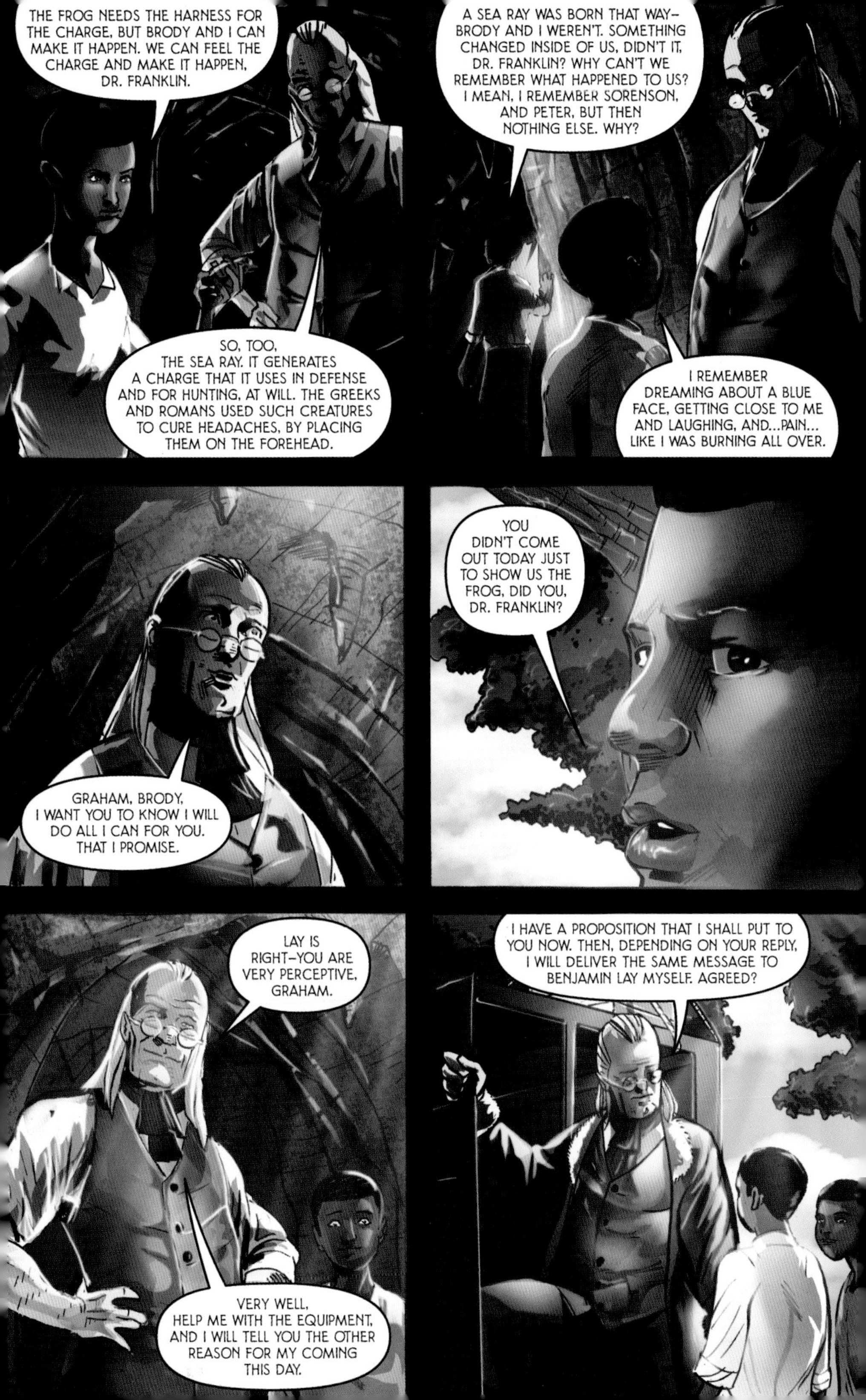
THE FROG NEEDS THE HARNESS FOR THE CHARGE, BUT BRODY AND I CAN MAKE IT HAPPEN. WE CAN FEEL THE CHARGE AND MAKE IT HAPPEN, DR. FRANKLIN.
SO, TOO, THE SEA RAY. IT GENERATES A CHARGE THAT IT USES IN DEFENSE AND FOR HUNTING, AT WILL. THE GREEKS AND ROMANS USED SUCH CREATURES TO CURE HEADACHES, BY PLACING THEM ON THE FOREHEAD.
A SEA RAY WAS BORN THAT WAY—BRODY AND I WEREN'T. SOMETHING CHANGED INSIDE OF US, DIDN'T IT, DR. FRANKLIN? WHY CAN'T WE REMEMBER WHAT HAPPENED TO US? I MEAN, I REMEMBER SORENSON, AND PETER, BUT THEN NOTHING ELSE. WHY?
I REMEMBER DREAMING ABOUT A BLUE FACE, GETTING CLOSE TO ME AND LAUGHING, AND...PAIN... LIKE I WAS BURNING ALL OVER.
GRAHAM, BRODY, I WANT YOU TO KNOW I WILL DO ALL I CAN FOR YOU. THAT I PROMISE.
YOU DIDN'T COME OUT TODAY JUST TO SHOW US THE FROG, DID YOU, DR. FRANKLIN?
LAY IS RIGHT—YOU ARE VERY PERCEPTIVE, GRAHAM.
VERY WELL, HELP ME WITH THE EQUIPMENT, AND I WILL TELL YOU THE OTHER REASON FOR MY COMING THIS DAY.
I HAVE A PROPOSITION THAT I SHALL PUT TO YOU NOW. THEN, DEPENDING ON YOUR REPLY, I WILL DELIVER THE SAME MESSAGE TO BENJAMIN LAY MYSELF. AGREED?

Abington

"OUR BUSINESS ENDEAVORS HAVE
RENDERED GOODLY PROFITS, MY BROTHERS.
YET USELESS THESE THINGS BE SHOULD
THE SOUL BE ECLIPSED BY THE SIN OF PRIDE."

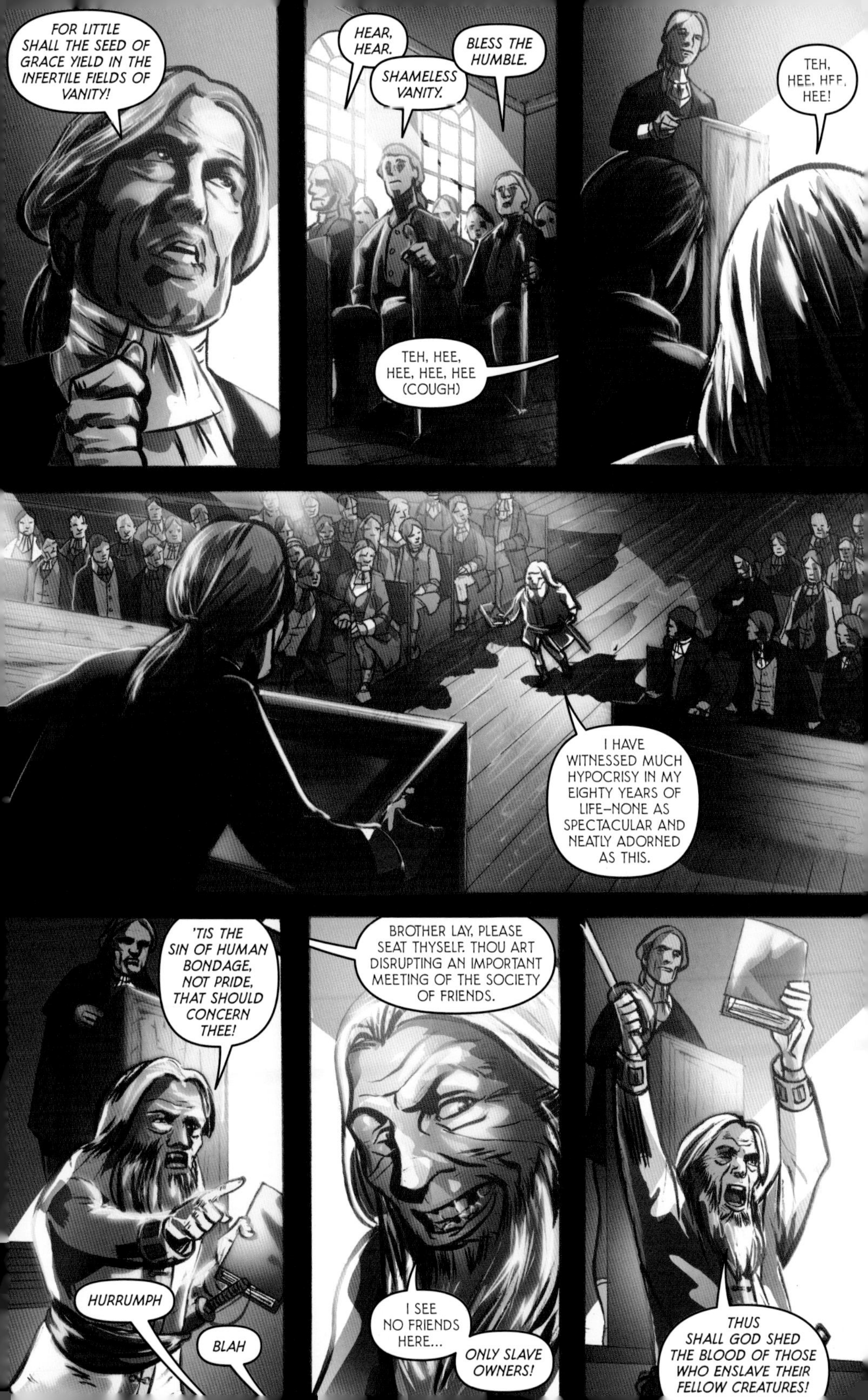
FOR LITTLE SHALL THE SEED OF GRACE YIELD IN THE INFERTILE FIELDS OF VANITY!
HEAR, HEAR.
SHAMELESS VANITY.
BLESS THE HUMBLE.
TEH, HEE, HEE, HEE, HEE (COUGH)
TEH, HEE, HFF, HEE!
I HAVE WITNESSED MUCH HYPOCRISY IN MY EIGHTY YEARS OF LIFE–NONE AS SPECTACULAR AND NEATLY ADORNED AS THIS.
'TIS THE SIN OF HUMAN BONDAGE, NOT PRIDE, THAT SHOULD CONCERN THEE!
HURRUMPH
BLAH
BROTHER LAY, PLEASE SEAT THYSELF. THOU ART DISRUPTING AN IMPORTANT MEETING OF THE SOCIETY OF FRIENDS.
I SEE NO FRIENDS HERE...
ONLY SLAVE OWNERS!
THUS SHALL GOD SHED THE BLOOD OF THOSE WHO ENSLAVE THEIR FELLOW CREATURES!

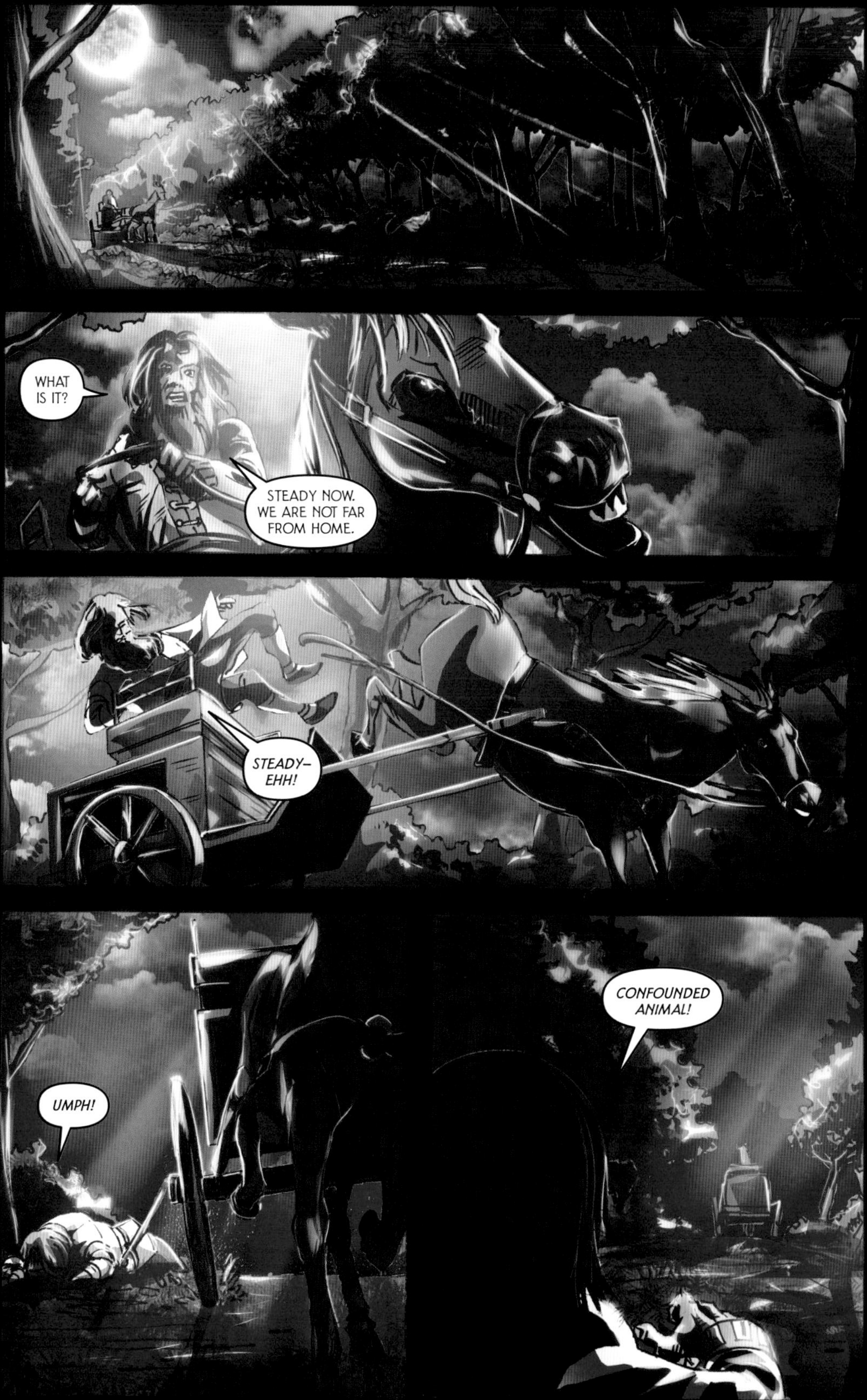
WHAT IS IT?
STEADY NOW. WE ARE NOT FAR FROM HOME.
STEADY—EHH!
CONFOUNDED ANIMAL!
UMPH!

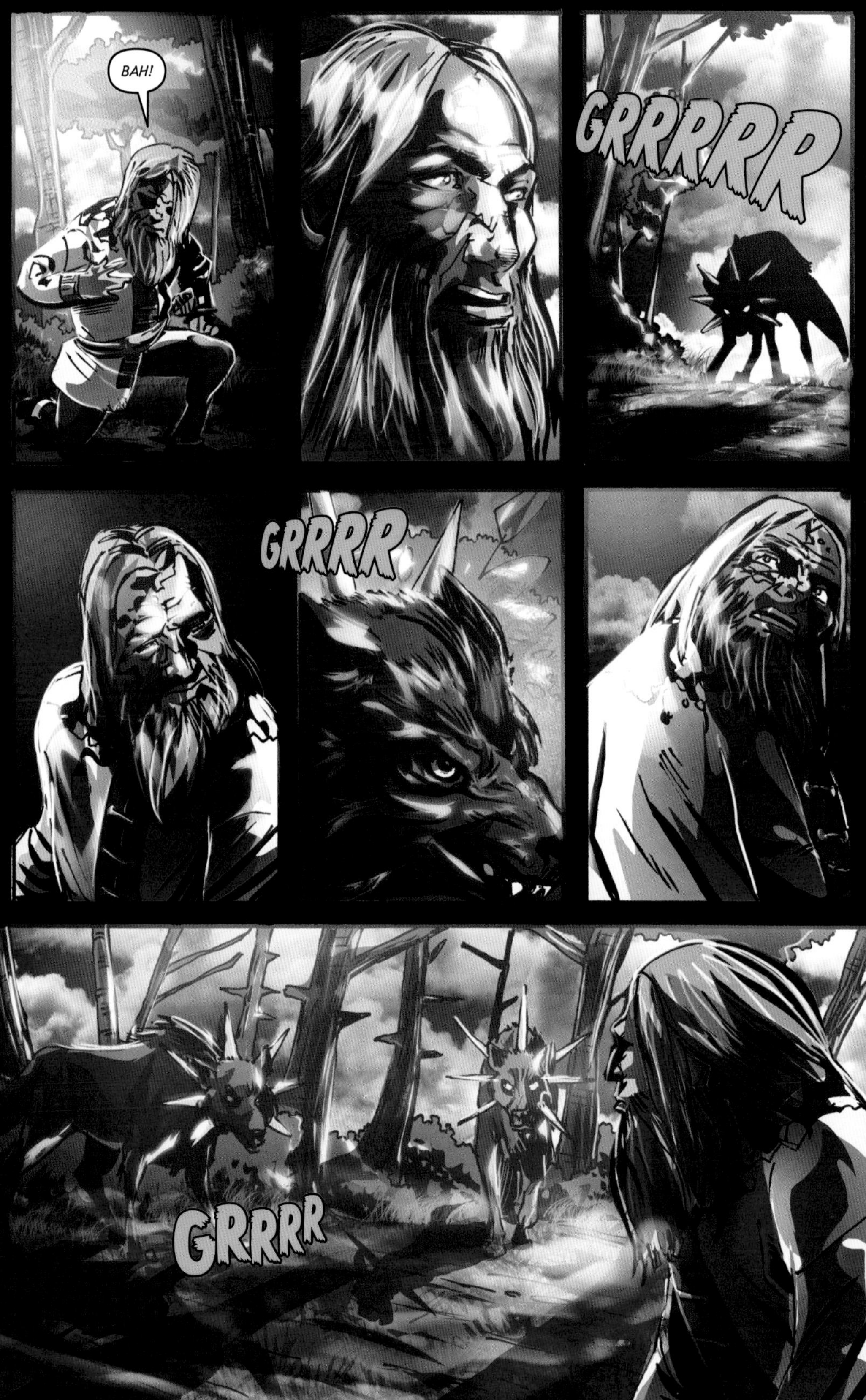
BAH!
GRRRRRR
GRRRR
GRRRR

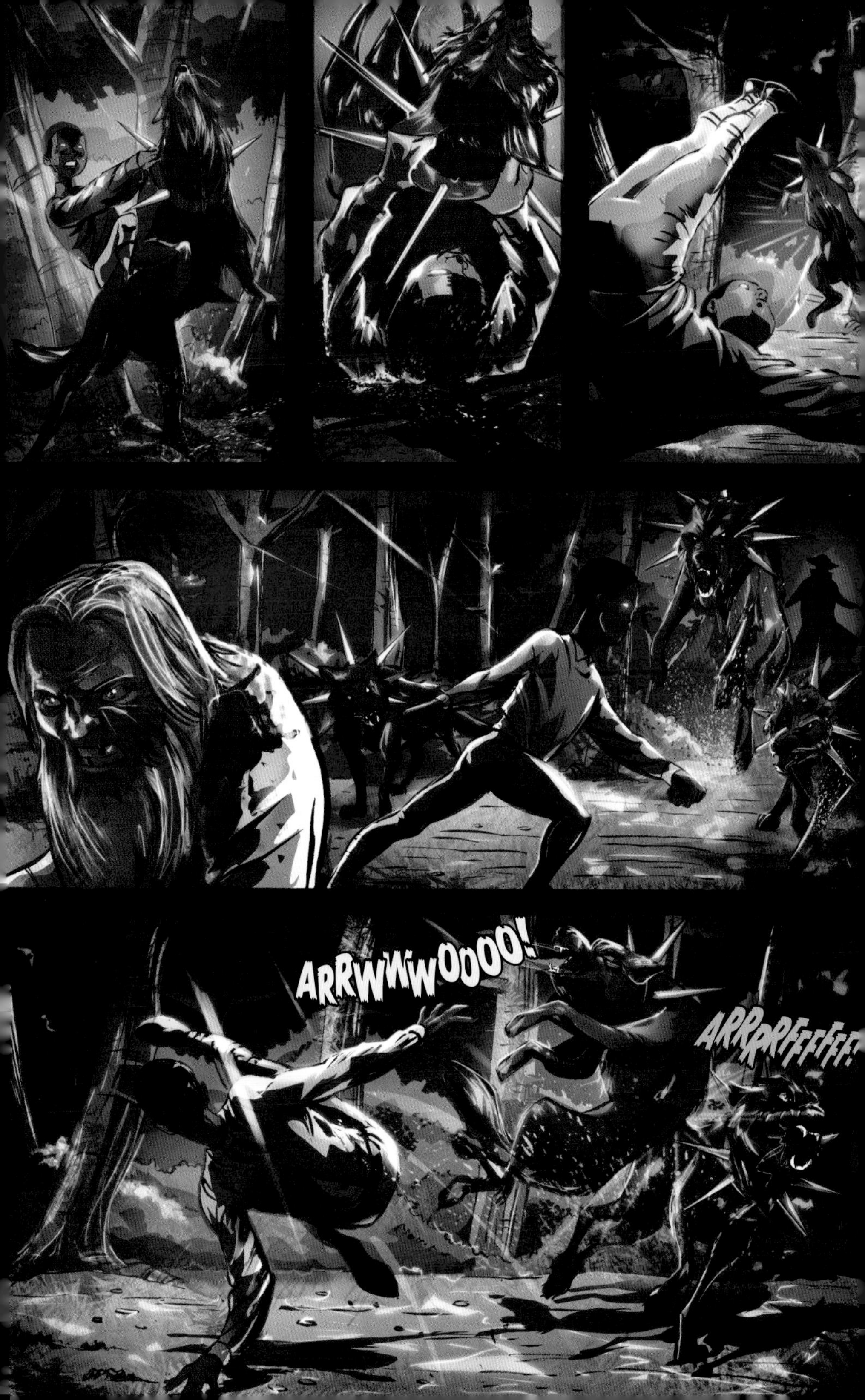
ARRWWWOOOO!
ARRRRFFFFFF!

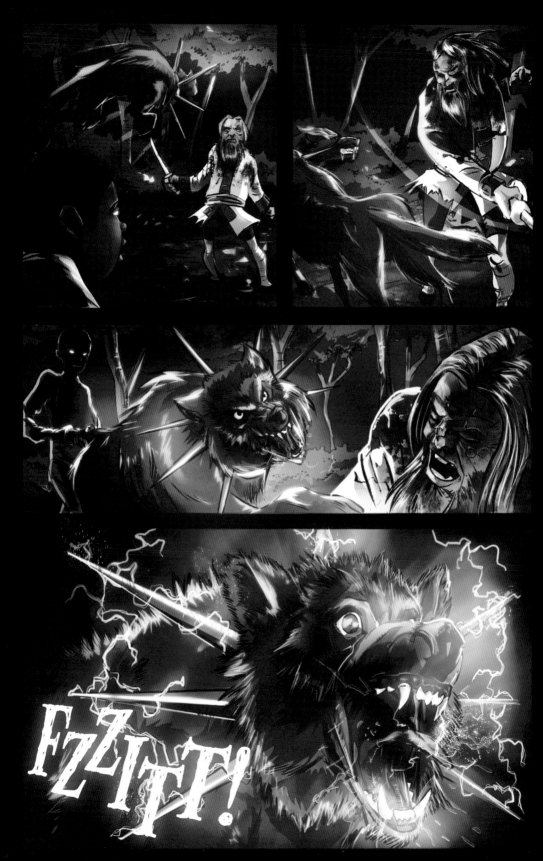

FZZITT!

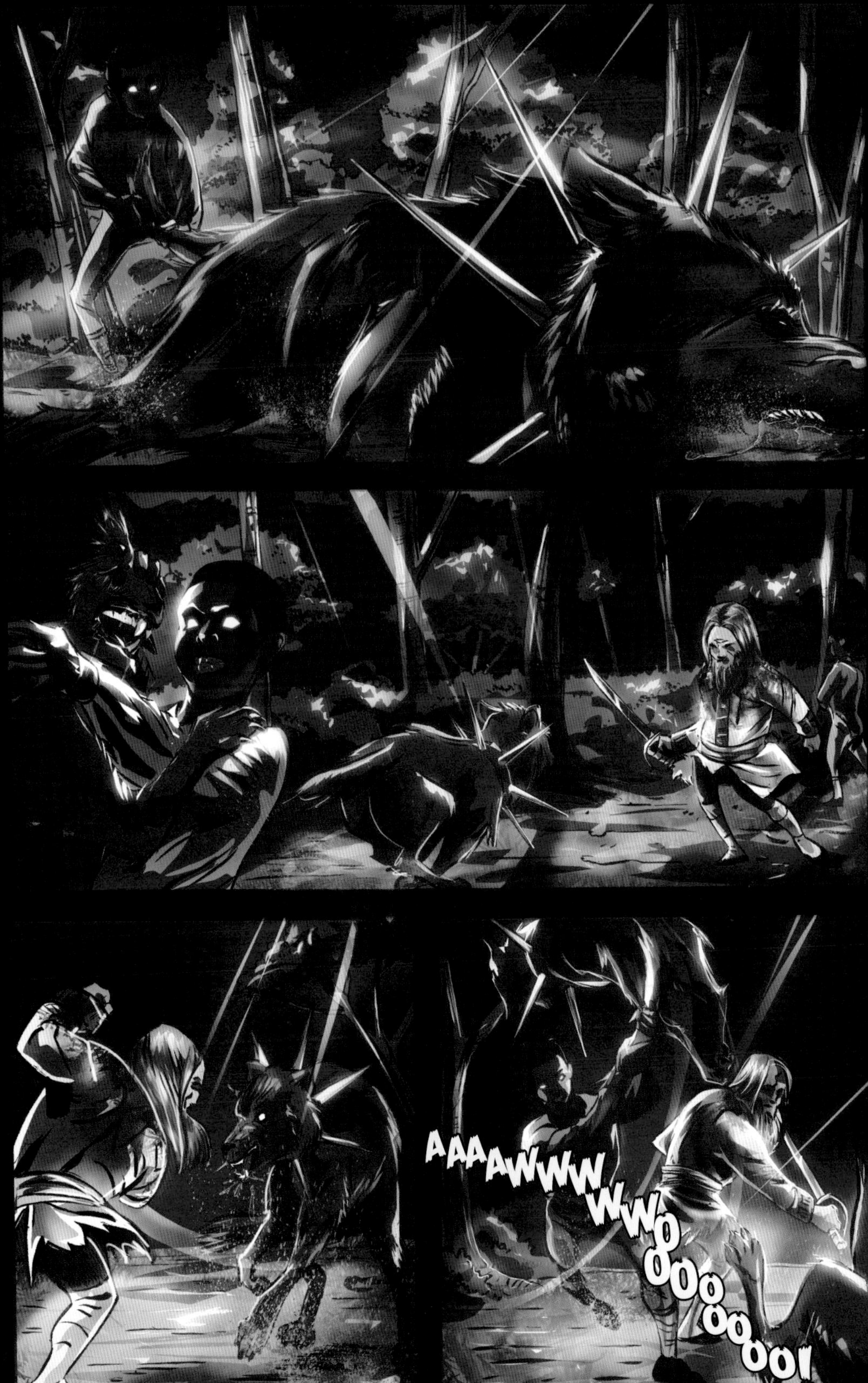
AAAAWWWWWOOOOOOOO!

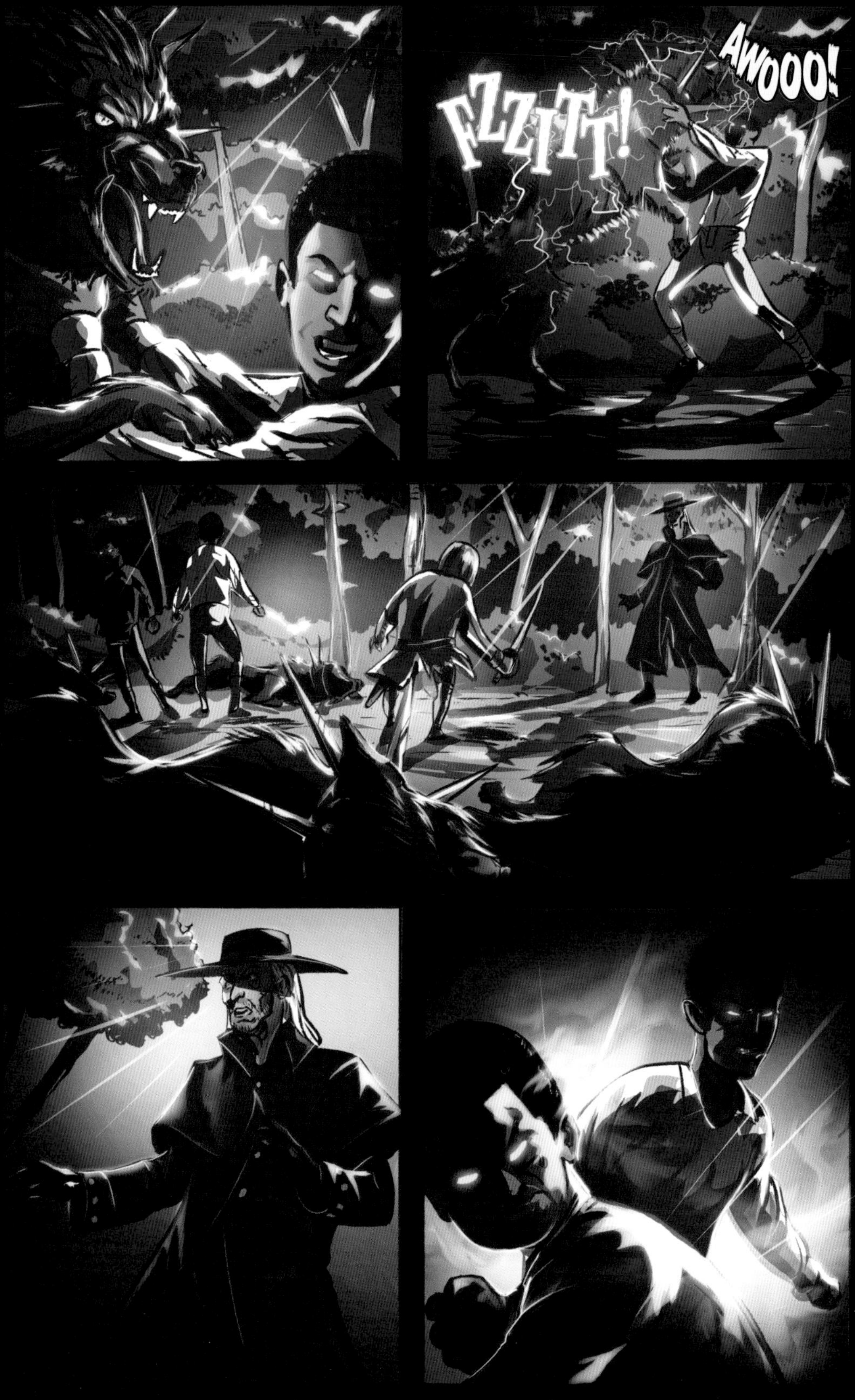
FZZITT!
AWOOO!

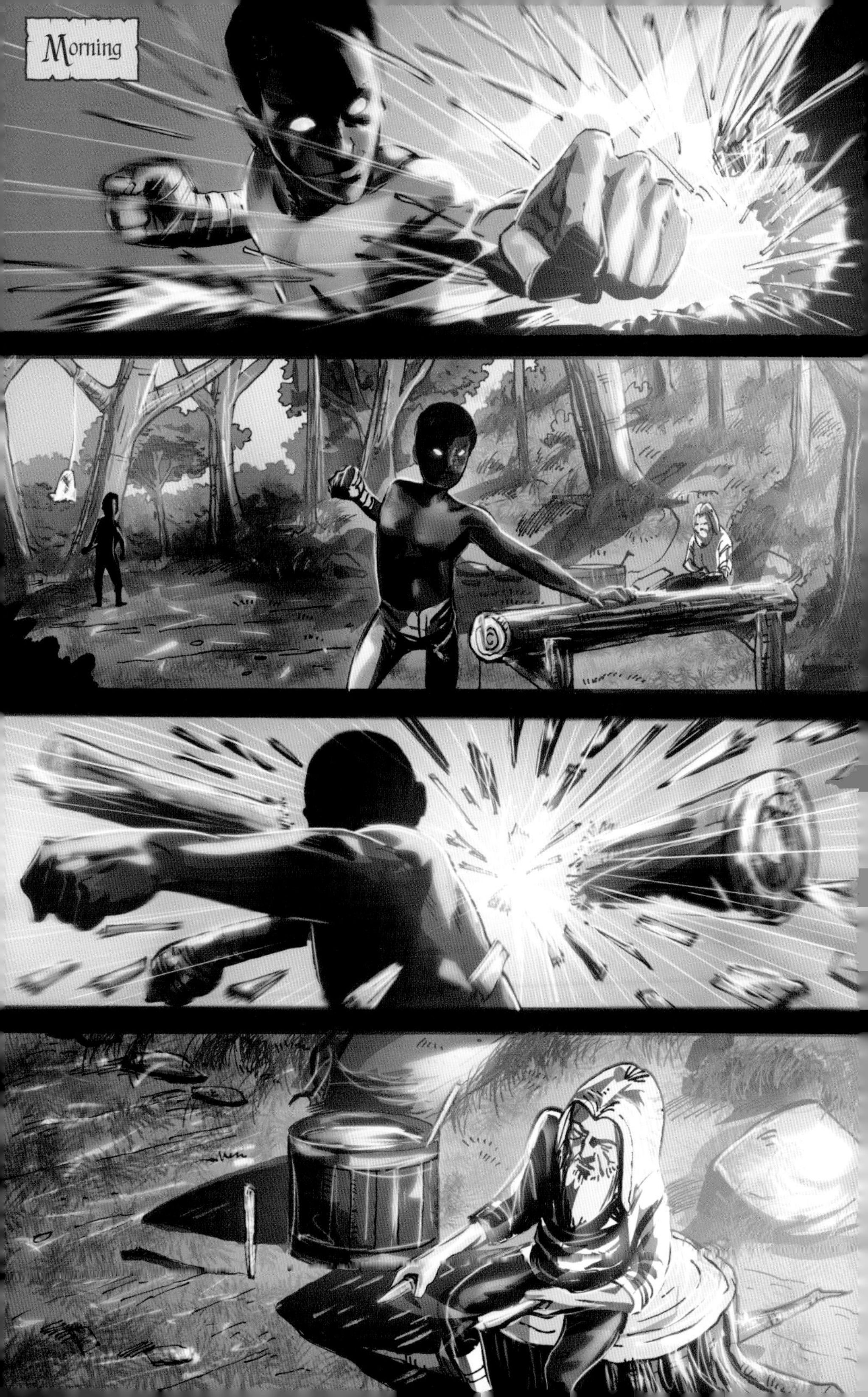
Morning

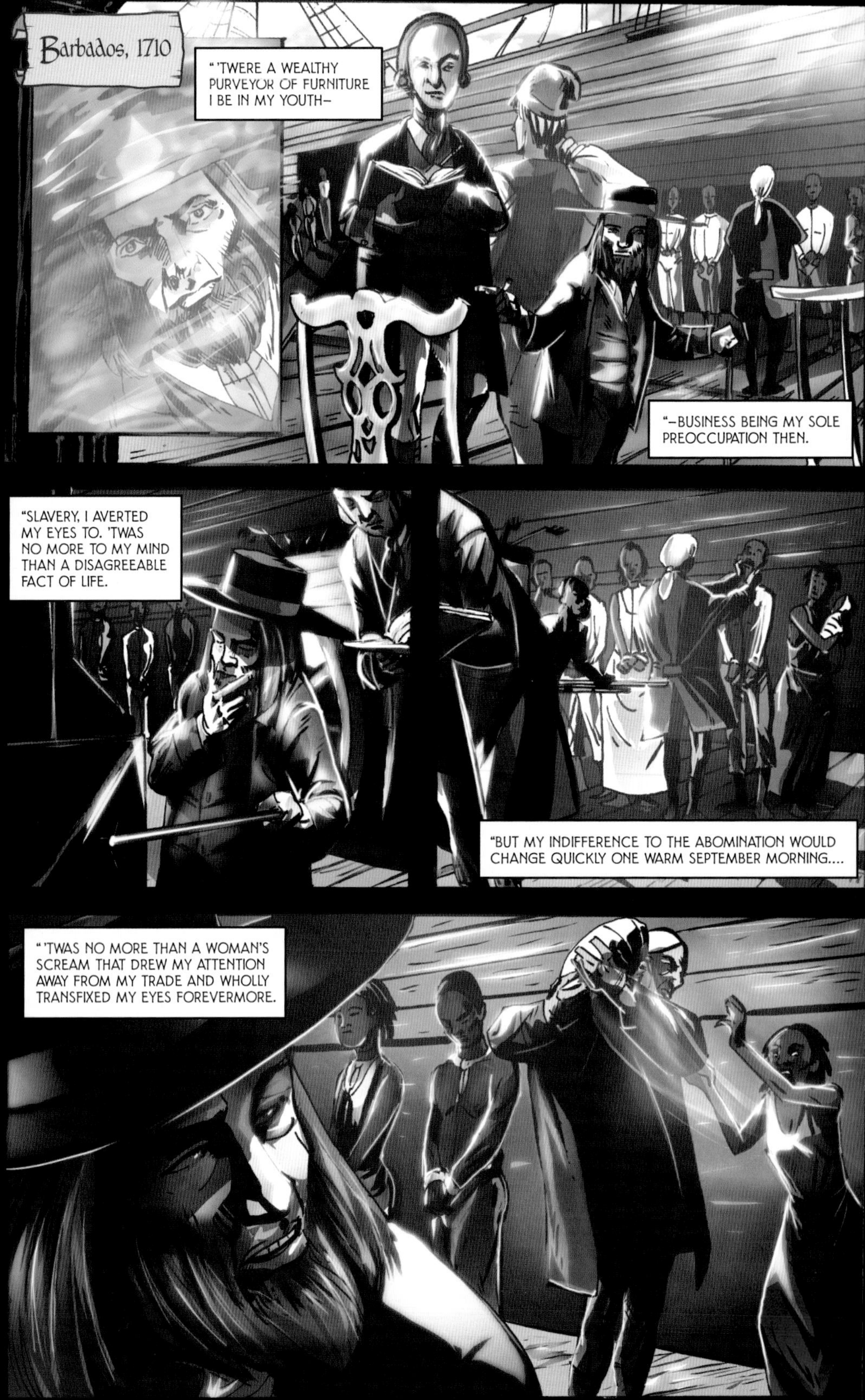
Barbados, 1710
"'TWERE A WEALTHY PURVEYOR OF FURNITURE I BE IN MY YOUTH–
"–BUSINESS BEING MY SOLE PREOCCUPATION THEN.
"SLAVERY, I AVERTED MY EYES TO. 'TWAS NO MORE TO MY MIND THAN A DISAGREEABLE FACT OF LIFE.
"BUT MY INDIFFERENCE TO THE ABOMINATION WOULD CHANGE QUICKLY ONE WARM SEPTEMBER MORNING....
"'TWAS NO MORE THAN A WOMAN'S SCREAM THAT DREW MY ATTENTION AWAY FROM MY TRADE AND WHOLLY TRANSFIXED MY EYES FOREVERMORE.

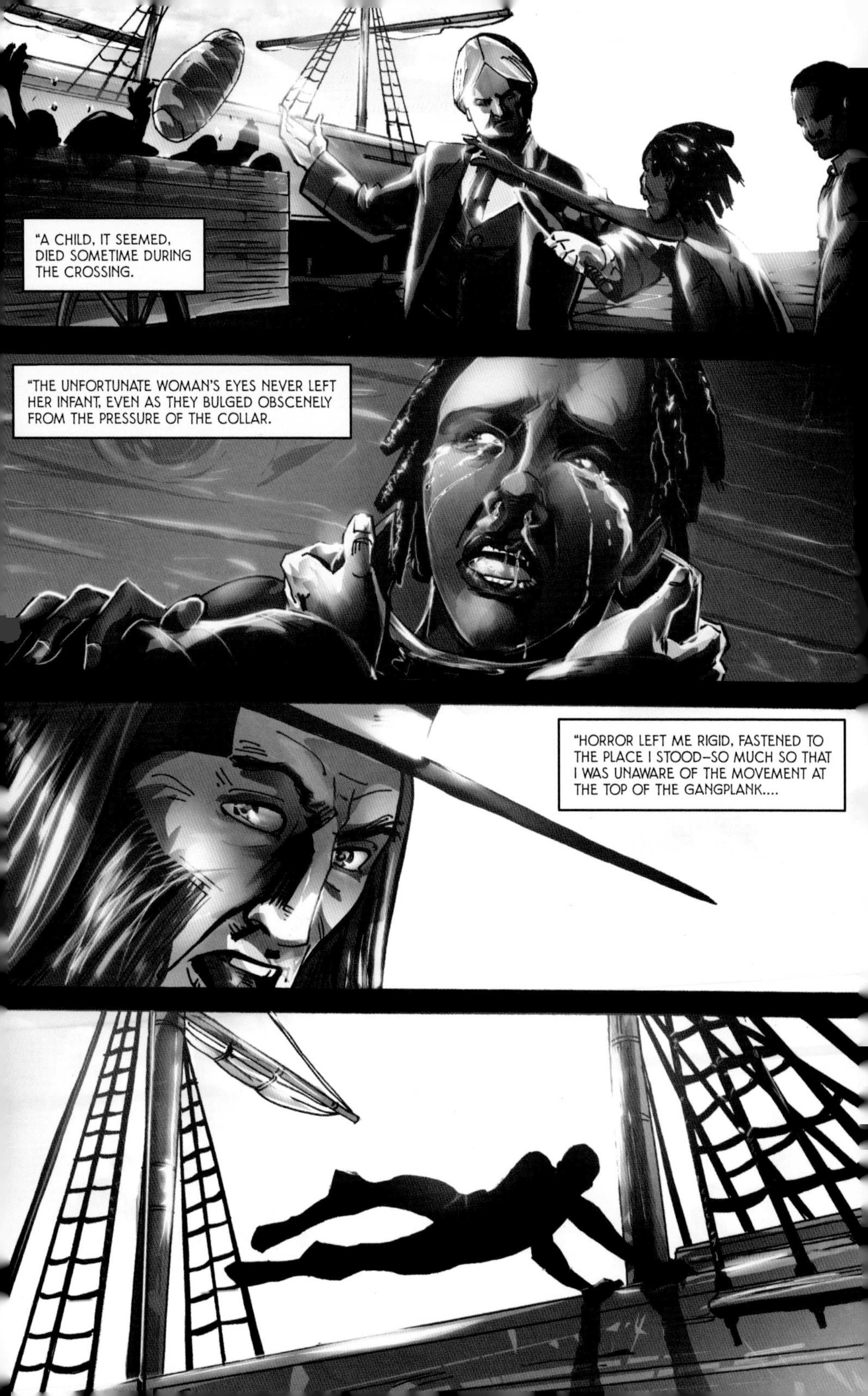
"A CHILD, IT SEEMED, DIED SOMETIME DURING THE CROSSING.
"THE UNFORTUNATE WOMAN'S EYES NEVER LEFT HER INFANT, EVEN AS THEY BULGED OBSCENELY FROM THE PRESSURE OF THE COLLAR.
"HORROR LEFT ME RIGID, FASTENED TO THE PLACE I STOOD—SO MUCH SO THAT I WAS UNAWARE OF THE MOVEMENT AT THE TOP OF THE GANGPLANK....

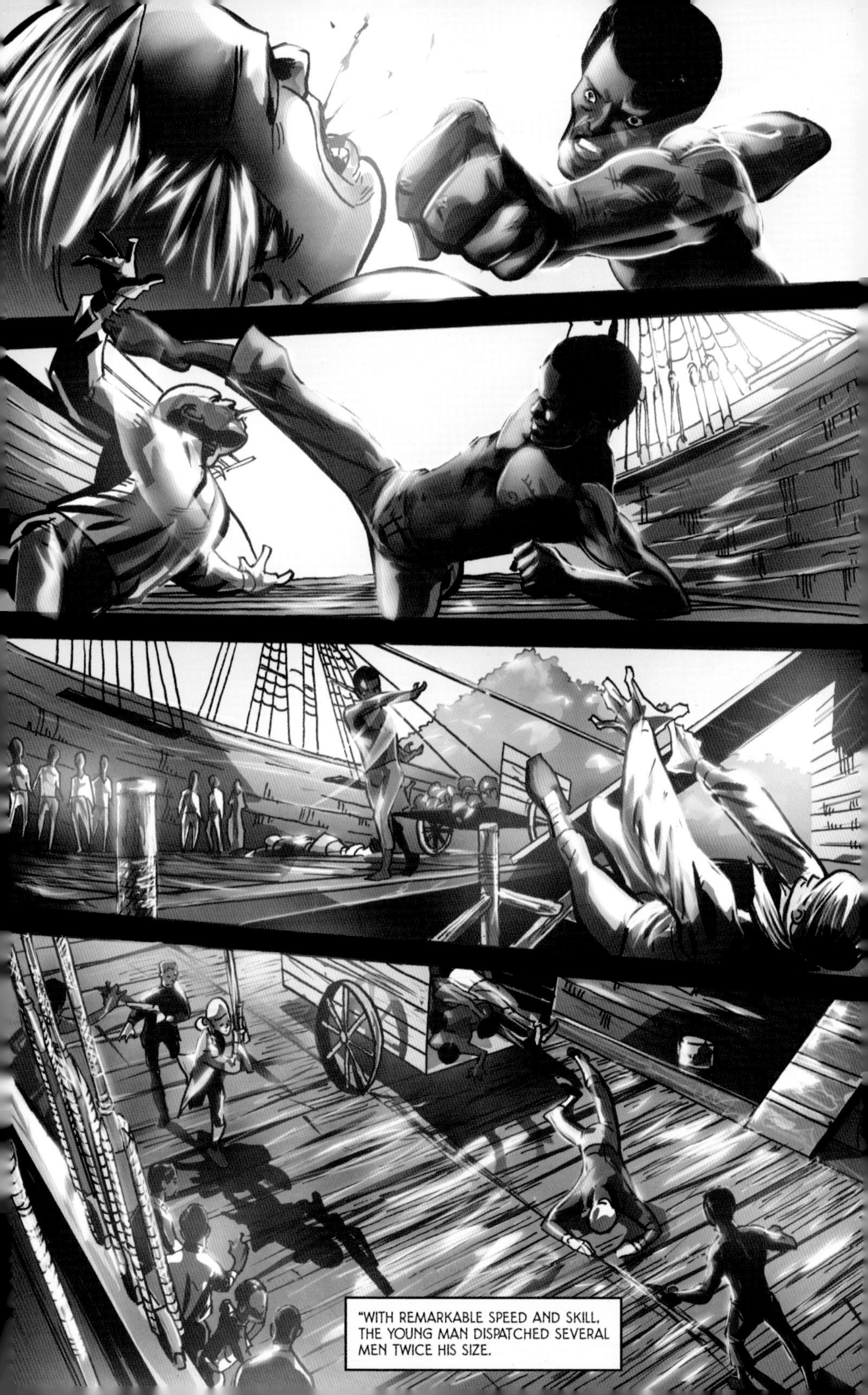
"WITH REMARKABLE SPEED AND SKILL, THE YOUNG MAN DISPATCHED SEVERAL MEN TWICE HIS SIZE.

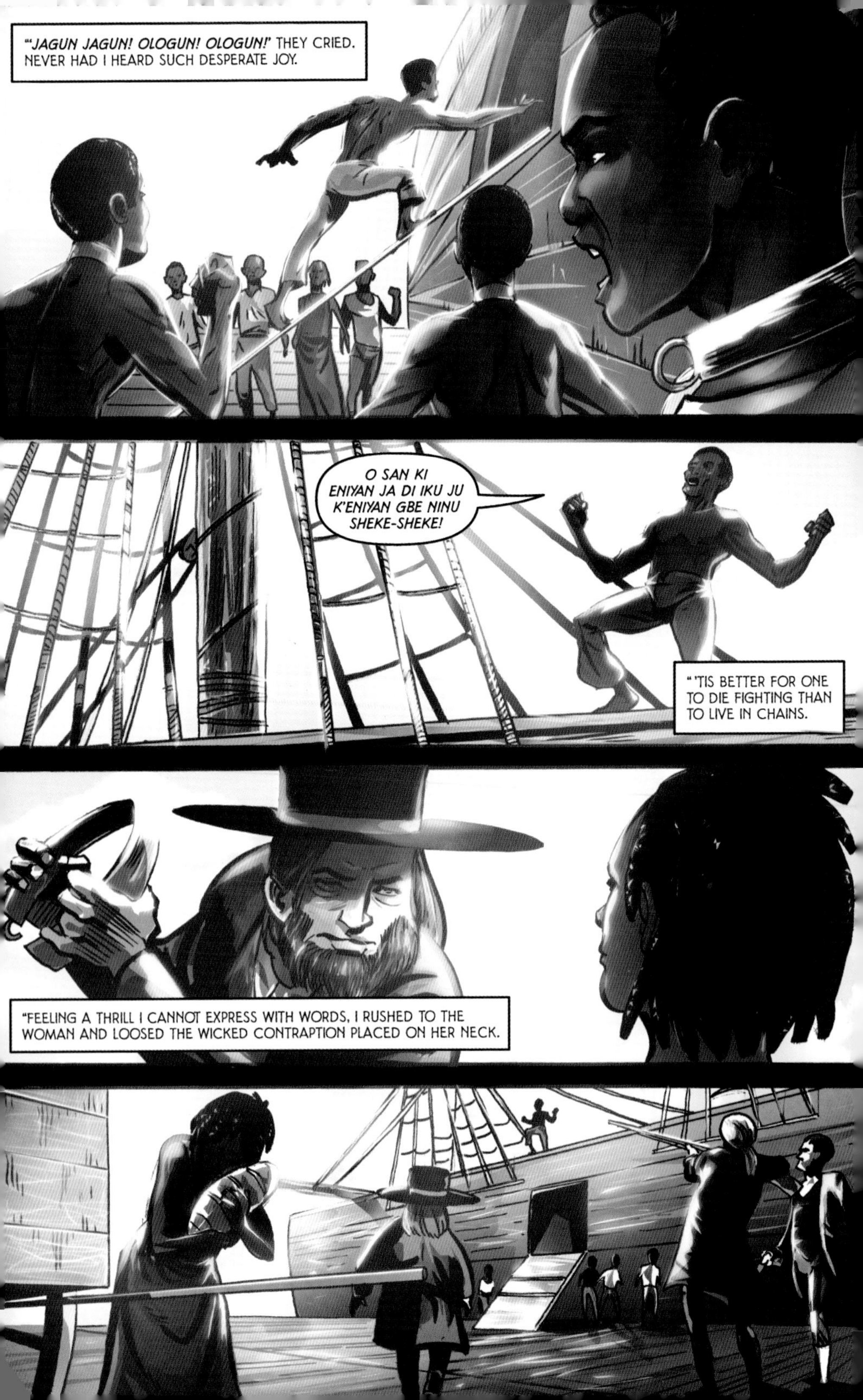
"'JAGUN JAGUN! OLOGUN! OLOGUN!' THEY CRIED. NEVER HAD I HEARD SUCH DESPERATE JOY.
O SAN KI ENIYAN JA DI IKU JU K'ENIYAN GBE NINU SHEKE-SHEKE!
"'TIS BETTER FOR ONE TO DIE FIGHTING THAN TO LIVE IN CHAINS.
"FEELING A THRILL I CANNOT EXPRESS WITH WORDS, I RUSHED TO THE WOMAN AND LOOSED THE WICKED CONTRAPTION PLACED ON HER NECK.

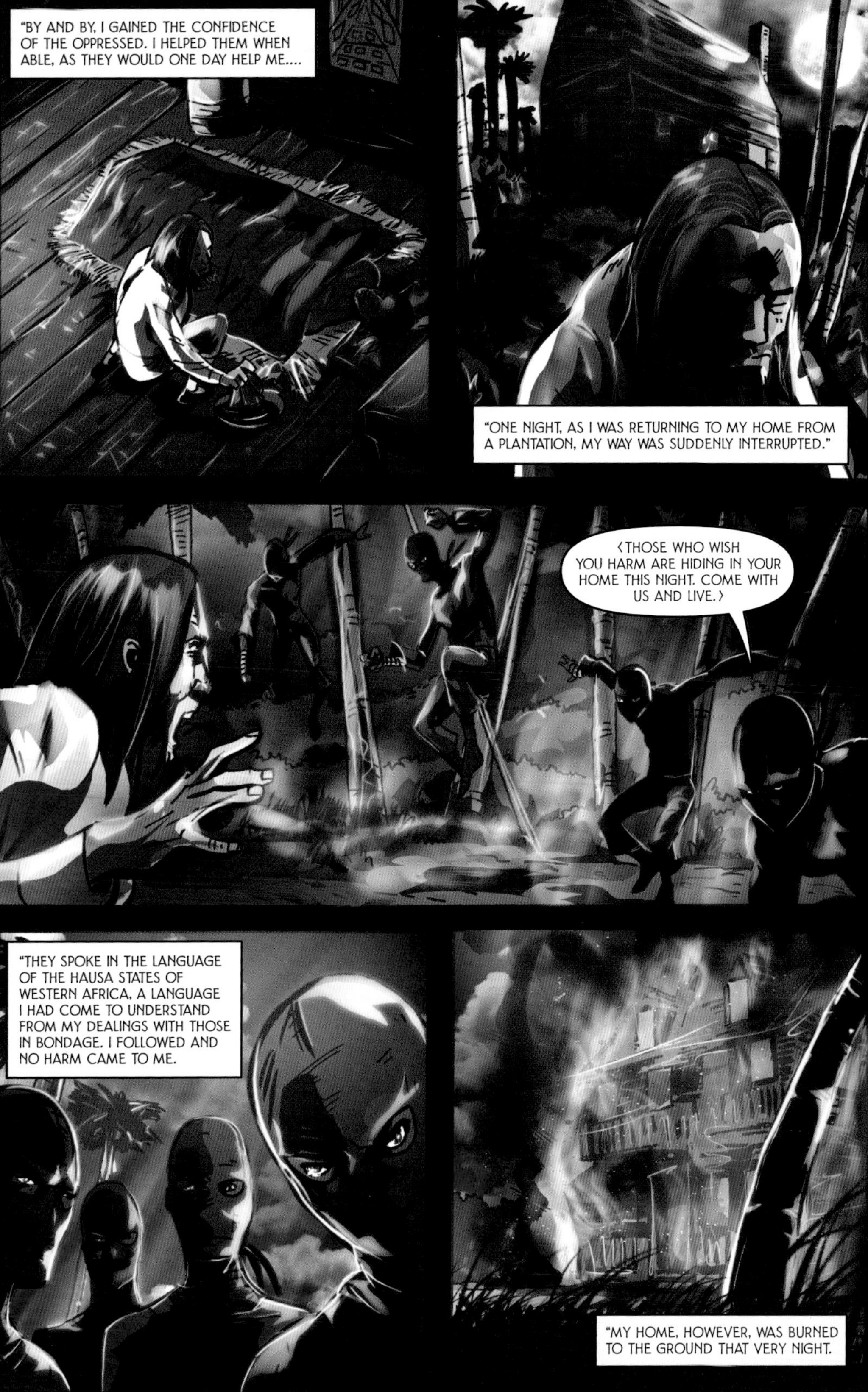
"BY AND BY, I GAINED THE CONFIDENCE OF THE OPPRESSED. I HELPED THEM WHEN ABLE, AS THEY WOULD ONE DAY HELP ME....
"ONE NIGHT, AS I WAS RETURNING TO MY HOME FROM A PLANTATION, MY WAY WAS SUDDENLY INTERRUPTED."
<THOSE WHO WISH YOU HARM ARE HIDING IN YOUR HOME THIS NIGHT. COME WITH US AND LIVE.>
"THEY SPOKE IN THE LANGUAGE OF THE HAUSA STATES OF WESTERN AFRICA, A LANGUAGE I HAD COME TO UNDERSTAND FROM MY DEALINGS WITH THOSE IN BONDAGE. I FOLLOWED AND NO HARM CAME TO ME.
"MY HOME, HOWEVER, WAS BURNED TO THE GROUND THAT VERY NIGHT.

"THEY IN TURN SELECTED AND TRAINED FOUR MEN EACH, AND THUS, BY AND BY, CREATED AN ARMY TO FIGHT FOR FREEDOM.

⟨WILL YOU JOIN US?⟩

"I DID.

"SOON I BEGAN TRAINING AND LEARNED DAMBE FROM THE GREAT MASTER. I WAS GIVEN THE NAME K'ANK'ANE ANNABI, 'LITTLE PROPHET.'

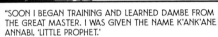

"I ALSO CONTINUED MY VENTURES TO PLANTATIONS, MUCH AGAINST THE WISHES OF OLOGUN. I EXPLAINED THE NEED OF HOPE FOR THOSE HELD CAPTIVE—HE EXPRESSED THE DANGERS OF IT.

"NO DOUBT, IT WAS FROM ONE OF THESE VISITS THAT I WAS FOLLOWED TO THE ENCAMPMENT BY A BRITISH SPY.

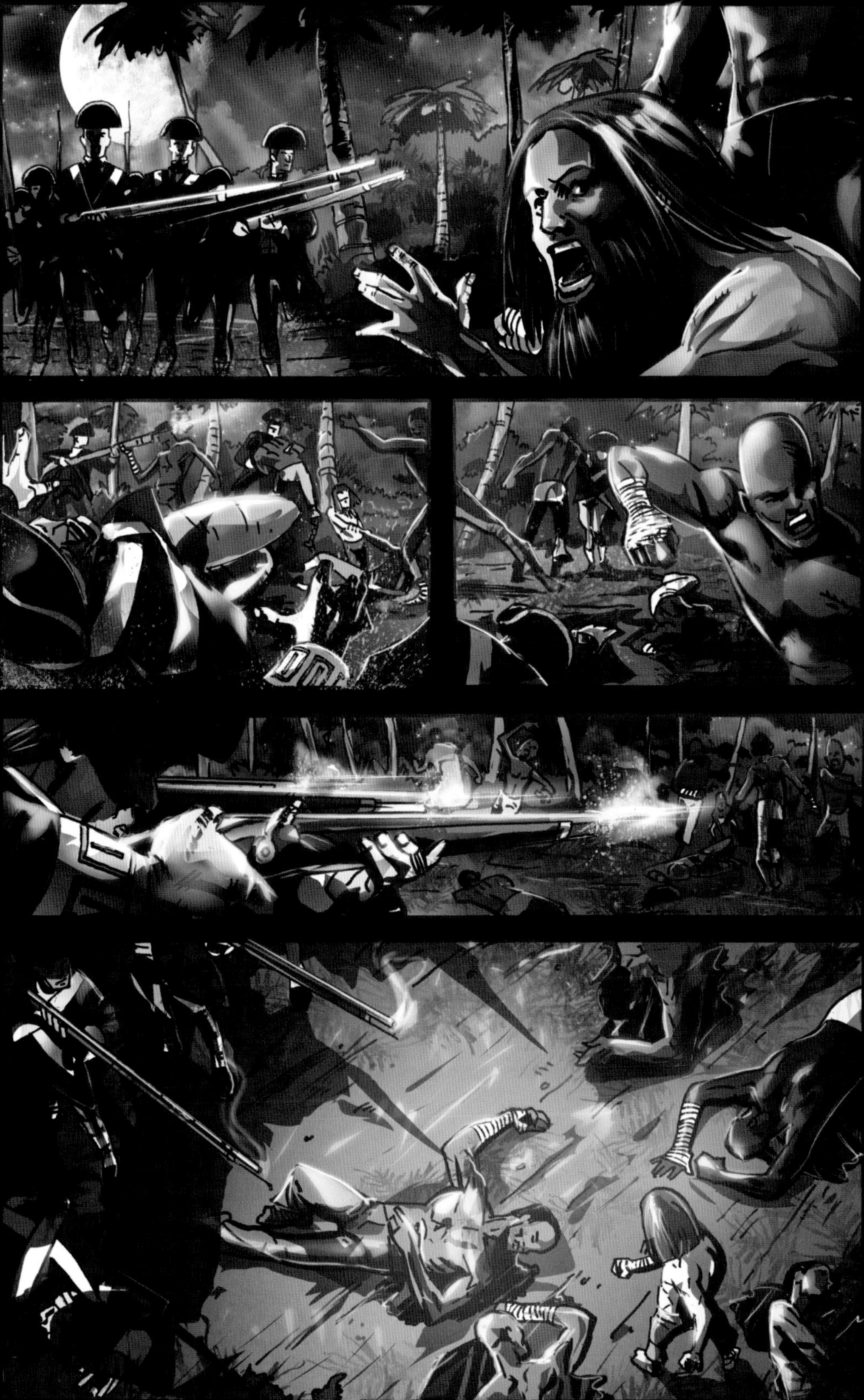

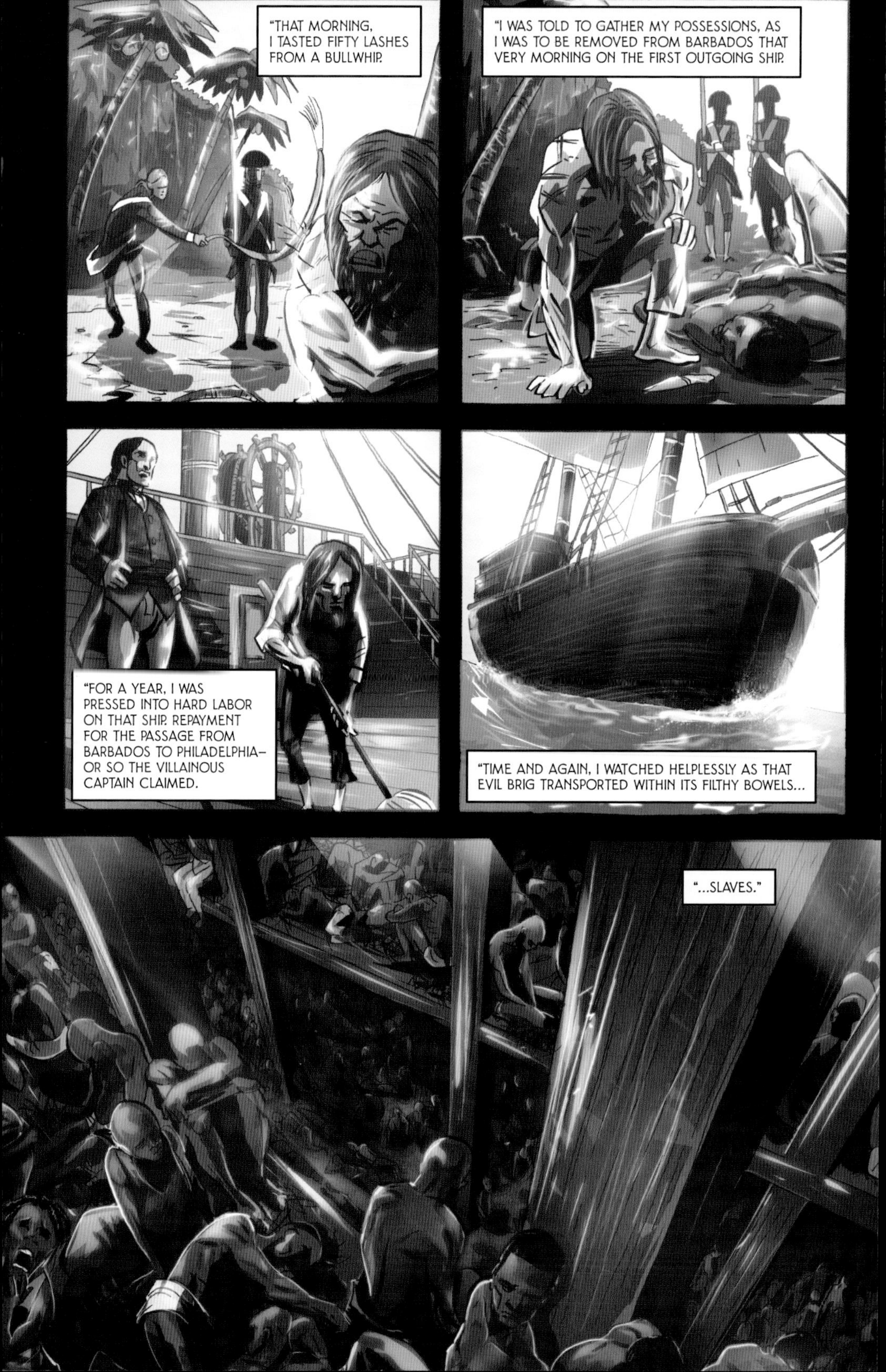
"THAT MORNING, I TASTED FIFTY LASHES FROM A BULLWHIP.
"I WAS TOLD TO GATHER MY POSSESSIONS, AS I WAS TO BE REMOVED FROM BARBADOS THAT VERY MORNING ON THE FIRST OUTGOING SHIP.
"FOR A YEAR, I WAS PRESSED INTO HARD LABOR ON THAT SHIP. REPAYMENT FOR THE PASSAGE FROM BARBADOS TO PHILADELPHIA– OR SO THE VILLAINOUS CAPTAIN CLAIMED.
"TIME AND AGAIN, I WATCHED HELPLESSLY AS THAT EVIL BRIG TRANSPORTED WITHIN ITS FILTHY BOWELS...
"...SLAVES."

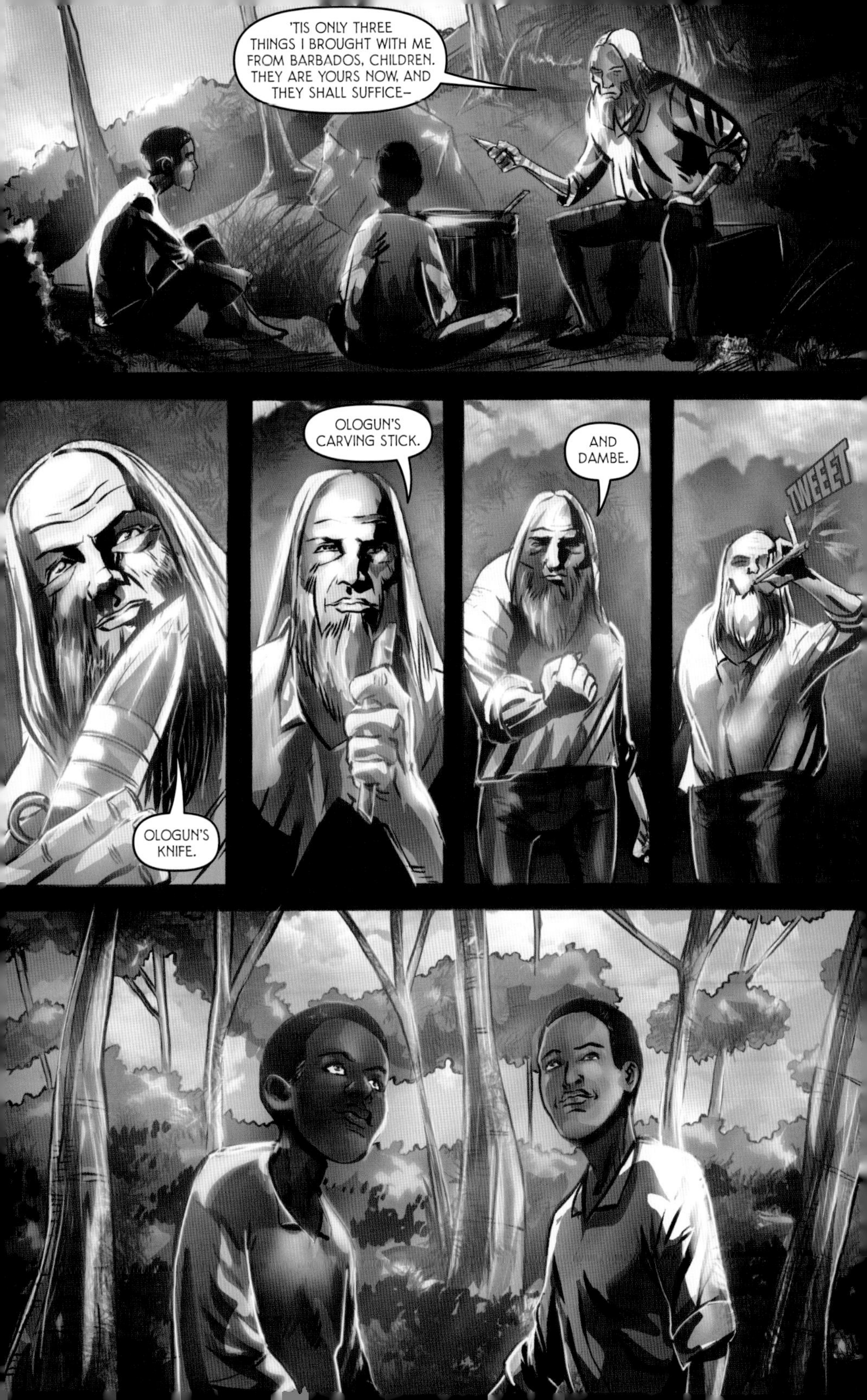
'TIS ONLY THREE THINGS I BROUGHT WITH ME FROM BARBADOS, CHILDREN. THEY ARE YOURS NOW, AND THEY SHALL SUFFICE–
OLOGUN'S KNIFE.
OLOGUN'S CARVING STICK.
AND DAMBE.
TWEEET

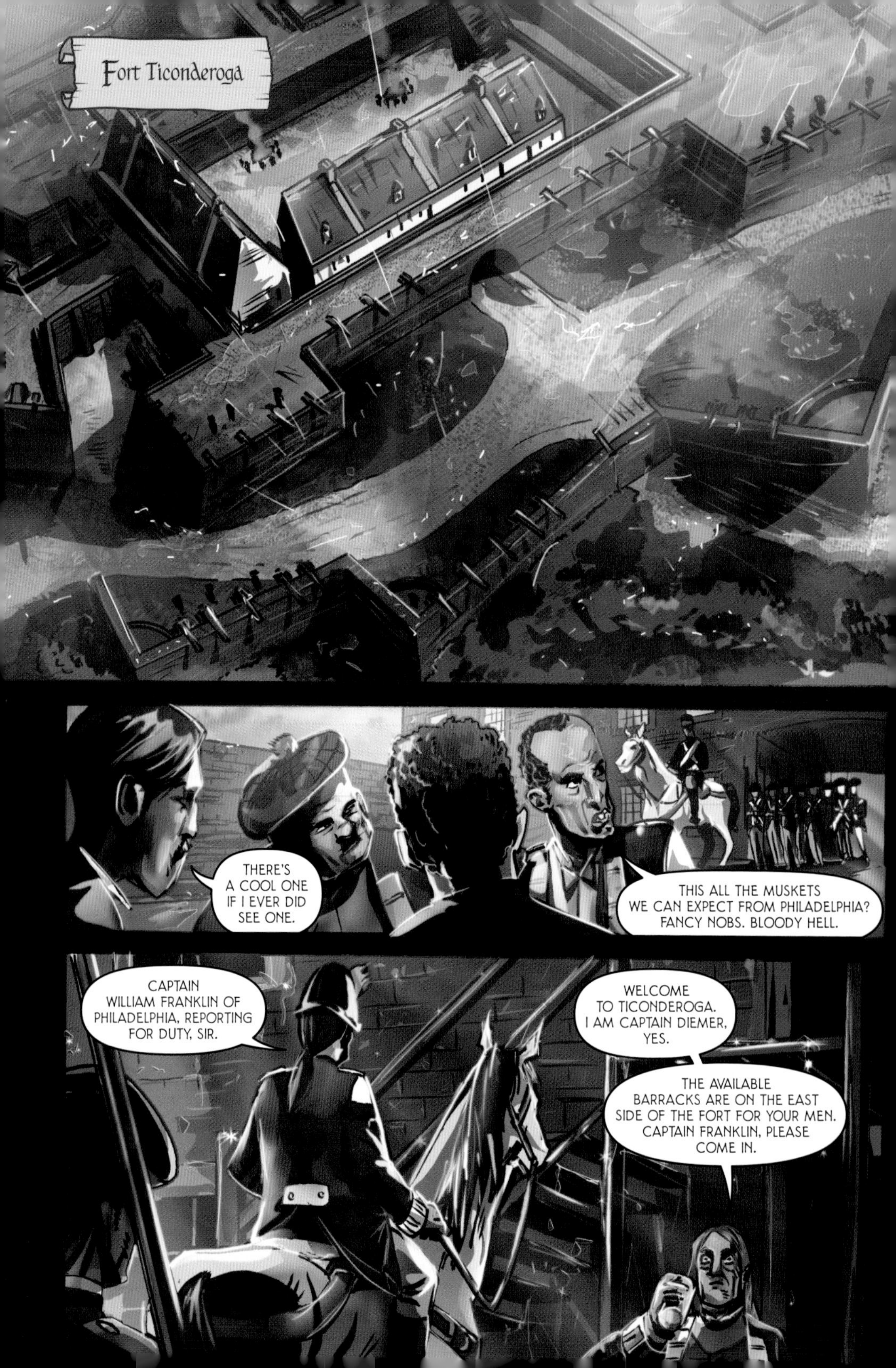

Fort Ticonderoga
THERE'S A COOL ONE IF I EVER DID SEE ONE.
THIS ALL THE MUSKETS WE CAN EXPECT FROM PHILADELPHIA? FANCY NOBS. BLOODY HELL.
CAPTAIN WILLIAM FRANKLIN OF PHILADELPHIA, REPORTING FOR DUTY, SIR.
WELCOME TO TICONDEROGA. I AM CAPTAIN DIEMER, YES.
THE AVAILABLE BARRACKS ARE ON THE EAST SIDE OF THE FORT FOR YOUR MEN. CAPTAIN FRANKLIN, PLEASE COME IN.

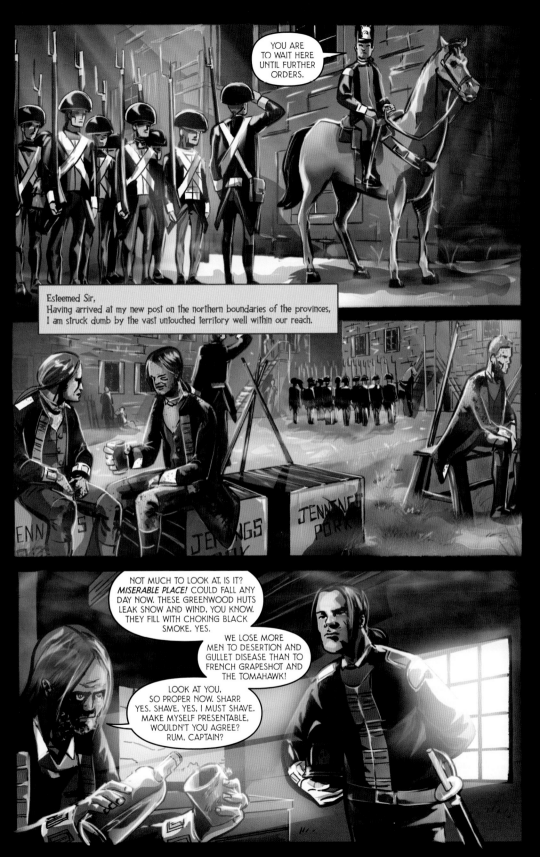

PLACE THIS MAN IN THE STOCKADE.

CROSS ME AGAIN, DOG, AND I WILL SEPARATE THAT WORTHLESS HEAD FROM YOUR BODY, UNDERSTAND?

AND ESCORT *THAT* OUT OF THIS FORT.

LIKE I SAID, THERE'S A COOL ONE IF I EVER DID SEE ONE.

BREACH!

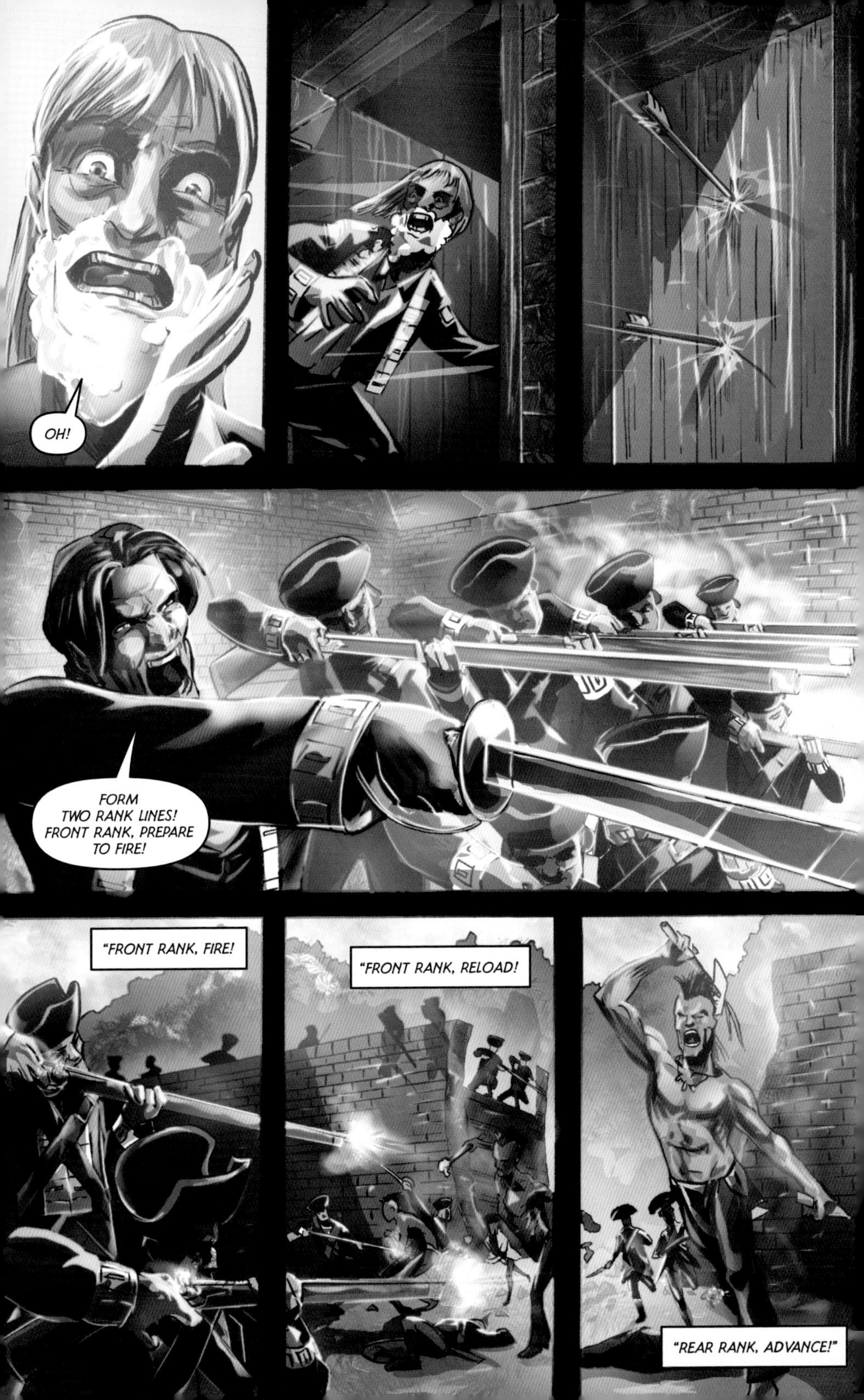
OH!
FORM TWO RANK LINES! FRONT RANK, PREPARE TO FIRE!
"FRONT RANK, FIRE!
"FRONT RANK, RELOAD!
"REAR RANK, ADVANCE!"

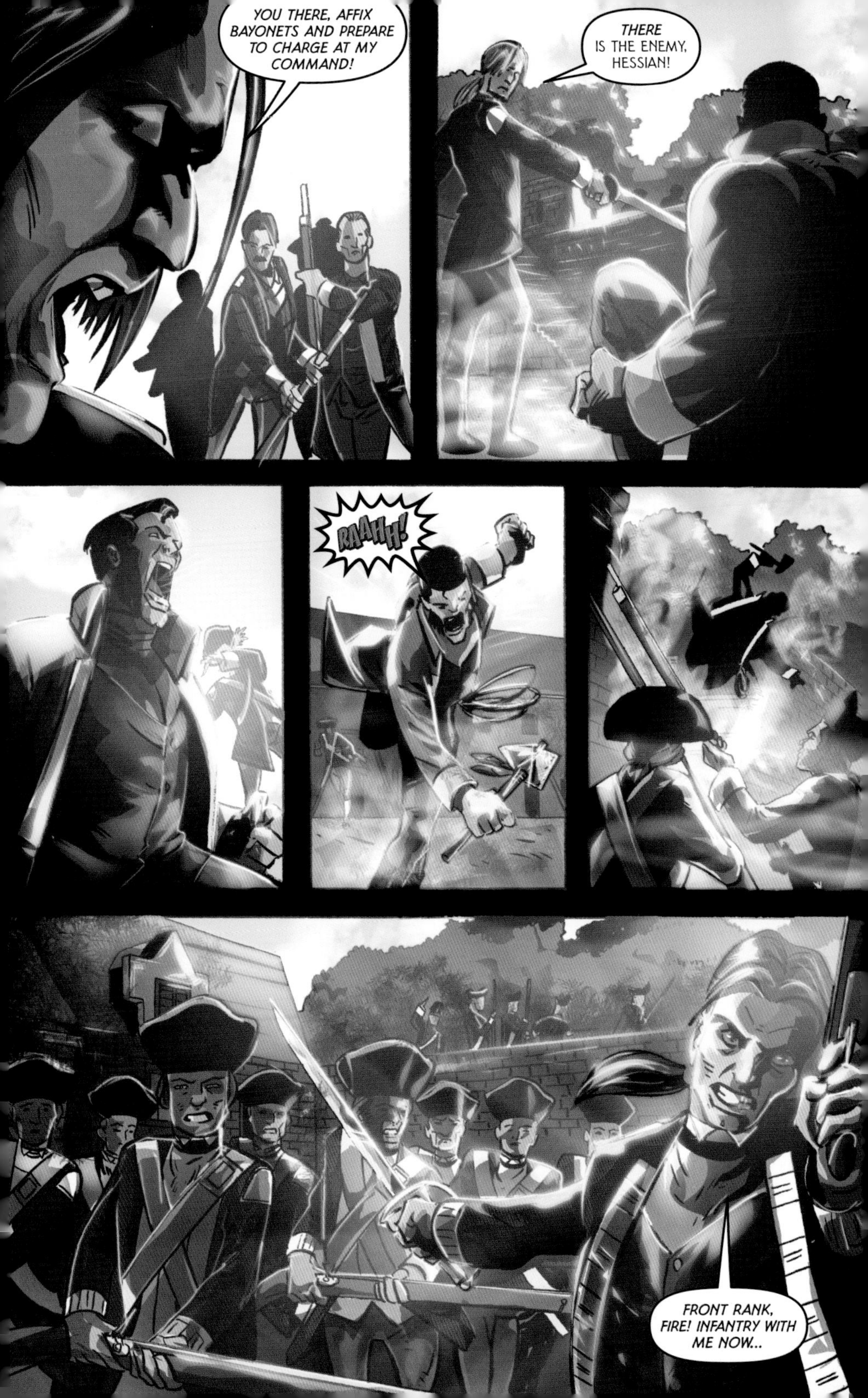
YOU THERE, AFFIX BAYONETS AND PREPARE TO CHARGE AT MY COMMAND!
THERE IS THE ENEMY, HESSIAN!
RAAHH!
FRONT RANK, FIRE! INFANTRY WITH ME NOW...

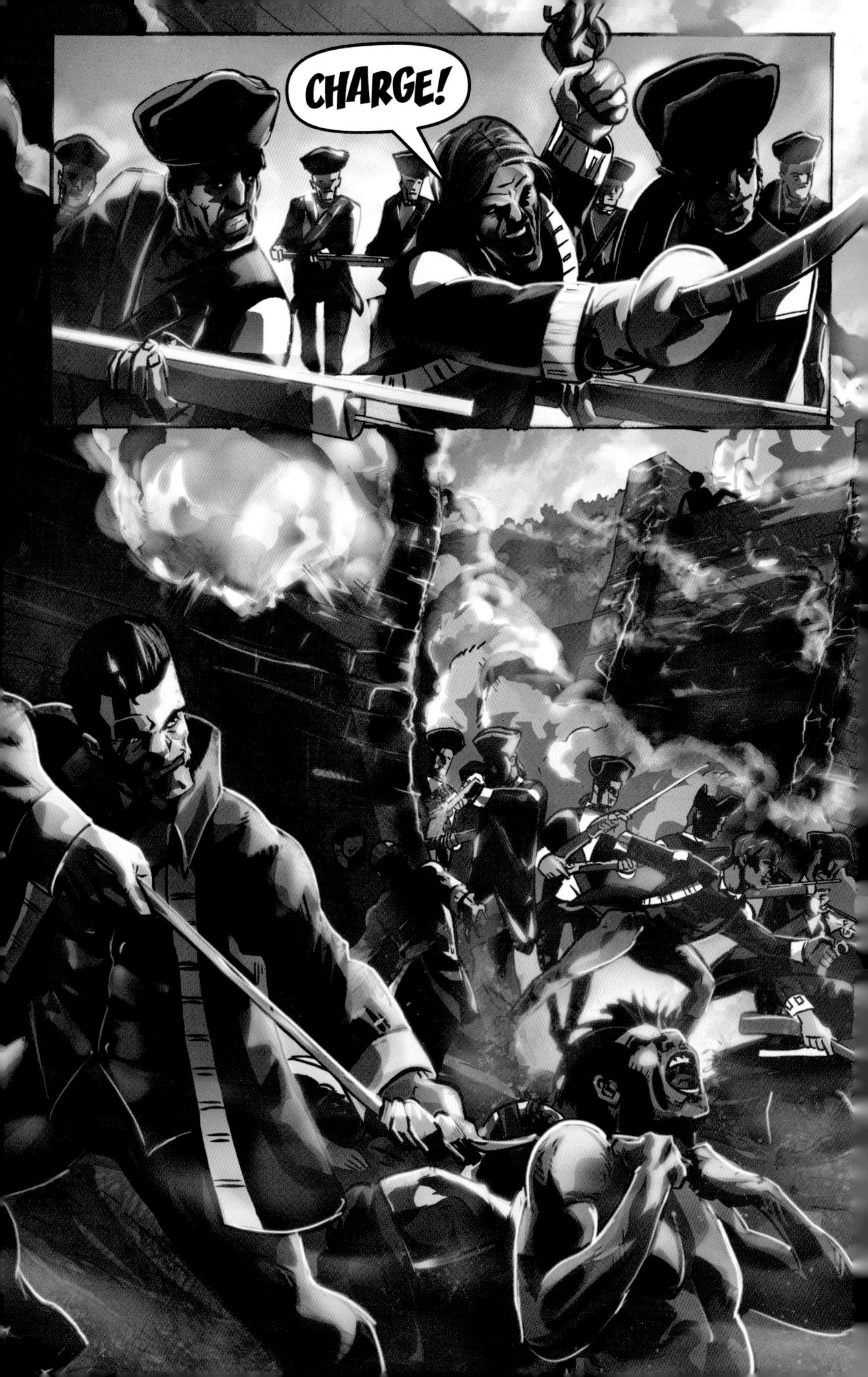
CHARGE!

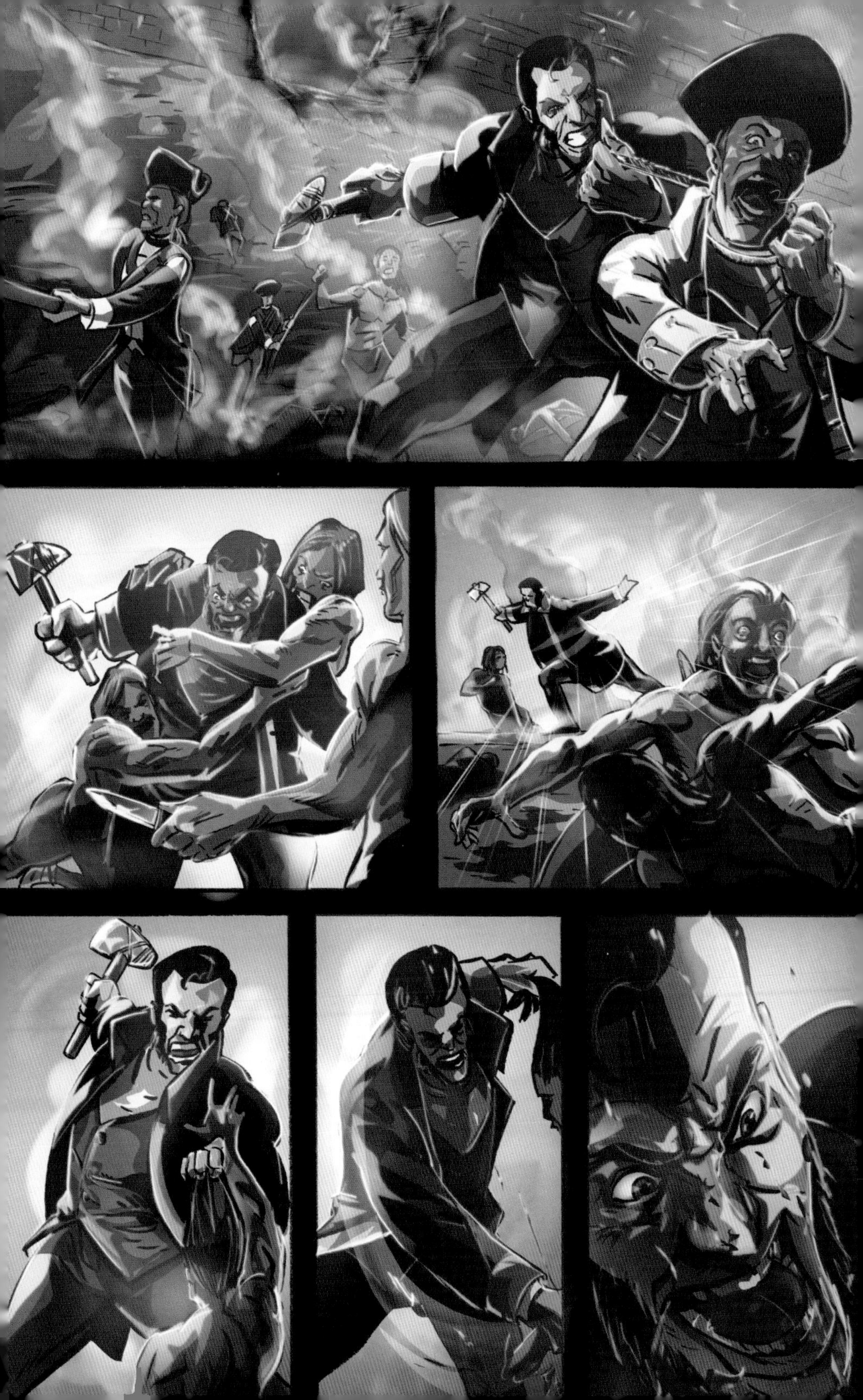

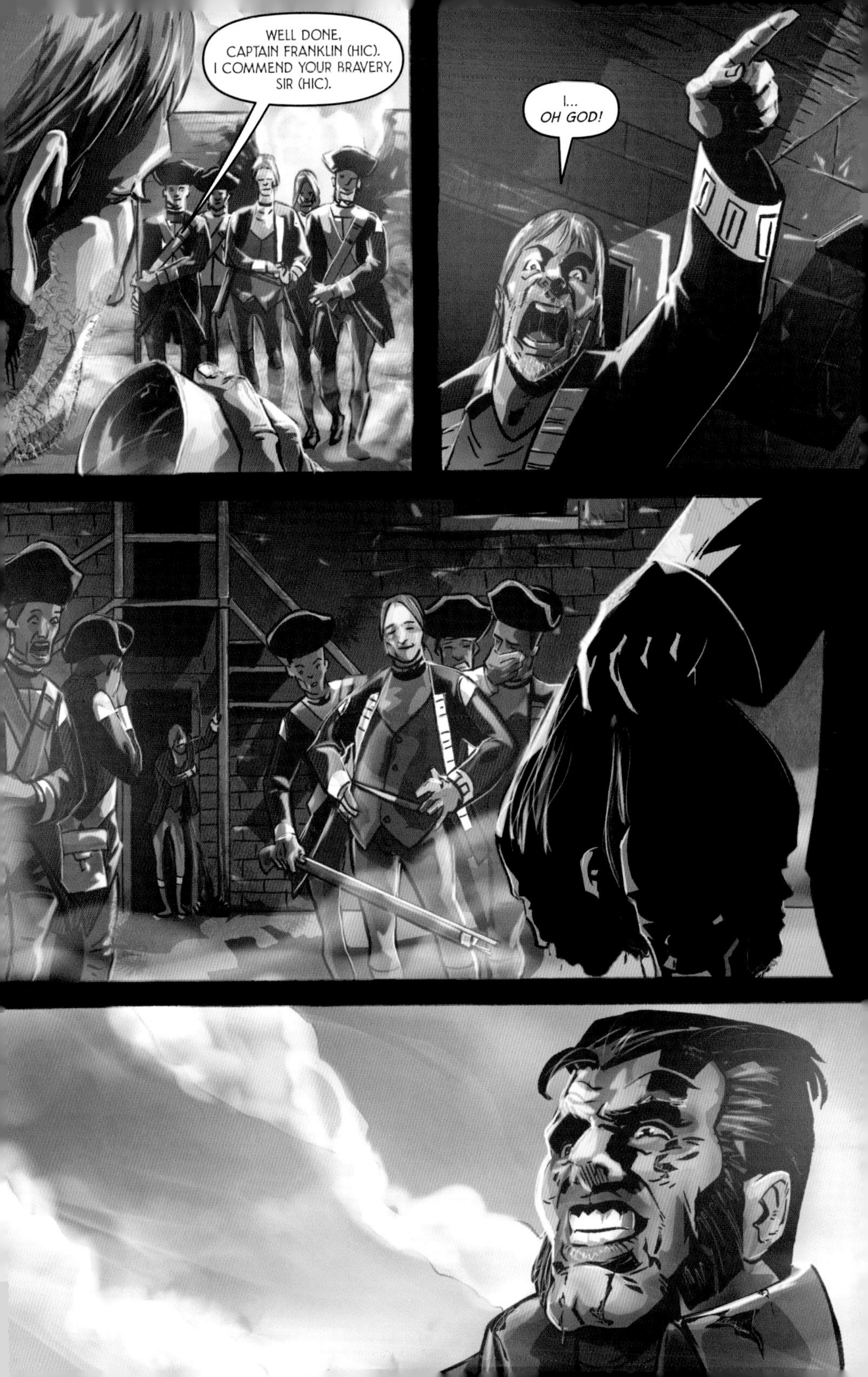
WELL DONE, CAPTAIN FRANKLIN (HIC). I COMMEND YOUR BRAVERY, SIR (HIC).
I... OH GOD!

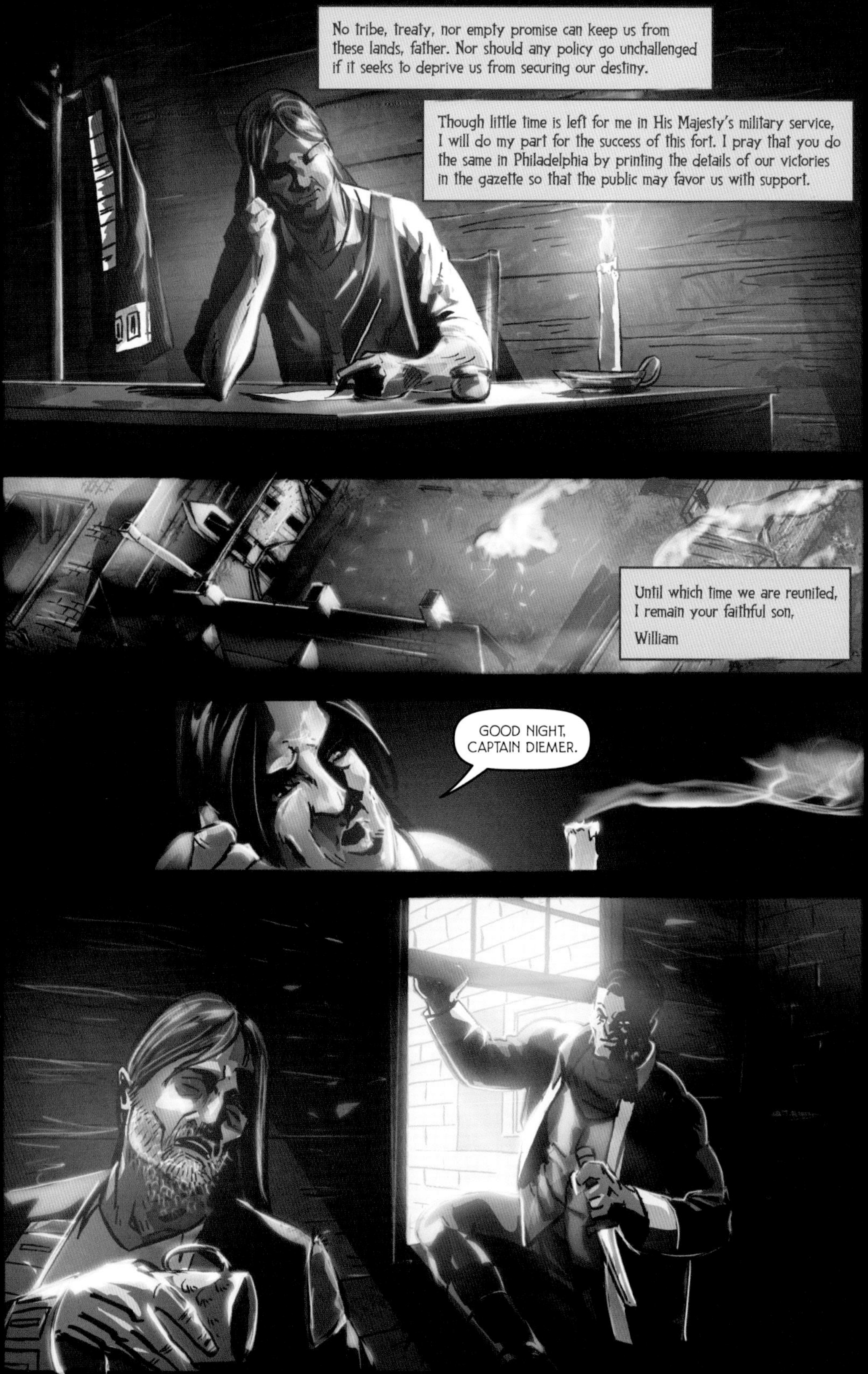
No tribe, treaty, nor empty promise can keep us from these lands, father. Nor should any policy go unchallenged if it seeks to deprive us from securing our destiny.
Though little time is left for me in His Majesty's military service, I will do my part for the success of this fort. I pray that you do the same in Philadelphia by printing the details of our victories in the gazette so that the public may favor us with support.
Until which time we are reunited, I remain your faithful son,
William
GOOD NIGHT, CAPTAIN DIEMER.

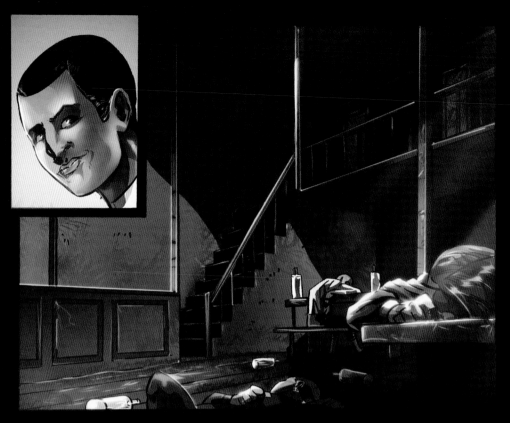

FWANKLIN ITH PAYING UTH MORE MONEY TO TAKE THEM, DEAR.

HOW MUCH MORE?

DOUBLE WATE FOR EACH.

WEII, THEN, THAT IS DIFFERENT.

GIVE THEM THE ROOM OVER THE WASHHOUSE. THEY CAN COME AND GO FROM THERE WITHOUT BEING SEEN BY THE OTHER GUESTS.

BE SURE TO SHOW THEM THE RULES, EZRA.

WULES. GLUG-GLUG-GLUG-GLUG.

'RULES OF THE TAVERN'
4 PENCE A NIGHT FOR BED
6 PENCE WITH POTLUCK
2 PENCE FOR HORSEKEEPING
NO MORE THAN FIVE TO SLEEP IN ONE BED.
NO BOOTS TO BE WORN IN BED.
NO RAZOR GRINDERS OR TINKERS TO BE TAKEN IN.
NO DOGS ALLOWED IN THE KITCHEN.
ORGAN GRINDERS TO SLEEP IN THE WASHHOUSE.

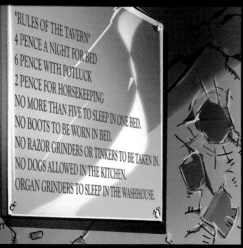

I KNOW YOU'RE WORKING FOR THAT PWINT THOP, BUT IF YOU HELP ME AWOUND HERE WITH MY WORK, TOO, I'LL PAY YOU EACH THREE PENTH A WEEK.

DO A LOT OF SHIPS' CAPTAINS STAY HERE?

CAPTHINS, THAILORS, AN' EVWEE TWADE THERE ITH.

BRODY AND I WILL HELP IN ANY WAY WE CAN, MR. JONES.

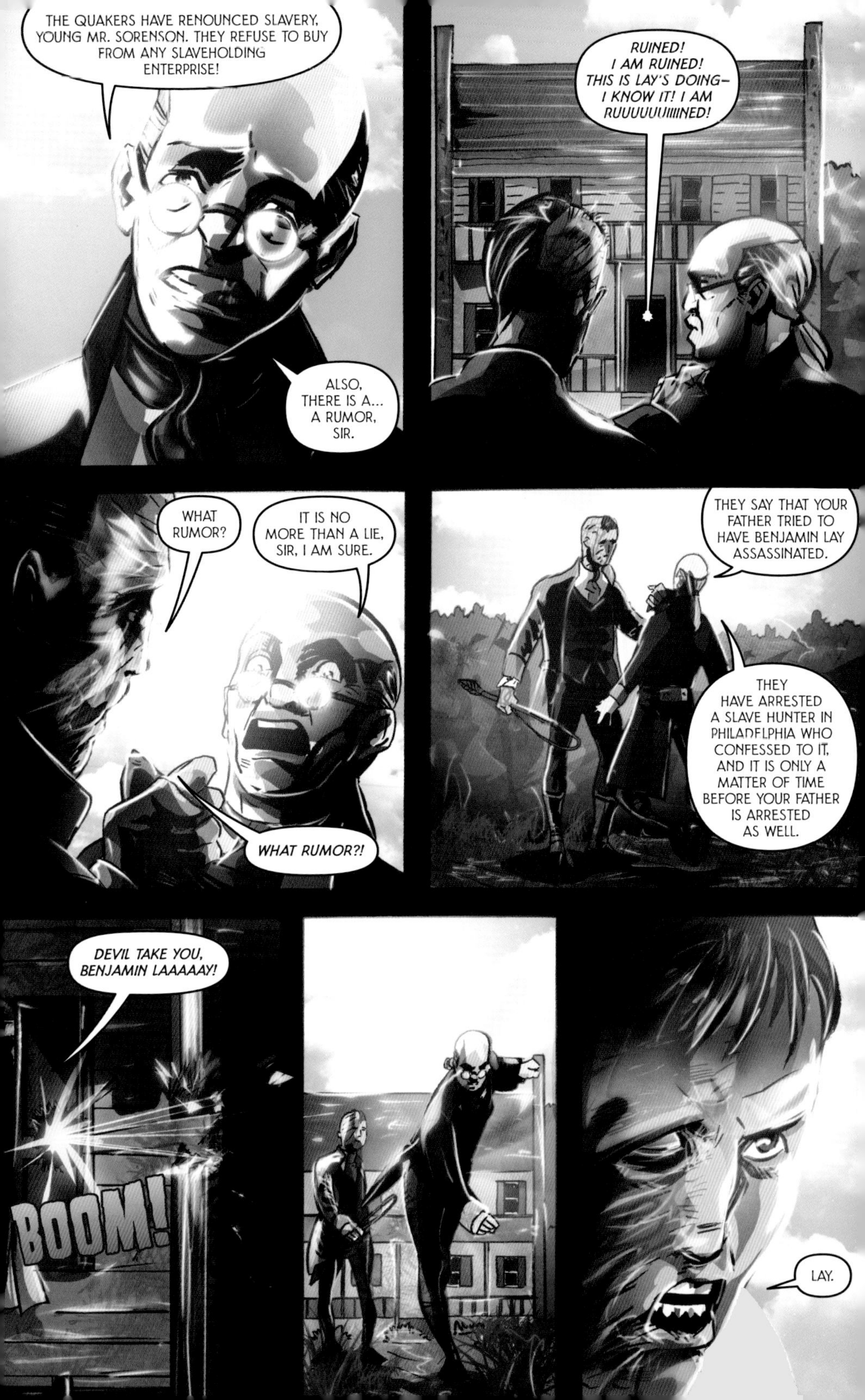
THE QUAKERS HAVE RENOUNCED SLAVERY, YOUNG MR. SORENSON. THEY REFUSE TO BUY FROM ANY SLAVEHOLDING ENTERPRISE!
ALSO, THERE IS A... A RUMOR, SIR.
RUINED! I AM RUINED! THIS IS LAY'S DOING— I KNOW IT! I AM RUUUUUUIIIINED!
WHAT RUMOR?
IT IS NO MORE THAN A LIE, SIR, I AM SURE.
WHAT RUMOR?!
THEY SAY THAT YOUR FATHER TRIED TO HAVE BENJAMIN LAY ASSASSINATED.
THEY HAVE ARRESTED A SLAVE HUNTER IN PHILADELPHIA WHO CONFESSED TO IT, AND IT IS ONLY A MATTER OF TIME BEFORE YOUR FATHER IS ARRESTED AS WELL.
DEVIL TAKE YOU, BENJAMIN LAAAAAY!
BOOM!
LAY.

WELL, FATHER, IF YOU HAD READ MY LETTERS INSTEAD OF BUNDLING THEM UP WITH TWINE, YOU MIGHT HAVE KNOWN THAT MY ACTIVE MILITARY SERVICE CONCLUDED TWO WEEKS AGO.

FRANKLY, I AM SURPRISED. I EXPECTED THE WHOLE OF PHILADELPHIA TO KNOW OF MY EXPLOITS IN TICONDEROGA BY NOW.

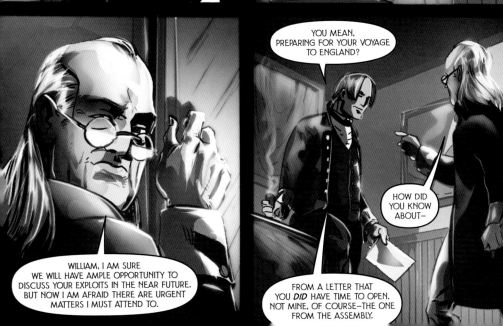

YOU MEAN, PREPARING FOR YOUR VOYAGE TO ENGLAND?

HOW DID YOU KNOW ABOUT—

WILLIAM, I AM SURE WE WILL HAVE AMPLE OPPORTUNITY TO DISCUSS YOUR EXPLOITS IN THE NEAR FUTURE. BUT NOW I AM AFRAID THERE ARE URGENT MATTERS I MUST ATTEND TO.

FROM A LETTER THAT YOU *DID* HAVE TIME TO OPEN. NOT MINE, OF COURSE—THE ONE FROM THE ASSEMBLY.

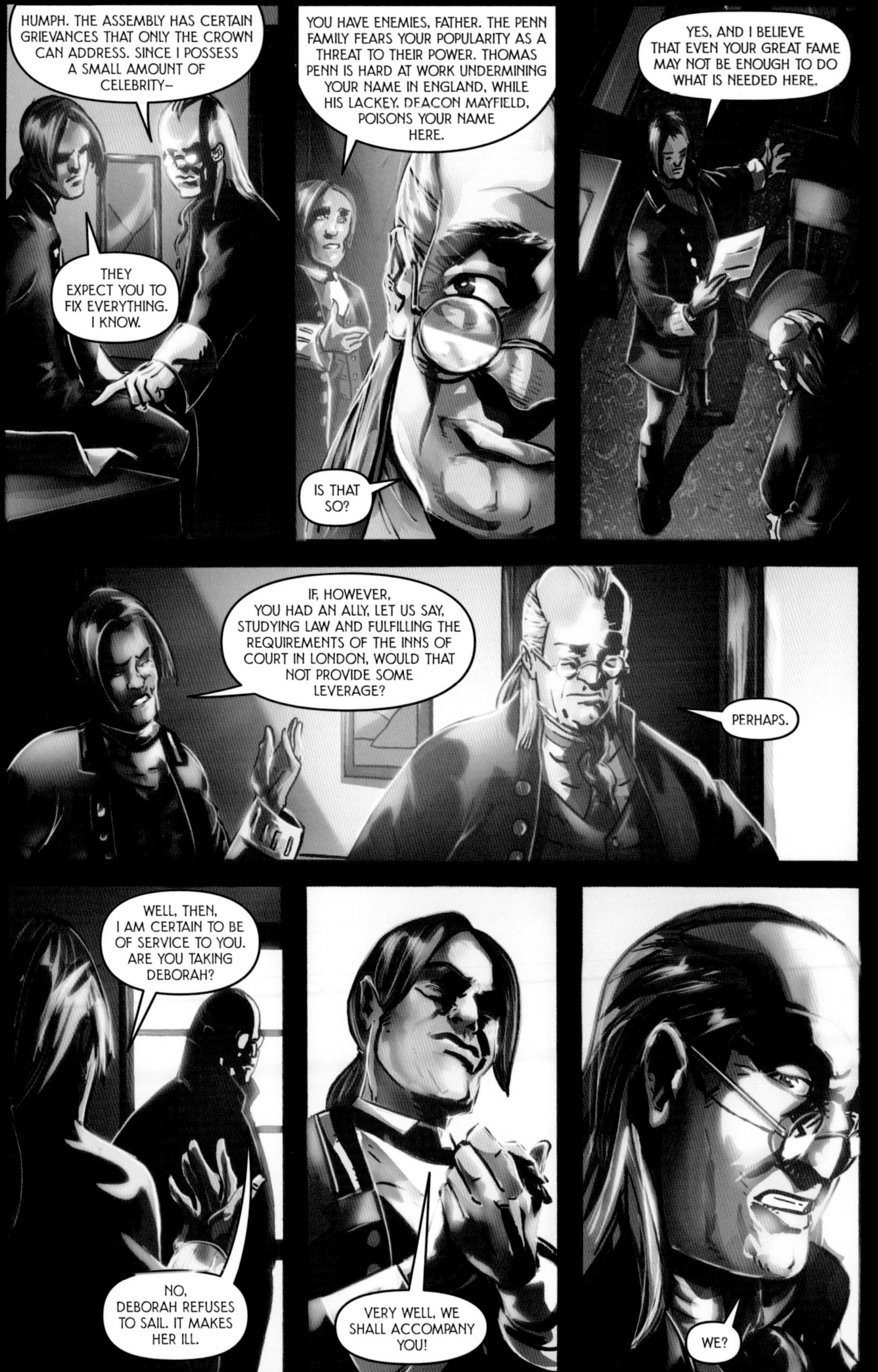
HUMPH. THE ASSEMBLY HAS CERTAIN GRIEVANCES THAT ONLY THE CROWN CAN ADDRESS. SINCE I POSSESS A SMALL AMOUNT OF CELEBRITY–
THEY EXPECT YOU TO FIX EVERYTHING. I KNOW.
YOU HAVE ENEMIES, FATHER. THE PENN FAMILY FEARS YOUR POPULARITY AS A THREAT TO THEIR POWER. THOMAS PENN IS HARD AT WORK UNDERMINING YOUR NAME IN ENGLAND, WHILE HIS LACKEY, DEACON MAYFIELD, POISONS YOUR NAME HERE.
IS THAT SO?
YES, AND I BELIEVE THAT EVEN YOUR GREAT FAME MAY NOT BE ENOUGH TO DO WHAT IS NEEDED HERE.
IF, HOWEVER, YOU HAD AN ALLY, LET US SAY, STUDYING LAW AND FULFILLING THE REQUIREMENTS OF THE INNS OF COURT IN LONDON, WOULD THAT NOT PROVIDE SOME LEVERAGE?
PERHAPS.
WELL, THEN, I AM CERTAIN TO BE OF SERVICE TO YOU. ARE YOU TAKING DEBORAH?
NO, DEBORAH REFUSES TO SAIL. IT MAKES HER ILL.
VERY WELL, WE SHALL ACCOMPANY YOU!
WE?

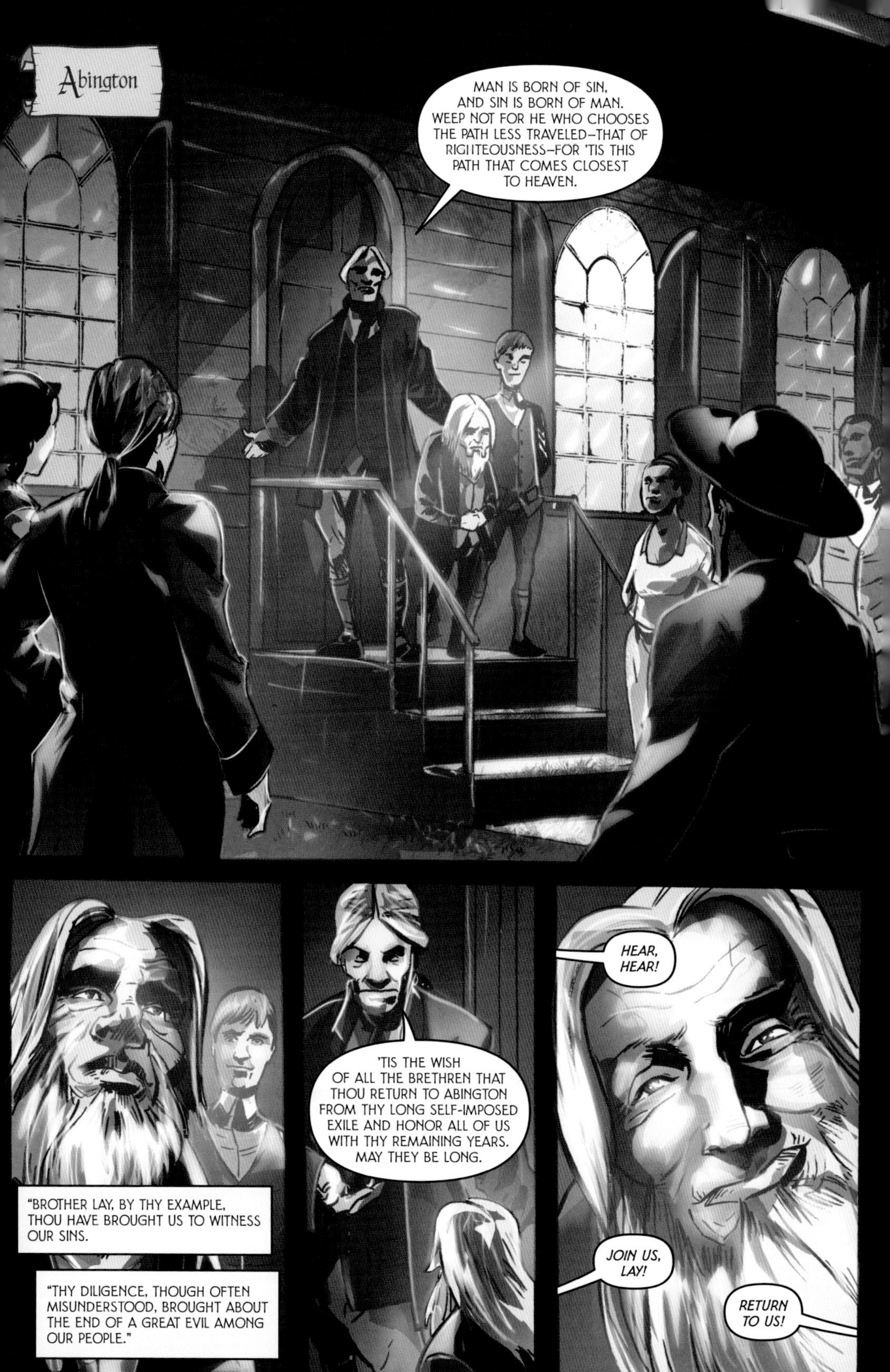
Abington
MAN IS BORN OF SIN, AND SIN IS BORN OF MAN. WEEP NOT FOR HE WHO CHOOSES THE PATH LESS TRAVELED—THAT OF RIGHTEOUSNESS—FOR 'TIS THIS PATH THAT COMES CLOSEST TO HEAVEN.
"BROTHER LAY, BY THY EXAMPLE, THOU HAVE BROUGHT US TO WITNESS OUR SINS.
"THY DILIGENCE, THOUGH OFTEN MISUNDERSTOOD, BROUGHT ABOUT THE END OF A GREAT EVIL AMONG OUR PEOPLE."
'TIS THE WISH OF ALL THE BRETHREN THAT THOU RETURN TO ABINGTON FROM THY LONG SELF-IMPOSED EXILE AND HONOR ALL OF US WITH THY REMAINING YEARS. MAY THEY BE LONG.
HEAR, HEAR!
JOIN US, LAY!
RETURN TO US!

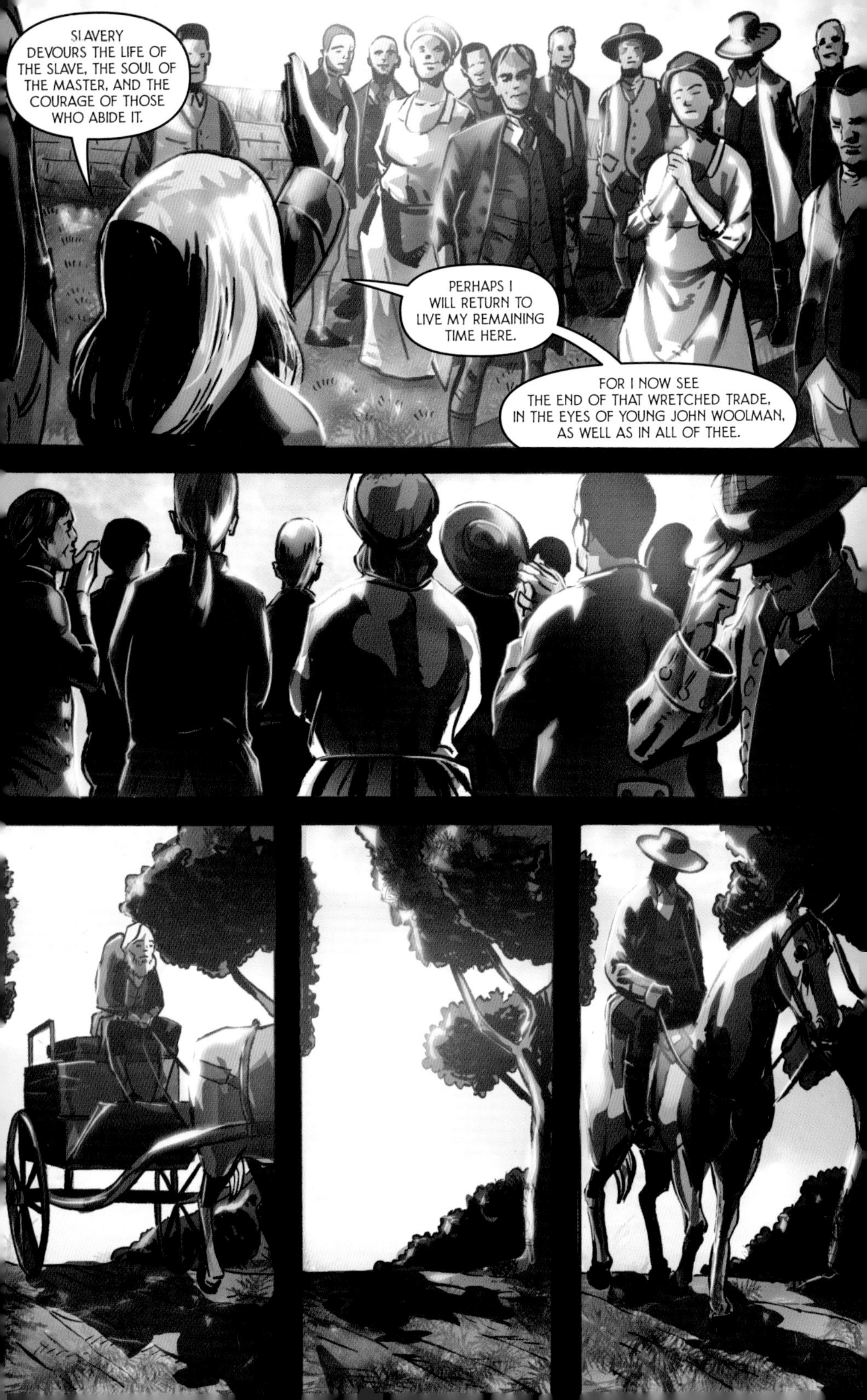
SLAVERY DEVOURS THE LIFE OF THE SLAVE, THE SOUL OF THE MASTER, AND THE COURAGE OF THOSE WHO ABIDE IT.
PERHAPS I WILL RETURN TO LIVE MY REMAINING TIME HERE.
FOR I NOW SEE THE END OF THAT WRETCHED TRADE, IN THE EYES OF YOUNG JOHN WOOLMAN, AS WELL AS IN ALL OF THEE.

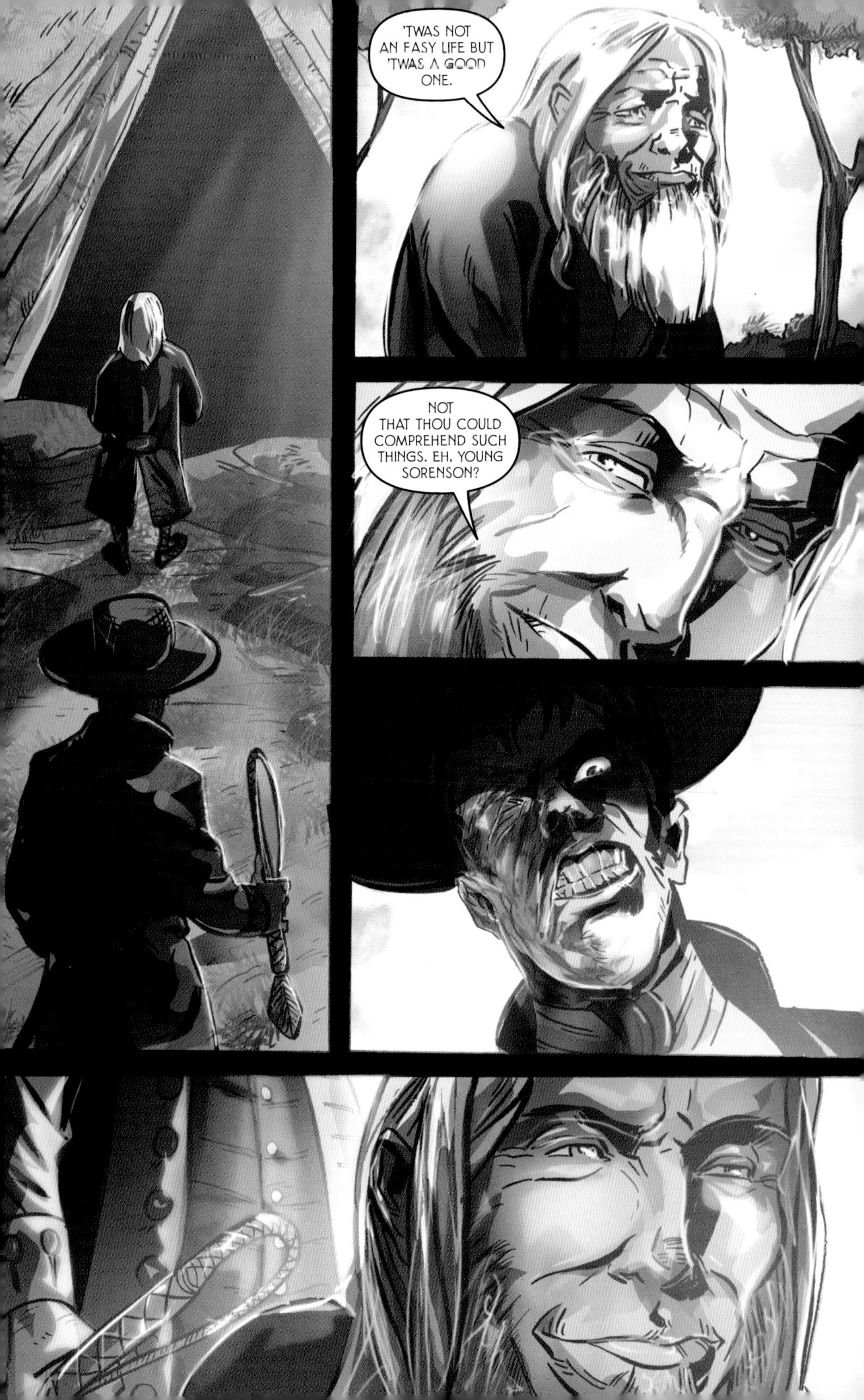
'TWAS NOT AN EASY LIFE BUT 'TWAS A GOOD ONE.
NOT THAT THOU COULD COMPREHEND SUCH THINGS. EH, YOUNG SORENSON?

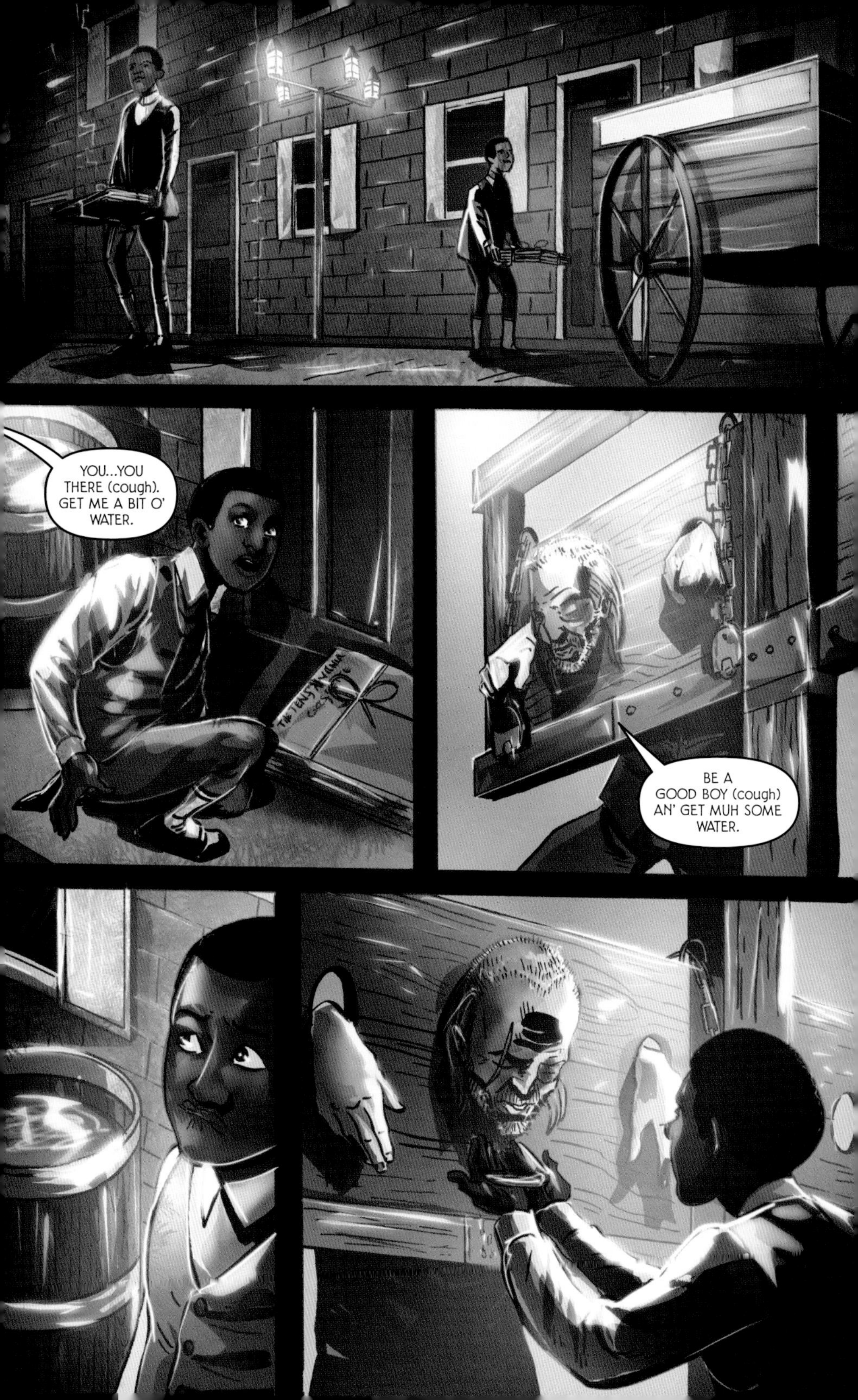
YOU...YOU THERE (cough). GET ME A BIT O' WATER.
BE A GOOD BOY (cough) AN' GET MUH SOME WATER.

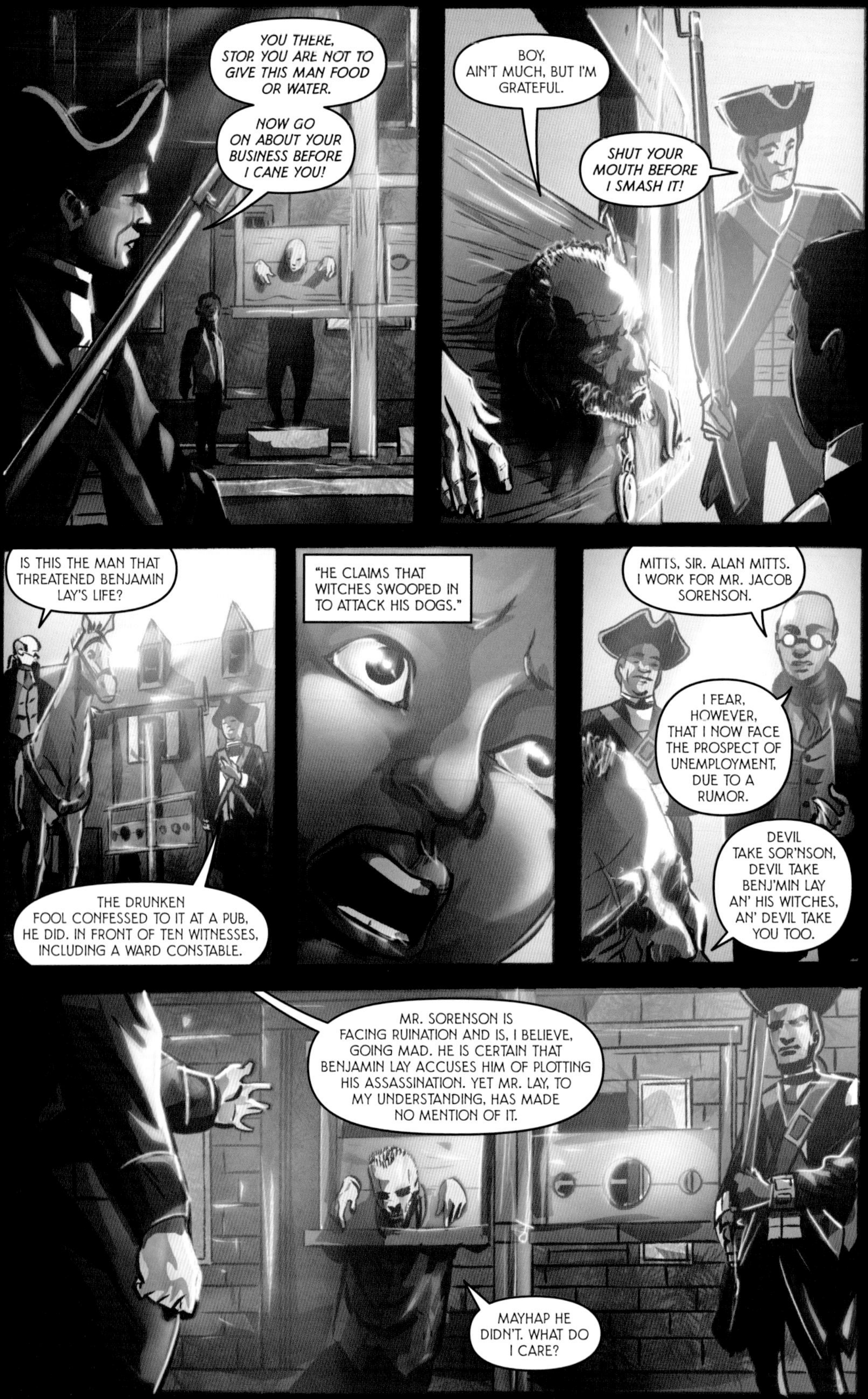

YOU THERE, STOP. YOU ARE NOT TO GIVE THIS MAN FOOD OR WATER.
NOW GO ON ABOUT YOUR BUSINESS BEFORE I CANE YOU!
BOY, AIN'T MUCH, BUT I'M GRATEFUL.
SHUT YOUR MOUTH BEFORE I SMASH IT!
IS THIS THE MAN THAT THREATENED BENJAMIN LAY'S LIFE?
THE DRUNKEN FOOL CONFESSED TO IT AT A PUB, HE DID. IN FRONT OF TEN WITNESSES, INCLUDING A WARD CONSTABLE.
"HE CLAIMS THAT WITCHES SWOOPED IN TO ATTACK HIS DOGS."
MITTS, SIR. ALAN MITTS. I WORK FOR MR. JACOB SORENSON.
I FEAR, HOWEVER, THAT I NOW FACE THE PROSPECT OF UNEMPLOYMENT, DUE TO A RUMOR.
DEVIL TAKE SOR'NSON, DEVIL TAKE BENJ'MIN LAY AN' HIS WITCHES, AN' DEVIL TAKE YOU TOO.
MR. SORENSON IS FACING RUINATION AND IS, I BELIEVE, GOING MAD. HE IS CERTAIN THAT BENJAMIN LAY ACCUSES HIM OF PLOTTING HIS ASSASSINATION. YET MR. LAY, TO MY UNDERSTANDING, HAS MADE NO MENTION OF IT.
MAYHAP HE DIDN'T. WHAT DO I CARE?

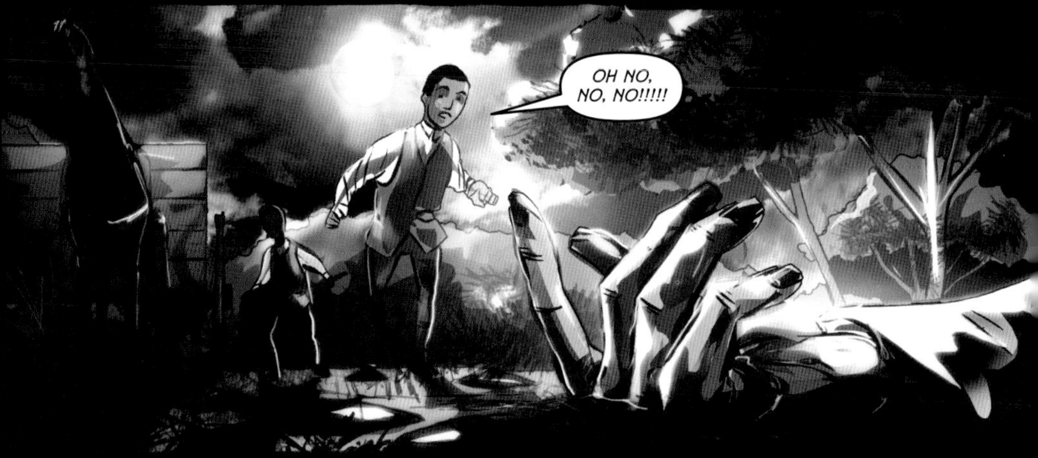
OH NO,
NO, NO!!!!!
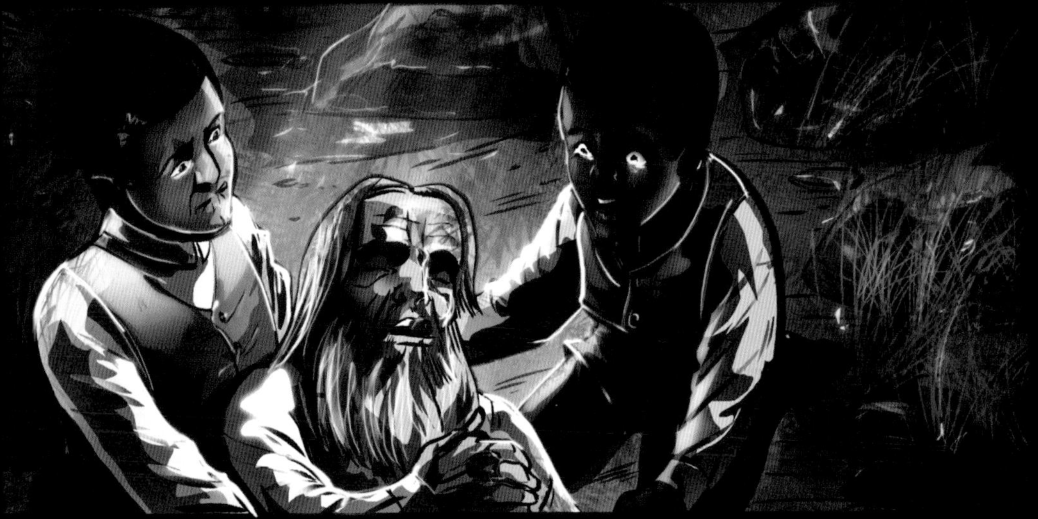
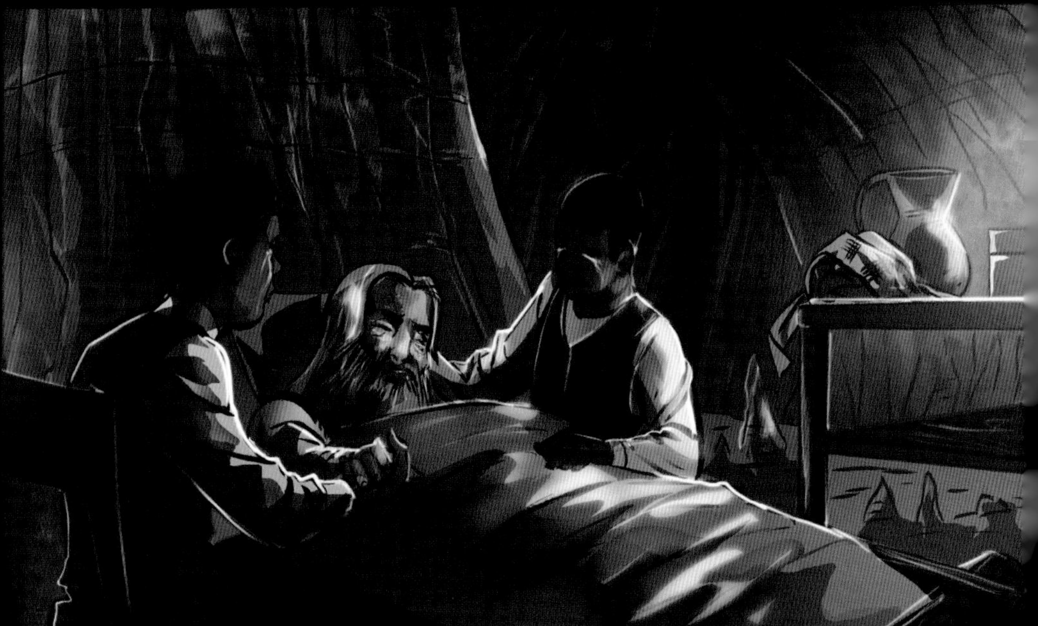

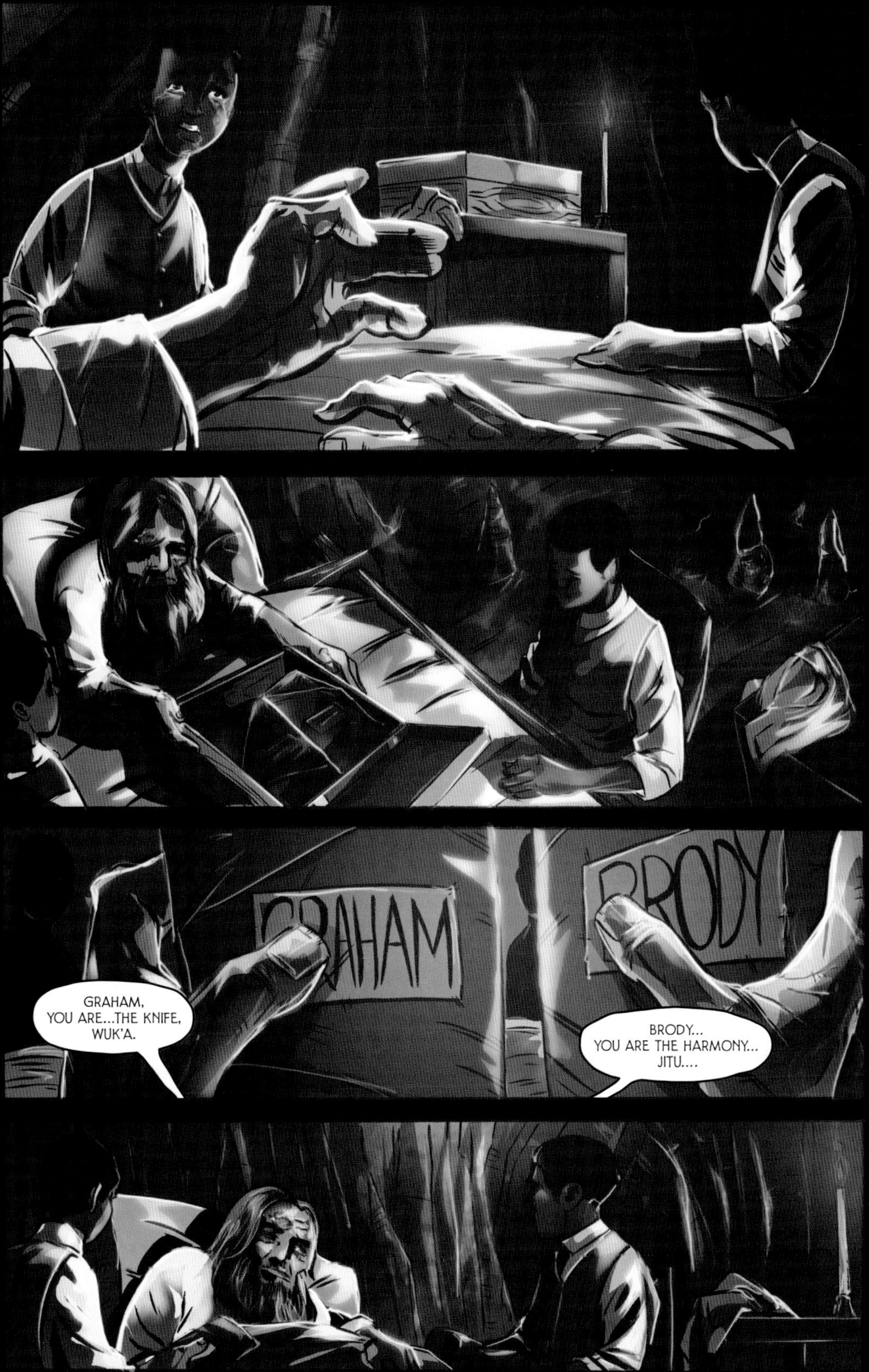
GRAHAM
BRODY
GRAHAM, YOU ARE...THE KNIFE, WUK'A.
BRODY... YOU ARE THE HARMONY... JITU....

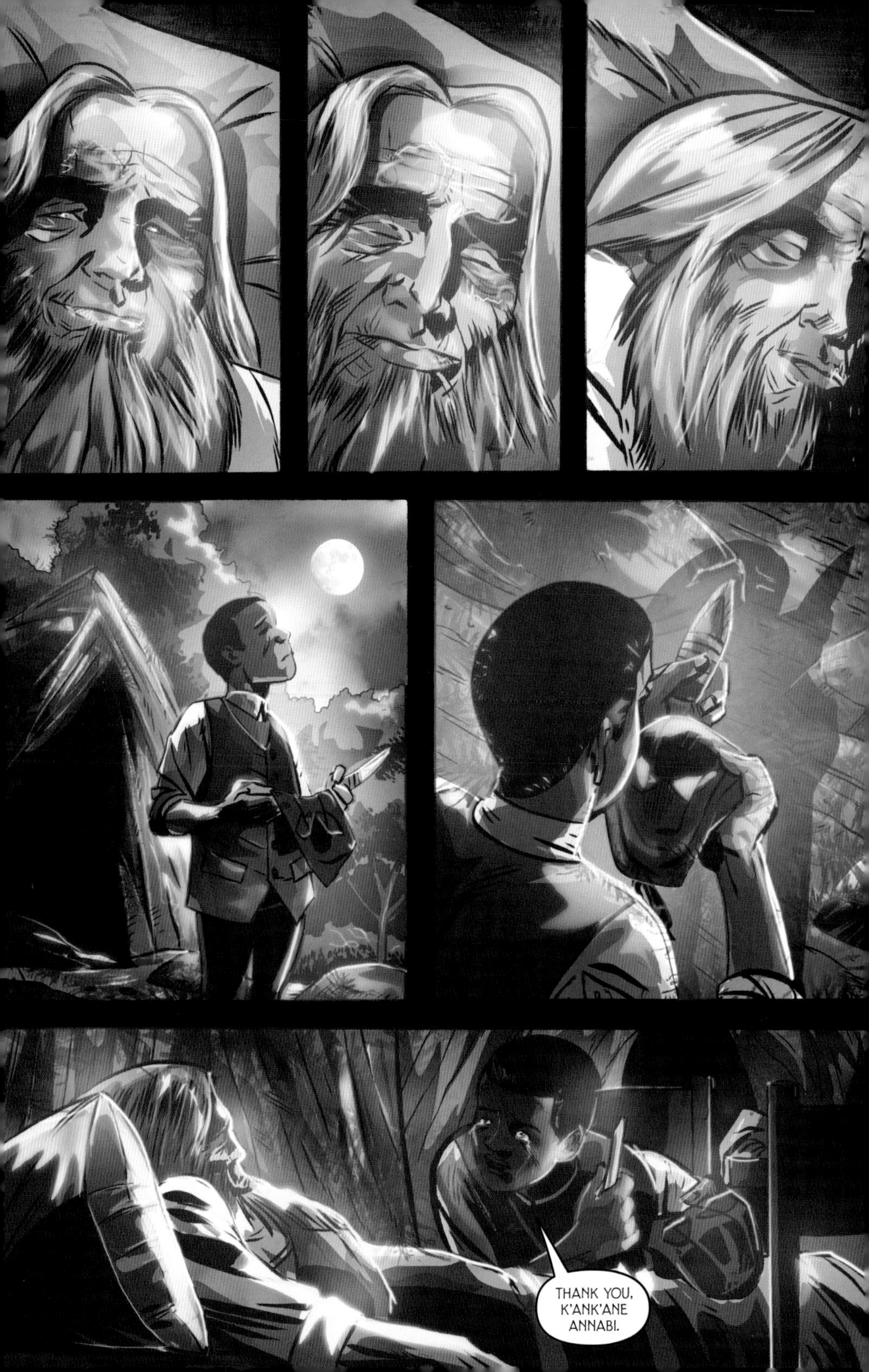
THANK YOU, K'ANK'ANE ANNABI.

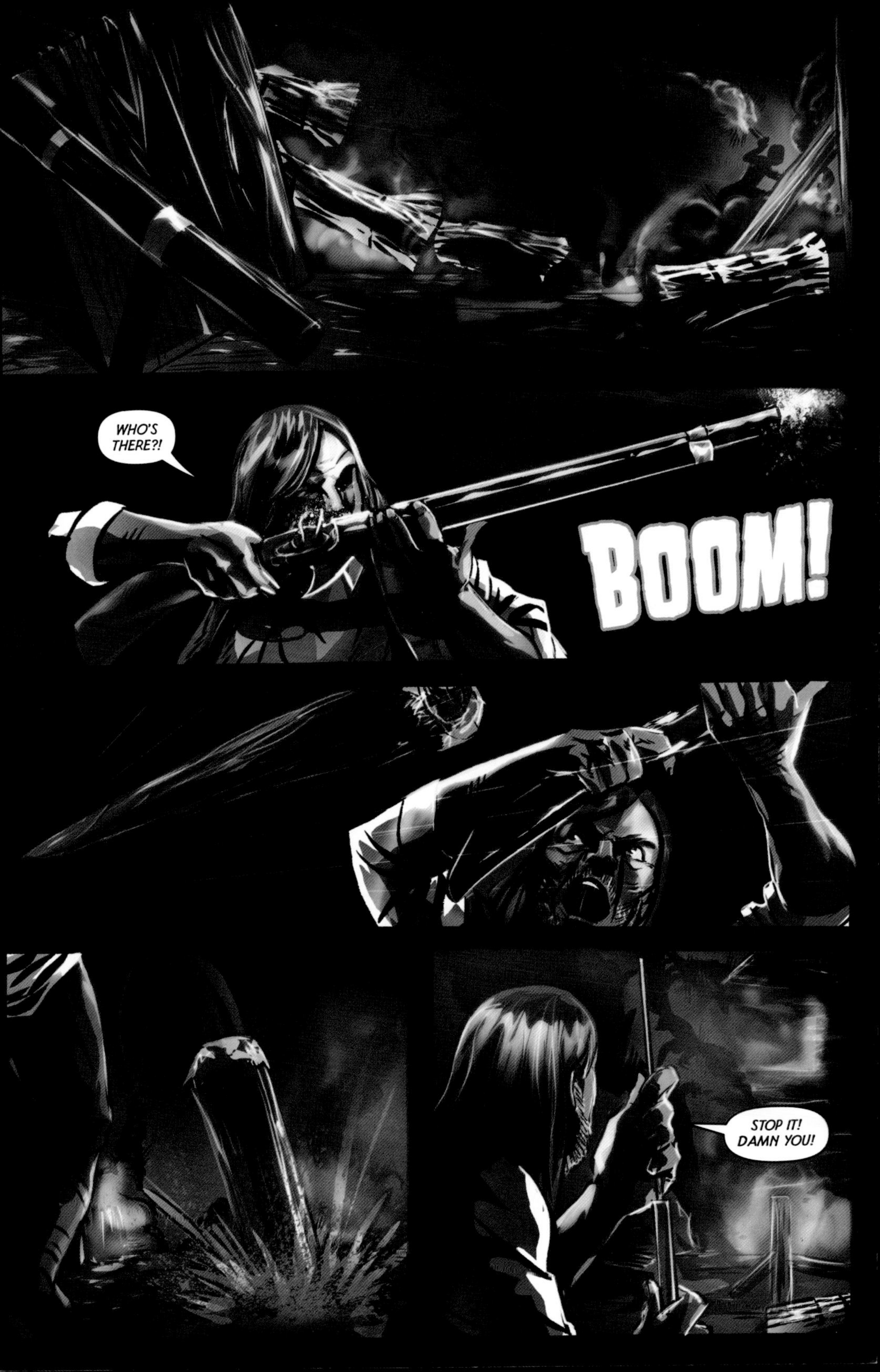
WHO'S THERE?!
BOOM!
STOP IT! DAMN YOU!

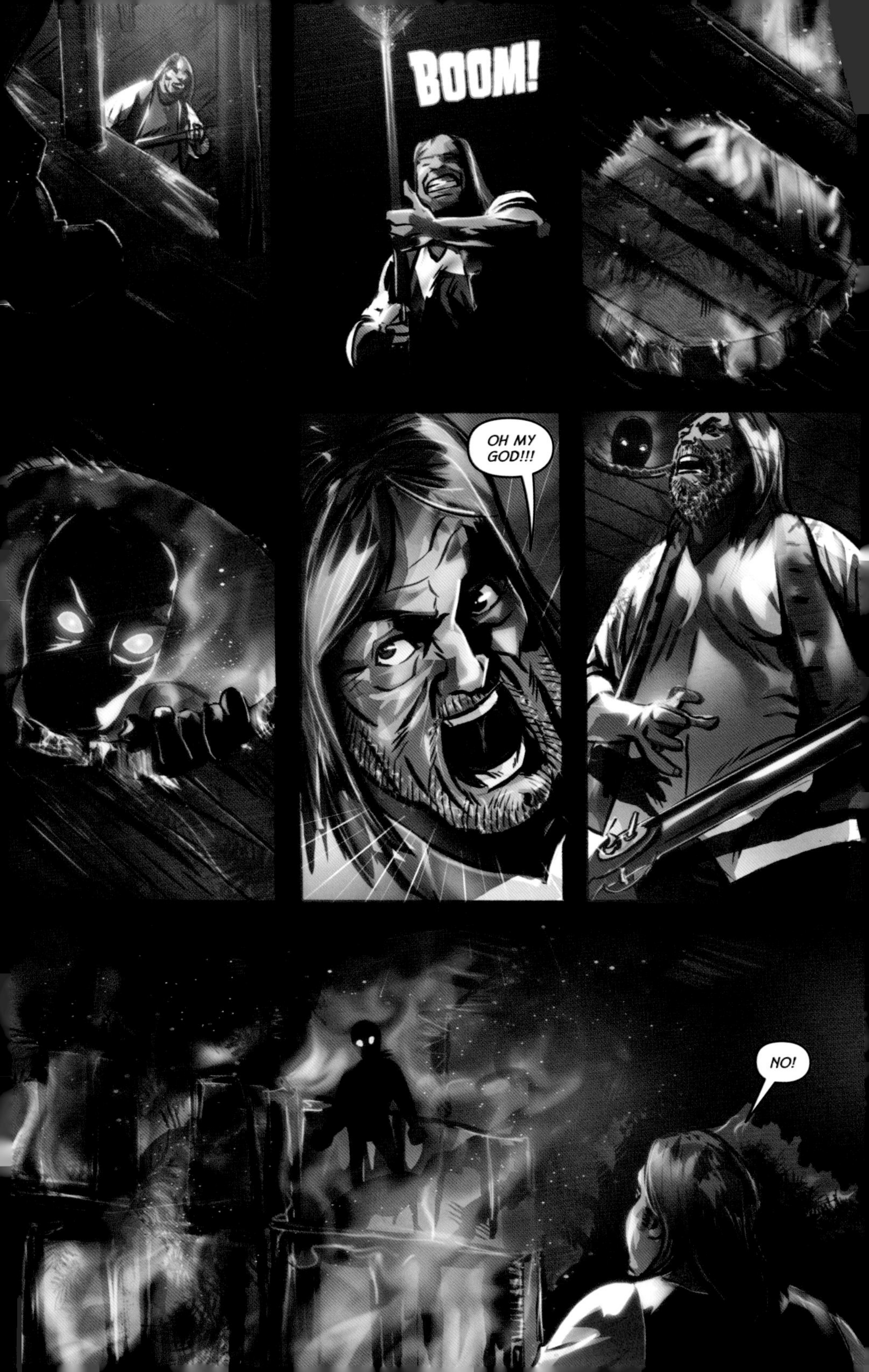
BOOM!
OH MY GOD!!!
NO!

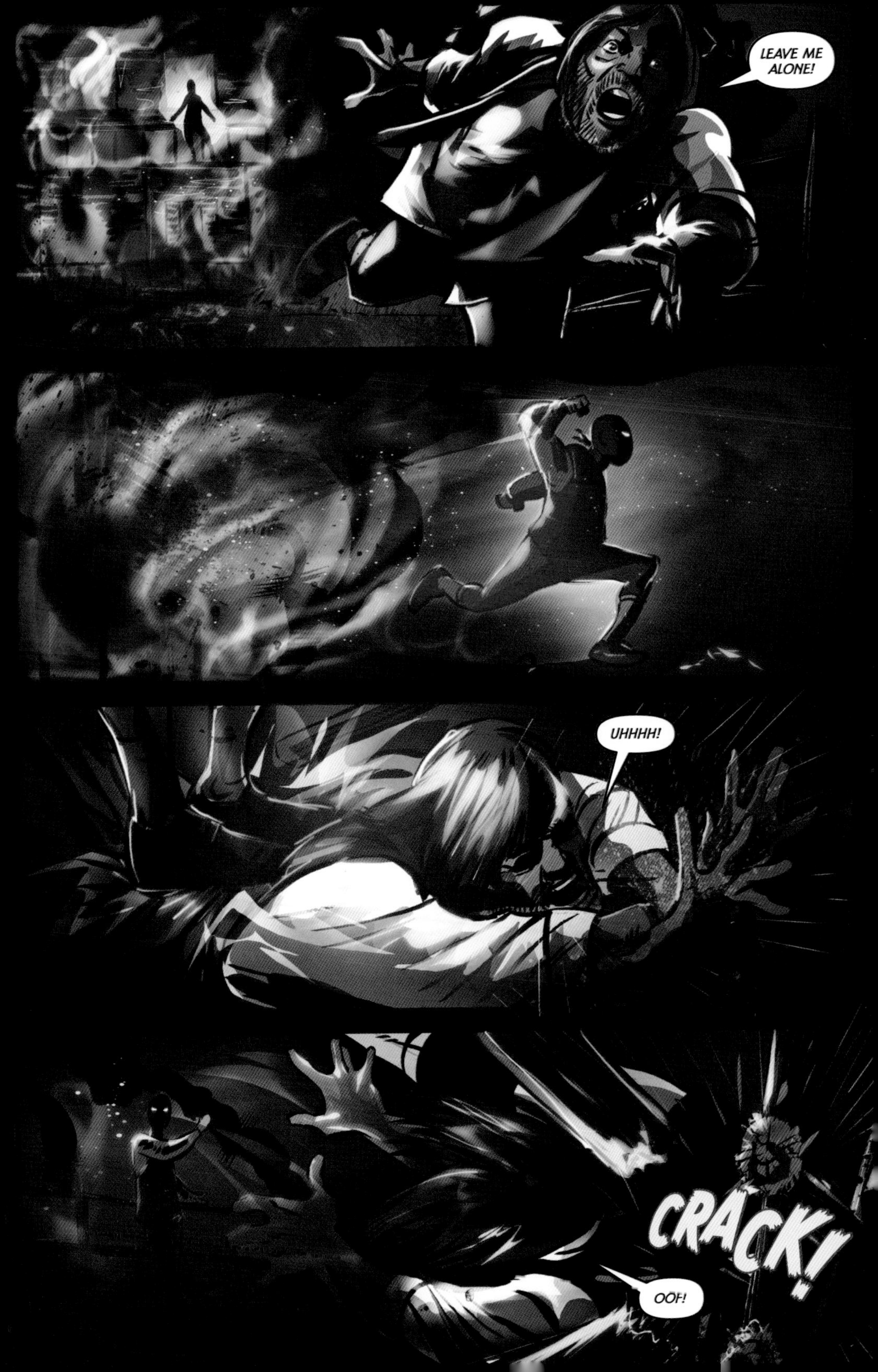
LEAVE ME ALONE!
UHHHH!
CRACK!
OOF!

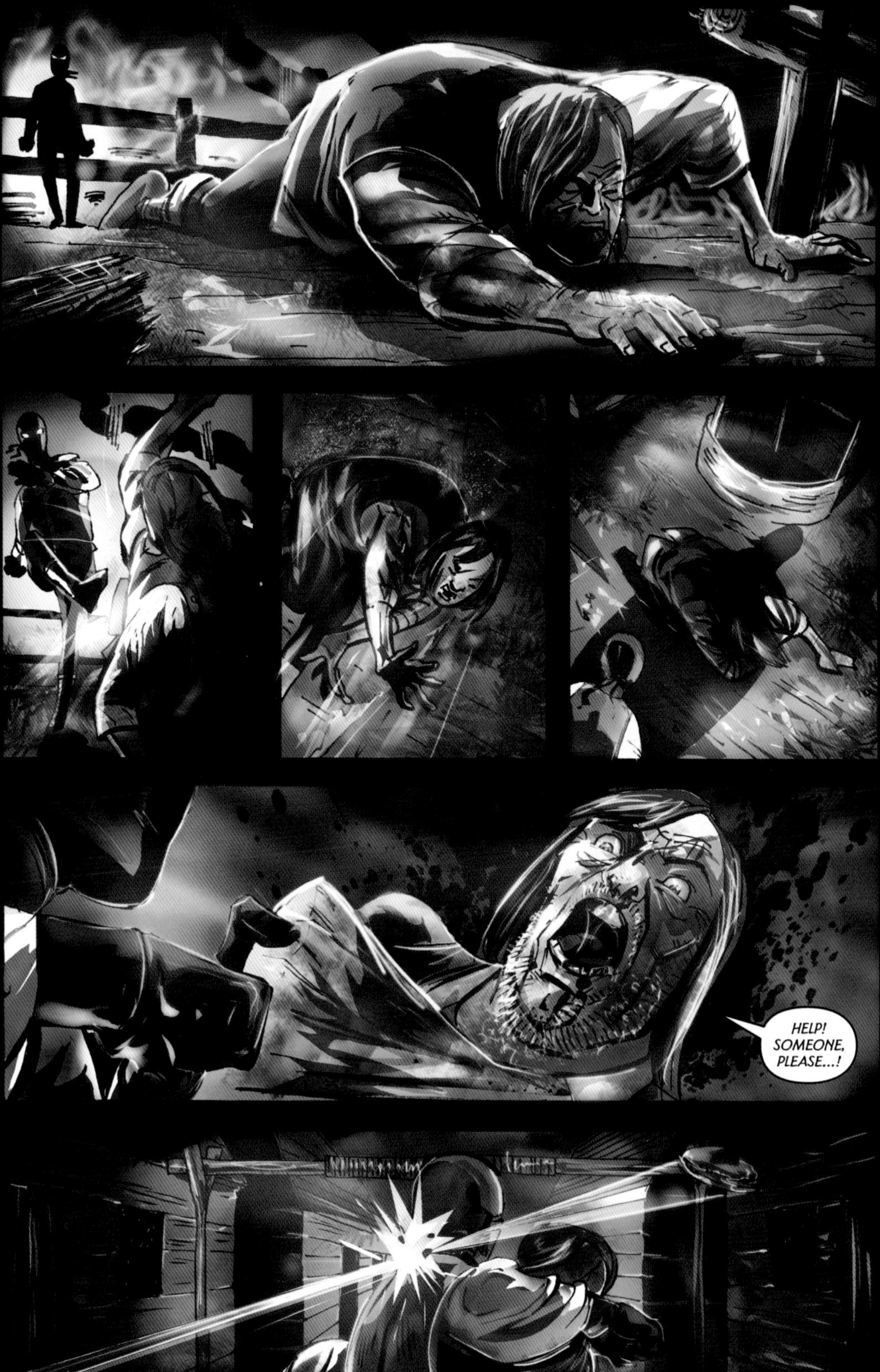
HELP! SOMEONE, PLEASE...!

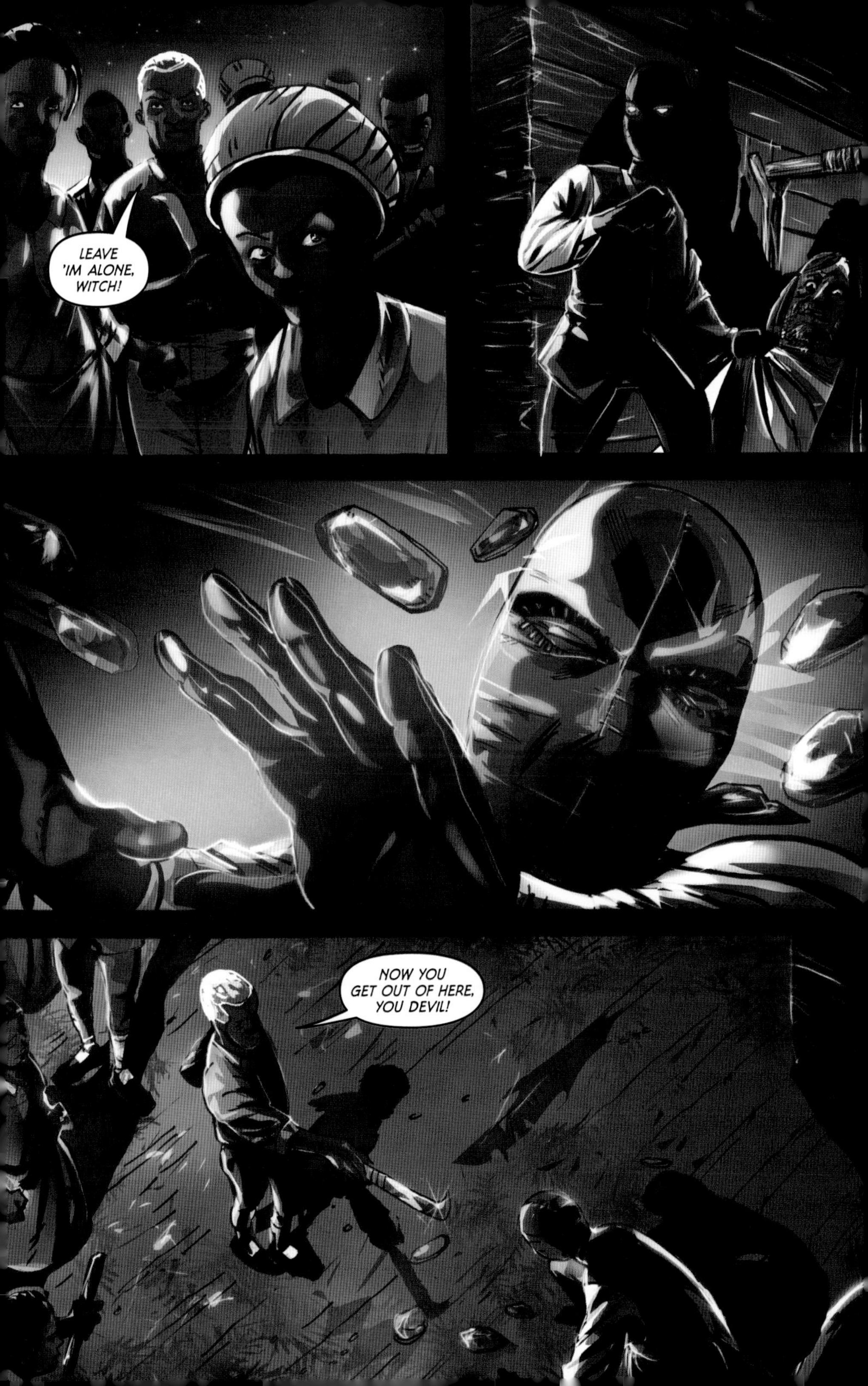
LEAVE 'IM ALONE, WITCH!
NOW YOU GET OUT OF HERE, YOU DEVIL!

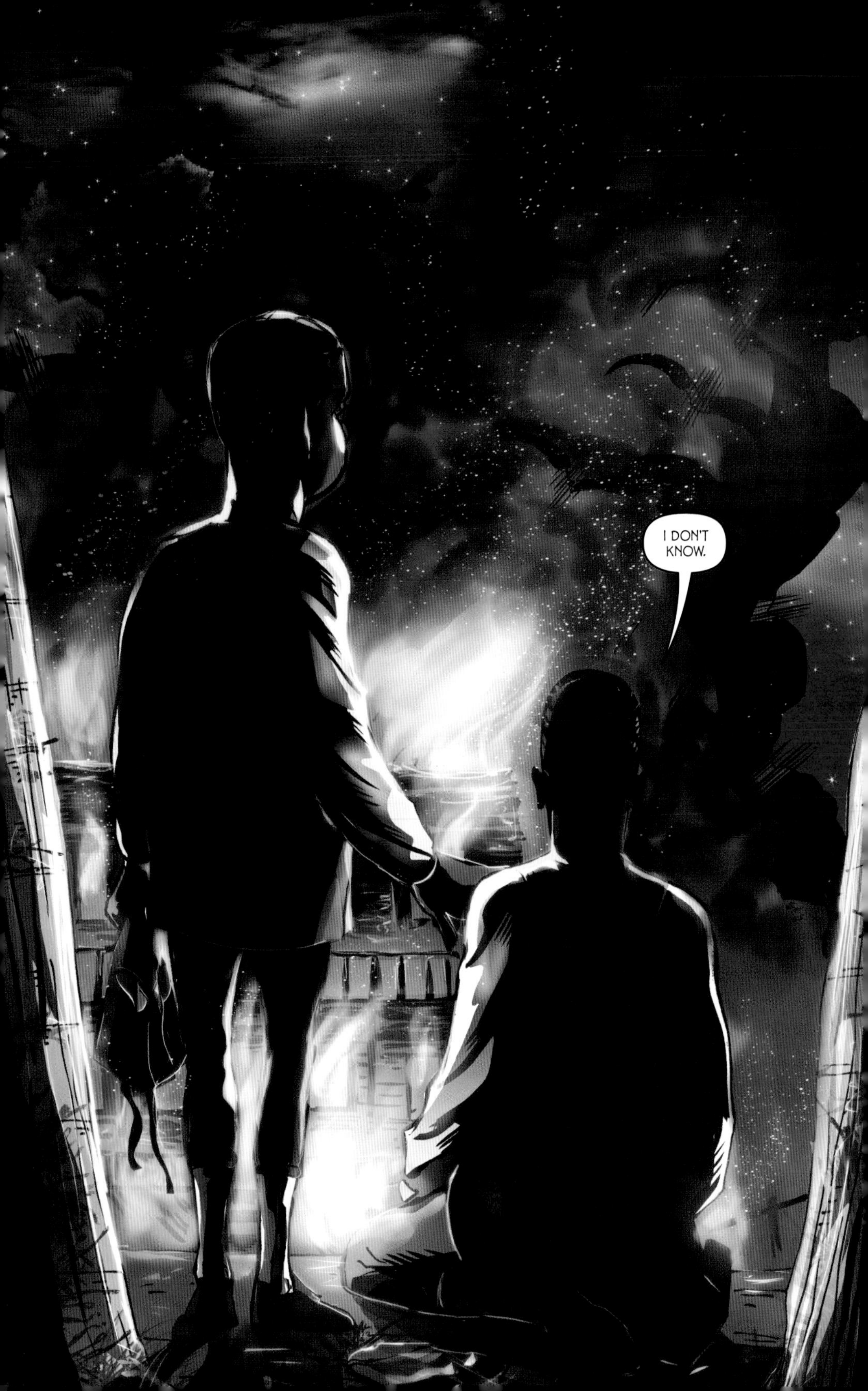
I DON'T KNOW.

EPILOGUE

"Anyone may steer a ship in a calm sea, my brothers....

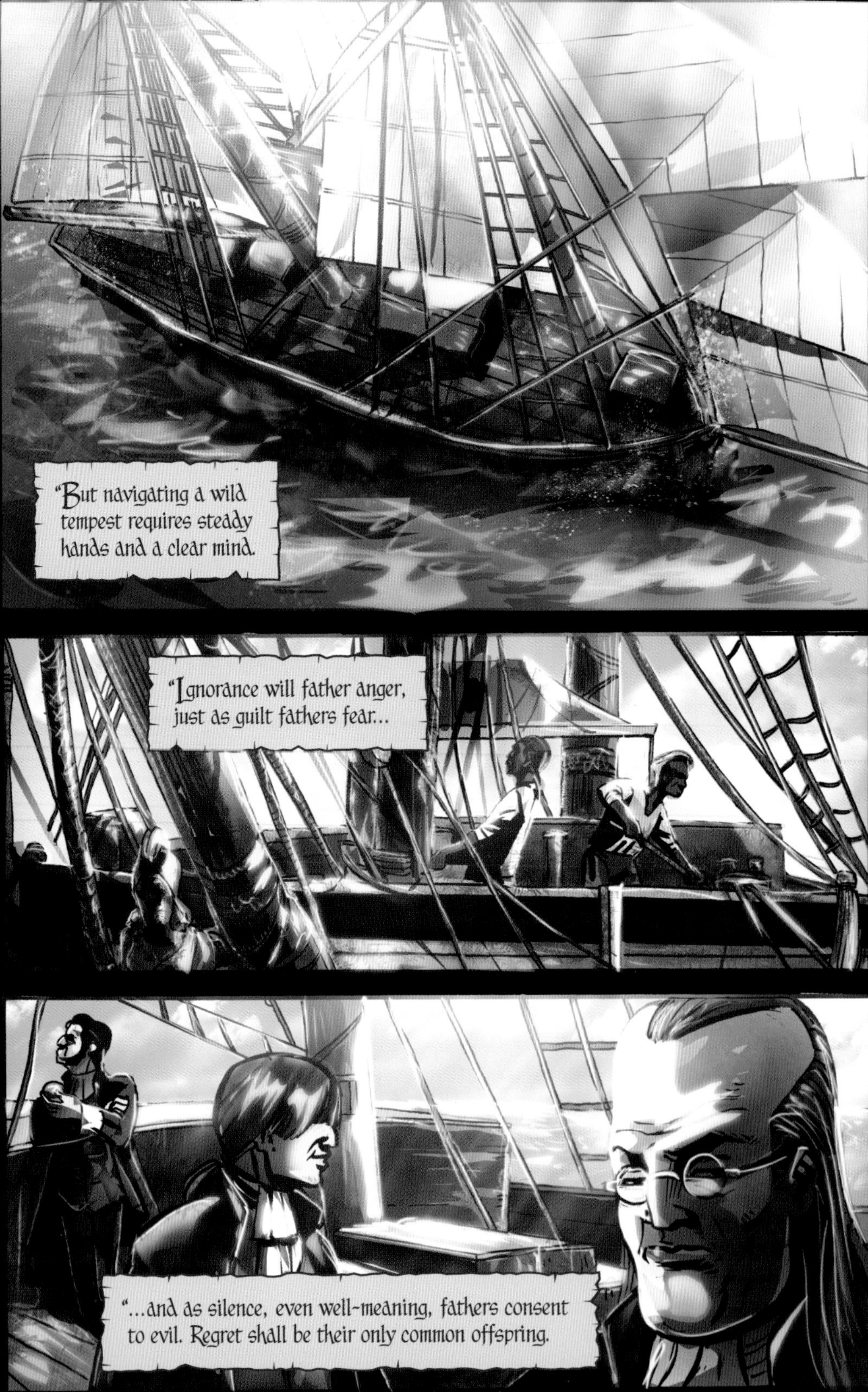
"But navigating a wild tempest requires steady hands and a clear mind.
"Ignorance will father anger, just as guilt fathers fear...
"...and as silence, even well-meaning, fathers consent to evil. Regret shall be their only common offspring.